Also by Elise Covert

Spring Break Renegade - available on Amazon Kindle

LINKED CIRCLES

Book One in the *Circles* Trilogy

Elise Covert

Adult Reading Material: The material in this book is intended for mature audiences only.

This novel has been a long time coming. It began in January 2013 and I finished it in a burst of furious typing in November of 2013. Thanks to all my writer friends who encouraged me. Thank you to my first readers Michelle, Shannon, Beth, and Chris. Your enthusiasm and sharp critique were gratifying and oh so valuable.

A big thank you to my editors - yes, it took more than one! - Jim Thomsen and Alan Riehl/Riehl Faith Productions. And many thanks to Kari Ayasha of Cover to Cover Designs for creating the beautiful cover.

And thank you to my husband, who, when I first asked, "What would you think about having a wife who is an erotica writer?" answered, "I think it'd be cool."

Dear Reader,

Thank you for picking up or downloading this novel. Opening the cover of a new book for the first time (or in today's world, clicking past the table of contents of your new e-book) is the first step into a journey. This journey might take you through shadowed woods, golden meadows, glassed skyscrapers, sweet small-town pathways, or the basement den of a madman. I, as the author, want to spark something in your blood or your mind, direct from my typing fingers to your eyes. We are communicating in the ancient art of story-telling, you and I.

My disclaimer: this is fiction, a fantasy, a story I have created from scraps of my imagination. Nic is a cautious girl, and we should all be cautious. Before ever putting yourself in a vulnerable position, please know and trust your partner.

I hope you enjoy this adventure. It has been an adventure for me to write it, as I spun various plot twists and scenarios, discarding and then re-examining them.

I sometimes imagine that after writing a story, I have left it on a small insignificant table in the corner of a room. It could be your office building lobby, or a bookstore in which you are browsing, or perhaps a hotel lobby. As you now walk by, you happen to spot this little volume and muse, "What is this?"

And then the adventure begins…

Elise Covert
September 2014

CHAPTER ONE

Nicole Simmons watched through the window as the dark-haired man whipped his silver Jeep into the parking lot below. He pulled into the vacant spot near the door, as if he knew it was available just for him. Nic tapped her pencil against the pile of reports in her arms. As the man strode to the entrance below her, she craned her neck to follow him as long as she could.

Then she turned back to the empty conference room and resumed her task of dropping a copy of the report at each chair. She glanced at the water pitchers. Yes, they were filled and jammed with ice cubes. Next she checked on the coffee. Also prepared, but the supplies were lacking.

Nic stuck her head out the door and called to Stephanie, the office assistant.

"Hey Steph, we need some Sugar in the Raw and some packets of stevia in here. Can you grab those?"

"Sure." Stephanie rose from her chair at the front desk.

The elevator doors opened and the dark-haired man stepped into the office lobby. Nic smiled and walked forward with her hand outstretched.

"Hello there. You're here for the community center meeting?"

"Yes, I am. Hello," the man said as he took her hand in his own. "I'm the architect, Jack LaTour."

His hand was warm and his fingers closed around hers. He gripped her hand firmly, holding it in his, but not aggressively. Nic noticed that the irises of his green eyes were rimmed with gold.

Green and gold eyes, like he's some kind of cat.

He was still holding her hand, a few seconds longer than was socially normal. While a formal smile curved his lips, a furrow between his brows gave her the impression of bemusement, as if he also wasn't sure why he was holding her hand like that. Nic didn't feel like pulling away and actually wondered if he would let go of her hand easily if she tried. She tilted her head at him and lifted one corner of her mouth, flashing what she knew was her slightly crooked, yet amused smile. He grinned back at her and let go of her hand, almost giving it back to her instead of dropping it.

"Hello, Mr. LaTour. I'm Nicole Simmons, the program coordinator for the Tyff Foundation. I'll be working with you on this committee for the new community center."

"Good."

Nic wondered what he meant by that. "Yes, uh, we'll be right in here." She nodded toward the conference room. "Take any seat. You're the first one here."

"I always am."

Jack LaTour entered the conference room and set his leather satchel onto the table.

He's sure of himself, Nic thought.

"Hello, Jack, so good to see you again."

Nic's boss, Frances, strode into the room. She was tall, with her short blonde hair tucked behind her ears. Her deep red lipstick matched the color of her nail polish. Nic always thought that Frances looked more like the editor of a fashion magazine than the Chief Community Officer of Tyff Tech Corp.

Frances shook Jack's hand and Nic noticed the familiarity between the two.

Once the manager and several board members arrived, everyone settled around the table and the meeting began. Nic took the floor first, going over the concept for the community center, the financing, and the vision of

Cedric Tyff, the founder of the corporation and the foundation.

"He doesn't want a building that looks like it is trying to make an artistic or architectural statement," Nic said. "He wants a building that looks like it belongs to the neighborhood which it will serve. It should look integrated, welcoming, and upbeat."

Her eyes trailed over the people around the table, finishing on Jack. He twirled his pen in his fingers and a smile took hold of his mouth, spreading slowly.

"Upbeat," he said. Nic had a vision of warm honey pouring from a bottle. His voice left a sweet taste in her mouth.

Then she realized that everyone was waiting for her response to what was, apparently, taken as a question.

"Uh, yes, upbeat. By that he means, uh," Nic looked to her notes although she knew the answer wouldn't be found there. She had to break eye contact with Jack to get her thoughts back together. "Upbeat. Positive. Optimistic. A place where the community will find the resources to improve and even remake their lives for the better."

Whew.

After a few more remarks, Nic returned to her seat and took notes on the comments and concerns. It didn't escape her that Jack took as many notes as she did, writing swiftly in a notebook.

After the meeting, Jack packed his satchel and slipped out the door while Nic collected the remnants of her report. She thought to call a goodbye to him, but when she lifted her head, he was already in the hallway. The thought of his hand, firmly holding her own, flashed through her mind. She wished that he had turned back, smiled or waved, given her some acknowledgement.

She left the conference room and headed for the lobby, with her arms full of throwaway papers.

In the lobby, Jack was talking on his cell phone, while looking out the bank of windows. He turned toward her.

Nic stopped, hesitating because he was looking at her so intensely, his eyes narrowed and unwavering. Jack flipped his phone closed and strode in her direction. When he reached her, he stood close, slightly too close for comfort, and Nic felt the urge to step back. But she deliberately didn't.

He has come this close. Let him deal with it, she thought.

She met his gaze and held it. After a few moments, he smiled. She realized that he had accepted her confrontation. She tilted her head to one side and smiled as well.

"Can I call you?" he asked quietly.

"Yes," she said. Her tone matched his.

His smile broadened and he turned to the elevators.

She chewed on the inside of her upper lip as she watched his smile disappear behind the elevator doors. Then she turned toward her office and dropped the papers into the recycling bin.

CHAPTER TWO

Nic picked up her phone after the first ring, noting who was on the caller ID. It wasn't Jack, but she wasn't disappointed.

"Hi," she said. Her lips softened into a smile.

"Hi there, my girl," Lawrence said. "I've been picturing you in my mind all morning."

Nic felt a warm blush spread throughout her body. "Oh? And just what picture do you have in mind?"

"You. Naked. On your back on the rug, in front of the fire. As I hope you will be later tonight."

She let her breath slip over her lips in a warm sigh. "Yes. I can make that happen."

"Good. Can we say nine tonight? I need to get a few things done first. At nine, however, I will have a chilled bottle of wine and a hot fire going."

"I'll be there. Nine."

"I'll send a taxi for you. You'll stay the night?"

She hesitated. "I have work tomorrow. I really can't."

"You know you can get to work in plenty of time from here."

Nic bounced on the toes of her feet. She loved waking up in Lawrence's bed. She hated waking up a half hour earlier than normal though.

"I'll stay over on the weekend."

"And tonight?" He was persistent.

"You don't make this easy."

"I intend to make it very difficult for you to say no to me."

She almost caved, but thought of the full day of work she had tomorrow. "I just can't. Not tonight. But I promise, Friday night I will."

"All right, I'll let you off the hook for tonight. I'm going to have you for breakfast Saturday morning. I hope."

Nic laughed and ended the call with a soft farewell. As she leaned back in her chair, she let herself enjoy the warm tingle for a few moments, smiling slightly.

"And what is pleasing you, Ms. Nicole?" It was Frances, her boss.

"Ah, just thinking of my plans for tonight."

"Seeing Lawrence, are you?"

Nic grinned and nodded, feeling her cheeks heat a little with a blush.

Frances smiled back with one eyebrow raised. "Oh, tsk. That pretty little blush is giving you away."

Nic knew she was blushing even more.

"Okay, enough of enjoying Nicole's blushing beauty. Now then, can we have that meeting recapping the to-do list today? Ten minutes and then we meet in my office. Tell Stephanie."

"Okay, I'll be there."

Frances turned away, then stopped. She rested her hand on the door handle and looked back at Nic.

"And Nicole," she said.

"Yes?"

"I expect you to be one hour late tomorrow morning."

* * * * *

Lawrence slid the button of her blouse through the hole, sliding the fabric apart against her chest. His silver hair glimmered in the firelight. Nic wove her fingers through the coarse strands as he lowered his head and kissed between her breasts.

“I’m glad you’re here.” His breath melted over her skin.

She tugged a lock of his hair. “Aren’t you always glad I’m here?” she teased.

“Most of the time.” She could feel the vibration of his answer against her ribs. “Sometimes you’re a pain in the ass.”

She laughed, pulling harder at his hair so that he raised his head. “Then why do you keep inviting me over?”

“Because ninety percent of the time you are lovely and laughing. And you give great blowjobs one hundred percent of the time.”

“But that ten percent? When I’m not lovely and laughing?”

“You get that stubborn look on your face that means you are about to say you can’t stay the night or can’t leave a toothbrush here or some other nonsense.”

She sighed.

She’d met Lawrence when she first went to work for the Tyff Foundation. Her background was in nonprofit management and he served on several charity boards. Having been an early investor in the software industry of the 1980s, he built on his already successful financial consulting career. His millions gave him the means to become active in the nonprofit community, while his innate generosity of spirit drove his passion to improve the lives of those less fortunate. Lawrence was on the board of several charities that the Tyff Foundation supported and their paths crossed often. A mutual appreciation bloomed, then a friendship. When he asked her out for a casual dinner, she assumed it was professional. When he poured her a glass of wine and then took her hand in his, she was taken by surprise. Lawrence understood. He knew that she didn’t expect someone so much older—fifty-one, in fact—to ask her out. He was a widower, having lost his wife ten years earlier to cancer. But he was so confident and easy of manner, that after the shared bottle of wine, when he kissed her outside of her apartment building, she found herself leaning into him. He was obviously pleased at her response, for his arms came around her, bending her back slightly, and his mouth covered hers more ardently.

Since then, they got together regularly, twice a week or so. The first time that he slipped Nic's clothes from her body, parted her legs, and pushed into her, she was left breathless. His touch was so experienced. His hands knew so many secret points of arousal. His whispered words of desire and encouragement induced so many new erotic feelings from her.

After a few dates, she found that she not only accepted his older age, but found his maturity and confidence to be an incredible turn-on. Along with those great sex tricks he seemed to have learned through the years.

He never pursued a commitment. He let her know that he enjoyed her company and found her to be sexy and exciting, but he didn't see a future with a woman so much younger than he. Although she was grateful that he didn't push her into something serious, Nic was confused in those first weeks, as they grew closer through conversation and love-making while he still kept her at arm's length. Eventually, she appreciated the relationship the way it stood: frequent evenings together, weekends sleeping at his house, a few dinners out, but no invitations to the charity parties and auctions he attended, no meeting his four grown children, no public hand holding or affection. She hadn't wanted any kind of serious relationship in a long time and resented the men who tried to assert a claim on her after only a few dates. This was refreshing. Freeing. It didn't require the depth of feeling that exclusive relationships demanded.

She didn't want to feel that depth of feeling again. The depth of love was usually met by the same depth of pain.

Lawrence let her know that he would be asking other women to accompany him to those charity and art galas, women more his own age, with similar social standing. He encouraged her to take advantage of any opportunities that came her way. By "opportunities" she knew he meant other men. So every once in a while, she accepted a casual date from some man or another. Even kissed a few here and there.

And always fantasized about Lawrence's touch as she rubbed herself to orgasm alone in her bed later that night.

They had already shared a bottle of crisp white wine tonight, over a plate of crostini that he prepared as a late supper. Then he led her to the familiar rug in front of the fire and kneeled, pulling her down with him.

Lawrence's fingers unbuttoned her blouse completely, pushing the fabric apart. He planted gentle kisses along the soft flesh of her cleavage. His tongue trailed between her breasts as one hand slid beneath the back of her shirt and expertly unsnapped the bra. He lowered her back on the rug and lowered his mouth to her right nipple, taking it past his teeth and suckling it. Nic groaned and her hands tightened in his hair.

Lawrence pulled away and rose to his feet. His shirt was already off. The firelight glinted off the silvery hair of his chest. Nic's eyes lowered from his chest to the impressive bulge in his pants. His body wasn't rock hard, but he looked at least ten years younger than he was. His face was worn and craggy, in the manner that made her think of Harrison Ford, Clint Eastwood, maybe Kevin Costner.

"Take off your jeans, Nic," he said. His hands flexed at his sides.

She complied.

"Take off your panties." A teasing smile curled his lips.

She complied with that as well.

She saw his chest rising and falling with his heightened breathing as his eyes roamed over her, lingering on her lips, her breasts, her pussy. He unfastened his trousers and a moment later, he was naked as well.

Nic caught her breath at the sight of his engorged cock. Lawrence lowered to his knees and slid up between her legs. He grasped her thighs and lifted them over his shoulders, his mouth inches from her hot pussy.

"My beauty. My girl. I want to taste you."

Nic nodded and caressed his cheek with the back of her fingers. "Please, Lawrence. Please do."

His head lowered and her eyes closed.

* * * * *

Later, Lawrence held her, his lips wandering up and down her neck. She could feel the heat of him inside of her as she crossed her ankles, savoring the feeling of the evidence of his release.

"You can't stay the night?" His hands traveled over her bare breasts.

Nic reflected on Frances's permission to be late in the morning. "No, I really can't. But maybe Friday?"

"Mmmmmm, yes, Friday. I can hold you in my arms all night."

"Yes, I'd like that."

"You would, wouldn't you. I enjoy our sleep-overs."

Nic bit her lip. "I enjoy you, and us."

"Mm, me too." He hesitated for a second, then continued to kiss her neck. "Nic—"

She waited for his words, but he was silent. "Yes?"

"Maybe someday - not now, but someday - you could stay here on a more permanent basis."

She shifted, turning to him. "What do you mean?"

He smiled and she turned her head to kiss his lips, unable to resist. As she pulled back he said, "Perhaps someday, I'll ask you to move some of your things here."

"You mean, live with you?" Nic pictured his large mansion as her own. The Lake Washington waterfront, the boat, the live-in housekeeper, the wine cellar and steam room and big plasma televisions.

"No. Neither of us want that. I would lay odds that you'll find the man of your dreams to marry in the next few years anyway. But having a few of your things here might be a practical idea."

She rested back against him again, quiet for some moments. She knew that Lawrence had no intention of ever marrying again and that didn't bother her at all. She didn't feel any need to be married, but his hurried definite statement about not wanting to live together, and assuming that she didn't want that either, rankled her. It shouldn't, she fully knew how he felt. Was it weird to like having a man keep her at arm's length? She held her distance from him just as much.

She brushed those thoughts away and said, "I love our arrangement. At least for now. It works perfectly for me and I think for you too."

"Oh yes. But I want you to know something." He tipped her chin up so she had to look at him. "If you ever need me, I'm always here. I will help you any way I can." His arms tightened around her. "I never expected to be involved with someone who is so much younger than me. But I find that I'm very happy about it."

Nic rubbed her cheek against his chest. "And I never expected to feel like this about someone so much older. But I do. And I'm happy about that too."

"Good."

His hand reached down and stroked the inside of her thighs. She watched his fingers tracing over her skin, and parted her legs further. When his fingers reached the smooth, soft lips of her bare pussy, he circled around the sides of them, tracing the curves. Nic began to hum. She felt his silent chuckle against her back.

He nibbled on her earlobe and whispered, “You are so hungry.”

Nic spread her legs wider. “Ravenous.”

CHAPTER THREE

She wasn't an hour late to work after all, but right on time the next day. The first phone call came in shortly after she arrived. She reached for her work phone, still flipping through her pile of things to get done for the day.

"Hello, this is Nicole Simmons."

"Hello, Nicole Simmons. This is Jack LaTour."

The phone slipped off Nic's shoulder. She barely caught it in her hand before it clattered to the top of the desk. She sat down in her chair, holding the phone to her ear.

"Yes, hello Jack. How are you?"

"Doing well, thanks." There was a slight hesitation. "I wanted to ask you out for a drink."

"Yes?"

"How about we meet for a cocktail somewhere? Sometime?"

Nic smiled and leaned back in her chair. "I'd like that."

"Good. So would I. Tomorrow night, perhaps? How about after work at the bar at the Mayflower Hotel?"

She picked up her pen and tapped it against the edge of the desk. "Yeah, I can do that. Maybe around 6:30?"

"I'll look forward to it, Nicole. And … if I could say something?"

Nic narrowed her eyes, bemused. What could he possibly have to say at this point?

"Yes?"

"When we met, the other day. At the meeting …"

"Yes?" She drew the word out a little longer this time.

Another pause. Nic wondered what he would say. That he was entranced by her? Found her to be the most stunning woman he had ever seen? Thought she needed a shower?

"You were wearing a pair of shoes … heels … and I just wanted to say … well … I liked them very much."

Nic thought for a moment about what she had worn that day. Her just-above-the-knee gray business suit, no hose, and the shoes? Ah, yes. The black leather heels, with the dainty metal links across the ankles. She didn't splurge on shoes, but those had cost a little more than she usually spent, and worth it from the compliments she had received about them. Now including Jack.

"Oh, those shoes. Let me think. Was I wearing the orange mules that day?" Nic pressed her lips together, wondering if her teasing would turn him off, but unable to resist.

If he didn't have a sense of humor, she wouldn't be interested for long anyway.

"Uh, no."

"Then it must have been my pink ballet flats." She held back her laughter.

"Nope. Definitely not pink ballet flats, whatever those are. Just how many pairs of shoes do you have?" She could hear the laughter in his voice now.

"Not many. Which narrows it down to those black ones that are much higher than I normally wear. Oh yes, and with the cute little chains around the ankles."

"Those are definitely the ones."

"And so, Jack," she said, drawing his name out. "Would you like me to wear those shoes tomorrow?"

"I would be very pleased if you wore those shoes tomorrow, Ms. Simmons."

"Would you really? All right, I'll keep that in mind," she said. She couldn't resist adding, "They'll look great with my torn denim skirt."

Jack was silent for a moment. Then he replied, "They'd look great with anything."

"Okay, Jack. I'm also looking forward to meeting you again."

"And Nicole, I am really looking forward to seeing those shoes on you again."

Nic laughed, murmured goodbye and hung up. Then she leaned back in her chair again and gazed at the ceiling. Her mind wandered back to Jack's firm handshake, his warm fingers, his sly smile. And those wicked green and gold eyes. She imagined them darkening, the green becoming the color of a deep jungle pond. With a sudden start, she realized just how turned on her body was, how her thighs pressed together and how her nipples were suddenly overly sensitive. She swore softly under her breath but smiled as well. Before she could turn her attention to the pile of tasks on her desk, she spent several minutes mentally exploring her closet, analyzing what she would wear with those shoes. It wouldn't be a denim skirt.

* * * * *

Nic walked into the lobby of the Mayflower Park Hotel a few minutes after six thirty. Using public transportation, in this case a bus, often meant that time was relative, or at least dependent on the whims of stop lights, traffic jams, and disruptive passengers. In this case, it was the passenger who got his bike stuck on the bus bike rack six blocks before this stop. Nic would perhaps have chosen to walk, as a few of the other riders decided, but not in tonight's heels.

She glanced around and found the discreet sign over the archway indicating Oliver's, the hotel bar. She smoothed her hands over her form-fitting deep red dress. The stretchy material was not restrictive, but it did show off her curves. The square neckline framed her cleavage nicely, but wasn't low enough to shock anyone. The hem ended about two inches above the knee. She had worn the dress to work today, but kept a conservative blazer over it.

The blazer now draped over her arm.

She willed her ankles not to waver in the high heels and then made her way to the bar. Just before she entered, she paused, stood up straight, lifted her chin just slightly higher than normal, and tilted her pelvis forward and up. There had to be some purpose to those inane modeling lessons her grandmother had encouraged her to take in high school. Supposedly she was to learn "deportment." In actuality, she learned how to walk with the elegance of a third tier fashion model.

Nic glanced around the dark and dignified bar, noting the table groupings, the dark wood and the formal tie-back curtains that framed windows looking out onto Olive Way. The murmur of civilized voices droned and the slightly pungent, slightly sour smell of expensive whisky scented the air. And now she knew she was standing, framed, in the entryway to the bar, posing like a perfume model.

So she continued on, entering the room and realizing that she was several years younger than everyone else there. Nic glanced around again and saw Jack lift a hand to her from a two-top table by the window. She licked her lips. He looked even better than she remembered. This man would definitely catch her attention no matter what room she was walking into with his casual classic look, but in the moody ambiance of the bar, he reminded her of a character in a movie, waiting for a secret rendezvous with a mysterious lover.

Would she be that lover?

"Hi," she said as she slid into the chair that he pulled out for her. A small candle flickered on the white tablecloth.

"Hi," Jack said as he took his own seat. "Thanks for coming."

"Elegant place. I haven't been here before."

"No? It's one of my favorite quiet bars in Seattle."

A favorite to bring dates? Nic wondered. She leaned forward, her hands clasped on top of the table, and studied his face.

His green eyes gleamed in the soft lighting. She knew he must be a good five years older than she, if the slight lines around his eyes and mouth were any indication. His dark hair was thick and slightly on the long side and Nic thought she detected a few gray hairs at the temples, unless it was just the candlelight. The top several buttons were undone on his white dress shirt. If she continued her inspection, she would need to bend her head to look under the table.

"Thirty-four," he said.

"What?"

"That's how old I am. I could tell I was getting the once-over."

"Oh, um, sorry. How embarrassing." Nic rolled her eyes.

"No, not at all. I was giving you the once-over as well."

"Okay." Nic knew her cheeks were pink, judging from their warmth. "I guess we're even then."

"Neither one of us seems to be leaving, so I guess we found the initial perusal pleasing."

She smiled. "Yes. Pleasing."

He laughed quietly and picked up the bar menu.

"Oh, wait," she said.

He glanced up.

"Twenty-seven."

"Twenty-seven? Oh, right. Very good. Now we are definitely even."

He asked her about her taste in wines. She deferred to him, beyond saying she didn't care for Zinfandels. He asked if she would like something to eat and together they decided on a small plate of tuna tartare terrine to share.

"You eat raw fish?" he asked.

"At the right time, yes."

"And what is the right time?"

"Sushi rolls at a nice restaurant. And something like tuna tartare as long as it is mixed with other things. I don't care for a big plate of raw fish. Do you?"

"Raw fish? At the right time."

Jack put in their order for a bottle of Syrah and the tuna. Then he sat back and looked at her with a smile.

"Well, we did get the initial inspection out of the way. But I have one more thing to check with you."

Nic felt her heart rate tick up, wondering what his playful tone might be suggesting. "You do?"

"I do. I caught a quick glimpse of those lovely feet of yours as you walked in, but I would like a closer look at your shoes. You wore them, I did see that."

"Yes, I did." Nic held out one foot from under the table, pointed in his direction. Jack held out a hand, then hesitated.

"May I?" he asked.

Nic narrowed her eyes, amused. "I suppose so."

Jack held her foot in one hand and played lightly with the thin silver chains around the ankle. The brush of his fingertips sent a little shiver up her leg. She saw his lips quirk.

"Thank you, Nicole. I wasn't sure if you would wear them or not. It could be seen as an unusual request on a first date."

"I figured it was just in fun. They are nice shoes."

Jack let go of her foot and she withdrew her leg back under the table just as the wine and food arrived.

Somewhat to Nic's surprise, they chatted easily about the community center, how she got into nonprofit work, and his work as an architect. She learned that he had designed the newest structure on the Tyff Corp. Campus. He had a condo on Queen Anne Hill. She described her modest but cozy apartment in Belltown.

The tuna tartare was delicious and Nic scooped another bit onto a piece of toasted bread. Just as she brought the piece to her mouth, she noticed that Jack was watching her, his hand idly curled around his wine glass. She prayed she would do this gracefully and then bit into the tuna and toast. Yes! Nothing lost, nothing crumbling in her hand. She chewed slowly, swallowed, ate the last half, and then took a sip of her wine.

"Tell me about yourself, Nicole."

She bit her lip and shrugged. "What would you like to know?"

"What kind of person are you?"

"I don't know." She couldn't think of a single self-descriptor on the spot like this. *Simple-minded?* "Is there anything specific you want me to describe? No tattoos, in case you were wondering."

He laughed and then leaned toward her, holding up one hand. "Give me your hand?"

She laid her hand in his. "Are you going to read my palm?"

"No." He studied her face. "You are a relatively serious person, I think. Capable of great and sophisticated humor, but not usually silly."

Nic thought of her tipsy laugh-fests with her friends and guffawed.

"Okay, maybe a few silly times. But overall, a woman of dignity and a fine sense of self-worth."

"You're making a lot of me after such a short time."

"I'm just guessing." His eyes glittered in the low light.

She cocked her head and shrugged. "Keep going."

"You are highly intelligent and always want to do a good job at everything you do."

"Are you describing me still? Or trying to make me sound like your dream woman?"

"We'll see." He lifted an eyebrow. "Now, to continue, you are devoted to your work, your tasks, whatever they may be, but have a hard time asking for help."

Nic frowned. That part was true, but how would he know that? Still guessing?

Jack stroked his thumb over her palm. She gasped quietly, then put her other hand over her mouth, trying to hide her reaction.

Jack leaned closer, his voice softer now.

"You are a very sensual woman. You are in tune with all of your senses. You feel things deeply, both emotionally and physically."

She nodded slightly.

Jack held her hand tighter. His face was close to hers and she realized that she was leaning in as much as he was. They were so close, she could feel the gentle warmth of his breath on her cheek.

He pressed his thumb to her palm, massaging a slow circle there.

Then he placed her hand on the table.

"That's all."

For a moment, Nic was left leaning forward, her hand on the table. She eventually sank back and dropped her hand into her lap and studied the candle flame.

"Nicole? Was I anywhere near accurate?"

She looked directly at him. "Uncannily so. I feel naked."

He laughed quietly. "Not entirely naked, but maybe partially so."

"You are sitting there fully dressed and I'm here in my panties." She used the word *panties* deliberately, wanting to provoke him.

"Hm, a nice image. Too bad it isn't so."

Nic picked up her wine glass and swirled it in her fingers.

"Do you have any questions for me?" he asked.

"Why yes, Jack, I do." She wouldn't let this opportunity pass.

"Shoot."

"Ever married?"

"No."

"Really."

"Yes." He grinned.

"And no girlfriend currently?"

"No. If I did, I wouldn't have asked you out for a drink."

"Good. I don't care for players."

"I can tell."

"You can tell a lot. Let's see what I can tell."

Jack leaned forward, resting his forearms on the table. "Yes, let's see."

Nic put her chin in her hand, resting her elbow on the table. "You are a successful architect. That's no secret. But I think you were successful at a relatively early age. Perhaps by your mid-twenties. This gives you confidence and surety in your own ideas that I saw at the meeting."

"Arrogant?"

"I'm getting to that." Nic was enjoying this. She felt that she was getting her turn to put him on the hot seat. "Arrogant," she mused. "No, I don't think that's the word. But I think you are incredibly self-confident. Is that warranted? I really don't know you well enough to know. But if I can hazard a guess, then yes, it is probably warranted. However," —Nic held up a finger— "you aren't blinded by your self-confidence. You are very observant. Not just to the physical, but to what makes people tick. And that, Jack, that is a rare talent."

"Oh, Ms. Simmons, well done." Jack clapped his hands.

Nic smiled and took another, larger, sip of her wine.

He leaned in again and took her hand as she set her glass on the table.

"What's your opinion of how we might be together?"

Nic shook her head. "Sorry, Mr. LaTour. I don't work that fast." But she didn't pull her hand back.

"You would like to take it slow."

"Let's get to know each other. You are very charming, and very attractive, and I will confess that I'm not immune to that. But" —she narrowed her eyes— "something tells me you could be dangerous."

"Dangerous?" He didn't look surprised at her word choice.

"Yes," she said firmly.

He smiled. "As you wish, Nicole. We take it slow." He stroked his thumb over her fingers.

She smirked and looked at his thumb. "Somehow, I think you aren't used to taking it slow."

He released her hand and signaled to the waiter. "Oh, I'll be as slow as you want."

Nic wondered if she really wanted him to go that slowly.

Jack paid the bill with a credit card. He shrugged into his jacket, then held her blazer as she slipped her arms into it. He smoothed it over her shoulders, his hands trailing down her arms. Nic was glad her face was turned away so she could bite her lip and stifle a shiver.

He led her out of the bar and into the lobby of the hotel. "How are you getting home?"

"Bus."

"Let me give you a ride."

"I actually could walk from here, but wouldn't in the dark. So yes, if it isn't any bother, I'll take the ride."

Jack held the lobby door open for her and then handed a ticket to the red-jacketed valet. The boy sprinted off down the street. Jack and Nic stood under the awning of the hotel. She shivered slightly in the cool air.

He took her hands, gathered them in his, and warmed them between his palms. He blew a soft heated breath into his hands. Nic drew in a deep breath of her own, feeling the gesture to be surprisingly intimate.

The silver Jeep came to a stop in front of them and the valet jumped out, rounded the vehicle, and swung the passenger door open for her. Jack handed her into the car and as Nic sat in the warm seat and drew her legs up, she saw the long line of her limbs and the shiny silver chains around her ankles.

Wow, these shoes really are that sexy, she thought.

Jack was an assertive driver, taking corners steadily, accelerating from stop lights and coasting to a smooth stop at red lights. It was approximately ten blocks to her building, a distance that was covered far too quickly. Nic didn't shy away from studying his face, the golden glow from the streetlights traveling over it. He was an amazingly handsome man, she concluded. And even more attractive to her after this evening.

He pulled in front of her building, in the loading zone, shut off the engine, and strode around the Jeep to take her hand and help her out. He led her up to the security entrance door.

Nic turned to him and found him standing pleasingly close. "Thank you, Jack. It was a terrific evening. And … intriguing I would say."

"You are intrigued, Nicole?"

"I am."

"Then I have accomplished my goal for tonight." He stroked a lock of her hair over her shoulder. "Or at least my primary goal."

"You have a secondary goal for tonight?"

"Mmmmmm, yes."

He leaned in closer then and Nic closed her eyes and lifted her mouth, meeting his kiss. His hand closed over her shoulder and slid down her arm as his lips met hers.

This was no simple kiss, the touch of lips on lips. *This was a union.* And then she thought of nothing else, only felt every dimension of this kiss. The pressure of his lips. The arousing smell of him. The caress of his hands over her arms. The pull as he brought her closer still and his hands slid around her lower back. Without thought and all on instinct, she felt herself bend into him, using the leverage of his hands to lean back, to bring her hips forward to press against him.

She felt the tingle as her nipples hardened inside of her bra and the sudden warmth of her panties against her sex.

She moaned.

He held her tighter and his tongue slid over the seam of her lips and slipped between before she had a chance to open her mouth. He held her so tight that their bodies melded together at chests, hips, abdomens. He inserted his leg between hers so that she was pressed to his thigh. Each movement was a thrill.

One of his hands caressed her back and then curved over her bottom, squeezing it slightly. And Nic realized that she was moving just barely on his thigh of her own accord, following the lead of his hand.

Shit, it's like I'm in heat.

He must have felt her stiffen because he drew back, breaking the kiss, withdrawing his leg, and pulling back so that his hands gripped her upper arms. They were both breathing hard.

Neither spoke for a long moment. Finally Nic ventured, "Some kiss." She heard the quaver in her voice. She couldn't bring herself to look him in the face.

"Some kiss," he echoed. With one finger, he slowly lifted her chin. "Look at me."

She did look at him then, into his eyes.

"Taking it slow," he said. She caught the glimpse of a smile as he lowered his head again and gave her a soft kiss.

"Thank God," she replied as he released her a long moment later. "I'm not sure I'd survive you any faster."

"Oh, Nicole." He took a few steps away, down the entrance stairs. "Yes, you would."

She hastily tapped in her entry code and caught the door as it clicked open. She turned back to find him at the door of his Jeep.

He was grinning.

"You would, Nicole." He opened the door and just before he got into his car, she heard a laugh. "And you will."

CHAPTER FOUR

"Hi, Jack. The flowers are lovely. And huge. I had to clear off my desk just to find a spot for them. Thank you very much." Nic paused, tapping her pencil on her desk, then continued, "I also enjoyed myself last night. The chat, the wine, the bar. Oh, and those last few minutes. Those were nice, too. Um, I'll talk with you soon."

Nic knew she was smiling from ear to ear as she ended the call. The flowers were indeed lovely, and indeed huge. A beautiful display of unusual flowers. No roses and baby's breath here. All were in bold colors of deep red, purple and green. Some of the flowers Nic couldn't name, but all were cradled in a wide crystal vase, supported by salal leaves.

She had to slide her files, phone, and messages to the far side of the desk to be able to set the vase down. Then she left the message on Jack's voicemail.

"Wow." Steph paused in the doorway to Nic's small office. "Holy wow! That's amazing. What did you have to do to earn that?"

Nic shrugged nonchalantly. "I guess I just charmed him."

"Uh-huh. Charm gets you a dozen roses from FTD. This is custom-made and I bet from one of the local flower artists."

Nic grinned. "Amazing what charm will get you."

"Mm-hm." Steph smirked and continued down the hall.

Nic settled in. Her eyes strayed to the flowers every few minutes. No heavy perfume emanated from the bouquet, for which she was grateful. She perused her e-mails, replied to the easy ones, took some notes on things to accomplish that day, flipped through a few documents that had been dropped on her desk, and then put her chin in her hand, studying the flowers and let her mind drift to last night.

Jack's fingers on the chains around her ankle. Jack's thumb stroking the palm of her hand. The taste of the wine and the background hum of the bar. His face illuminated in the candlelight, the crinkles around his eyes when he smiled, those striking green and gold eyes and the wide mouth. His hands, neither soft nor rough but full of strength and something else she couldn't quite name as they held hers. His grip didn't need to be hard to be felt.

That kiss. Good God, that kiss. Nic shivered and felt the physical response flow through her.

She straightened up in her chair and turned her mind to her work, which went smoothly till around ten o'clock. Her cell phone pinged quietly, indicating a text message.

Huge? You intimidated by size?

Nic gaped at the message, seeing that it was from Jack's cell number. *Oh, he thinks he's funny,* she thought. Before she could think of a reply, her phone pinged again.

TY for the message, btw. I'm in meetings & can't call.

Nic quickly thumbed a message in reply.

YW. Not intimidated. Am impressed.

She had only seconds to wait for the response.

Good. I aim to please.

She replied,

So far so good.

Nic set the phone aside but it pinged again a few minutes later.

Must pay attention here. May I call later?

Yes. Be good. Pay attention.

Hm. You sound like my 5th grade teacher.

Shhhhhh. Or I'll have to confiscate your phone.

The messages from him stopped after that, so Nic punched in a quick-dial number and waited while the phone rang.

"Hello, long-lost bestie. You don't call, you don't text …" Evi answered her phone.

"Yes, I know. I haven't returned your message from last night. I forgot to check my phone before bed." That wasn't true. She had checked her phone and had seen the text from Evi asking about the date, but just hadn't felt like talking about it yet. She had still been drifting on the high from the kiss.

"Oh? Did you have company?"

"No. I was just tired."

"Right. Now do you have a few minutes to tell me aaaaaaallllllll about it?"

"Just a few." Nic sighed. "He was great."

"Uh-oh. I heard the sigh. How great?"

"As in wow great. Fireworks great."

"I checked him out on the internet. He's cute. He's a little older. But you like those."

"Yeah, I guess so." Nic lowered her voice, conscious of the open door. "He's not as old as Lawrence."

"Not by a decade or so, at least. So what was so great?"

"Everything. I met him at the Mayflower Hotel."

"Convenient choice."

"At the bar there. And we talked easily, it wasn't hard, you know? And then he read my fortune and held my foot."

"What?"

Nic laughed. "He admired my shoes and touched my ankle. Then he held my hand and told me about myself."

"Because he knows you so well. What shoes were you wearing?"

"The black leather ones with the chains."

"I should've known. Foot fetish."

"Probably, but I don't care."

"Do you have any idea what men with foot fetishes want you to do with your feet?"

"A vague idea. He had real insight into me when he described what I was like."

"Like what?"

"Like I was intelligent and thoughtful and sensual."

"Uh-huh. He was just flattering you."

"Is it not true?"

"Oh, it's true. What else did he say?"

"That I am dignified and work hard but have a hard time asking for help."

"He's right there, but it might be a lucky guess. Did he tell you that you also have a difficult time returning messages?"

Nic thought of their flurry of texts that morning. "Ah, no."

"See, he doesn't know you so well after all, does he."

"Not yet."

"Hm. I get the feeling he's going to know you much better. But what about Lawrence?"

Nic tapped a pen against the top of the desk and sighed. "I've dated other guys since I've been with Lawrence. He's fine with it. Or at least he's always said that he doesn't want to hold me back from meeting someone else. He's always been clear about that. He dates other women sometimes too."

"I've never understood this part of your relationship with him. You see him almost every weekend and you guys talk on the phone every day. He gives you fantastic and expensive gifts. So why isn't this a boyfriend/girlfriend thing? You aren't just fuck buddies."

"No, we aren't. We haven't ever really defined what we are. We just started dating and found out that we really like to be with each other."

"And fuck each other."

"Yes, and *mmmmmmf* each other." Nic glanced through her door and down the empty hallway.

"Damn, Nic, the man is old enough to be your dad. No wait, Lawrence is old enough to be your grandfather," Evi said, before continuing with the obvious question. "Is the sex really that good?"

"Fantastic, Evi. Really. Lawrence is amazing. He does things to me that guys my age have never done."

"You'll have to tell me sometime what these 'things' are. Or better yet, tell Saul."

Nic laughed at the idea of giving some of Lawrence's incredible cunnilingus tricks to Evi's boyfriend. "Anyway, Lawrence knows that sometimes I date other guys. He really is okay with that, but doesn't ask for details."

"Do you think it would bother him that some guy is fondling your ankles under the table?"

"That would be one of those details I wouldn't mention."

"What happens when you fall in love with someone else?"

Nic hesitated then. She hadn't really thought about falling in love with someone else in the last few years. She didn't want to fall in love with anyone at all. Not anymore. Not after Tom.

She didn't often think of Tom these days. That was way behind her, back in the college years. She knew how love turned out. Disappointment all around, for everyone.

Everything felt so right when she was with Lawrence, but she didn't try to imagine a future with him. Nothing permanent.

"I suppose if I ever fell in love with someone else, I would let Lawrence know when it got to that point." Nic tapped her pencil again. "I respect him. I do. I would never want to hurt him, but we just enjoy each other without putting all kinds of rules into the equation. Don't you think that's okay in this situation?"

"I'm just curious, Nic. 'Cause I think you might have a conflict in your near future if you start seeing this guy Jack. Especially if it goes beyond the kiss and tit squeeze that you've gotten from most other guys in the last two years."

Nic sensed that her friend might be right.

"Which, by the way, you haven't said if you got a kiss from Jack. And/or a tit squeeze."

"Um, yes. A kiss." Nic thought again of the kiss, of the feel of Jack's arm tight against her lower back, of the pressure of his mouth on hers, leaning into his arm as his body aligned with hers, the sudden invasion of his tongue past her lips, the way she felt she was melting into him, that he was absorbing her almost. "An amazing kiss. It started off like normal, you know? But then ..." she trailed off.

"Then?"

"Then his kiss became … well … hot. Maybe 'urgent' is a better word. I didn't mind at all. In fact, I completely caved in. With some other guy I might have felt like pulling back or getting him to back off a little. But this kiss … wow, Evi. I felt it all through me."

"Commanding."

"What?"

"He sounds commanding. You know, in charge."

Nic thought about that word, about what being in charge might mean. She thought of the way he had held her hands at the table and how she hadn't been able to think of the right word to describe it besides *strength*.

"Commanding. Yeah, that's a good word."

"Watch it, Nic. Commanding men always want to be in charge."

"You know me. You know that I don't put up with that shit."

"Not yet. Hey look, I gotta go. It is a work day, you know."

Nic glanced at her watch. "Oh, right! I've got a lot to do, including a meeting this afternoon. I gotta go too. Call you tonight?"

"Yeah. See ya, chica."

Nic was able to settle into work after her chat with Evi and was prepared for the afternoon meeting with Frances and Steph and the few other members of Frances's staff. Frances closely followed her agenda, hitting each point and discussing each issue in turn. She marked off each completed item with a flourish of her purple pen.

When it was Nic's turn to present her information, she had everything at the ready. She had collected some information on successful internships for high school students and came up with ten essentials. She then reviewed the synopsis of her findings. Frances asked a few questions, then asked for an outline of a proposed internship program.

After the meeting, Nic dropped her materials on her desk and then reached for the phone to check the voicemails. Just as she lifted the receiver, Frances stepped into her office.

"Gorgeous," she said, as she fingered one of the round green leaves. "Absolutely gorgeous. I think you lucked out with Lawrence."

Nic hesitated. "It wasn't Lawrence."

France's left eyebrow lifted into a high arch. "Really. My word, Nic, aren't you the popular girl."

Nic wondered if her tone was teasing or more pointed. "It's just a gesture, I think."

"A gesture." Frances continued to rub the leaf between her thumb and finger.

"Yes, a thank you, just for an evening out."

Frances leaned down slightly and looked at the florist's name on the invoice. "*Green Designs*. I know them. Very expensive." She smiled at Nic, her eyes slightly narrowed. "Would you be able to get that outline on the internship program on my desk the day after tomorrow?"

"Oh yes. I'm very interested in getting that started." Nic just about had the outline in her head already.

Frances finally let go of the leaf and turned to the door before tapping a nail against the doorframe. She looked at Nic over her shoulder.

"Were these from Jack LaTour?"

Nic knew that was really none of Frances's business and she shouldn't be asking about the flowers, but she had chatted with Frances about her love life before and didn't want to look as if she was hiding anything.

"Yes, they are. We had a drink and dinner last night."

There was the eyebrow again. "I wouldn't have imagined that you and Jack were suited."

Nic shrugged. "Maybe we aren't. It was just a casual thing."

"Oh, Nic, these" —Frances gestured to the flowers— "these are not casual. Jack is telling you he is interested."

Nic felt a warmth at that comment. "You know him, don't you?"

"Yes, I do. Quite well. And no" —she shook her head— "we never dated. He isn't my type."

"Is there anything I should know about him?"

"There is a lot you should know about him, but they are things he should tell you himself. But you, Nic," Frances tilted her head, "you intrigue me."

"Me?" Nic was surprised. "But you've known me for over a year now."

"I thought I did. I think I may have missed something. Something Jack saw in you the moment he met you. Interesting. And Lawrence? What does he think of this?" Frances waved her hand at the flowers.

"He doesn't know. Yet. But I'll tell him. We have an … uh … understanding relationship."

Frances laughed quietly. "You might see just how far Lawrence's tolerance extends."

Frances left. And Nic wondered what the last five minutes had been about.

CHAPTER FIVE

Nic took a taxi over to Lawrence's house the next night, after packing a bag. The little yellow car, a Toyota electric hybrid as were many of Seattle's taxis, whisked her over the bridge, the streetlights zipping through the windshield and racing over her again and again. She shivered a little and pulled her enormous shawl around her.

Lawrence had given the shawl to her for her birthday the past summer. At the time, she thought it beautiful, but she couldn't appreciate the warmth it would bring to her during the chilly winter months. The shawl was soft and furry and a beautiful shade of blue-green. She brought it to her cheek, and thought of purring as she rubbed against it.

The taxi turned off the road and stopped at the double-iron gate. There was a slight pause and then the gates swung slowly inward. The car coasted past the gates and up the long cobbled drive to the brightly lit two-story home. The multitude of windows gave the house an airy feel. Nic could see straight through the home from the front windows to the lights of boats bobbing on Lake Washington on the other side.

The door opened just as the taxi pulled to a stop. Lawrence strode across the shallow porch and down the few steps. Nic opened the door to the taxi and Lawrence pulled her to him, his arm around her shoulders, his kiss planted on her cheek. She smiled and dropped the weekend bag from her shoulder to wrap both of her arms around his neck.

"Hi there," she whispered.

"Hi you," he murmured back, his eyes crinkling as he smiled at her. "Come on." Lawrence pulled her along with him, scooping up her overnight bag as he turned and entered the house. "What did you bring? This thing weighs a ton!"

"I never know what to bring for a weekend with you. Sometimes we stay here. Sometimes we go out."

"You can keep a spare change of clothes here. I've plenty of closet space."

Nic answered his grin with one of her own. "Maybe."

"Oh? Maybe? Of course you can, but don't plan on moving any furniture yet. Now then." Lawrence turned and smoothed his hands over her hair, then cradled her face in his palms. "How about you go get into something comfortable and then come meet me at the Jacuzzi. You look to me like a woman who could use some pampering."

"Mmm, perfect. Yes, I could."

Nic dashed up the winding staircase and headed for Lawrence's suite of rooms just to the left. She crossed the small sitting room, opened the door to the bedroom, and tossed her bag on the chair by the window. She quickly changed into the white robe Lawrence provided for her. Barefoot, she returned down the stairs, wrapping her hair into a knot on the top of her head. She made her way through the house, past the kitchen where she could see the cook, Sasha, busy with some culinary task.

They exchanged greetings as Nic continued out the back door to the swirling Jacuzzi. Lawrence was already seated in the hot water, his arms stretched along the tiled edge.

Nic glanced over her shoulder. Not seeing anyone, she dropped her robe to the ground and stepped into the steaming water. Lawrence lifted his hands to her, settling them on her waist as she drew close, then turned her around and pulled her back to sit between his legs. His fingers pressed into her shoulders, massaging her.

Nic dropped her head a little, inhaling the steam, and closed her eyes. Relaxing.

"How was your week?" Lawrence asked.

"It's ending nicely."

Lawrence laughed softly and massaged her back with his strong fingers for several more minutes, before his touch drifted over her shoulders to cup her breasts.

Nic leaned back against his shoulder and stroked his thighs beneath the warm bubbling water. She could just glimpse a few shivering stars through the trees. Her breath curled in the air before her, weaving with the steam of the hot tub.

She shuddered with a loud gasp as Lawrence tweaked one of her nipples. Immediately, she felt a heat flood throughout her, radiating to her face and hips.

Lawrence nuzzled her ear. "Your breasts are incredible. The perfect size for my hands," he whispered, "Pinching your nipple is like pushing your on button."

"No joke! Mm, what that does to me."

"Want to know what it does to me?"

Nic squirmed her hips back, feeling his erection, hard and thick, nestled between her buttocks. "What do I win if I can guess?"

"I think tonight we both win."

Nic stood and turned to face him. She looked into his blue eyes. Every line around them was dear to her as a mark of his experience and his hard-won life. His hair brushed over his forehead in a way that might be considered boyish if it wasn't for the silver tint. "That sounds very fine indeed," she said, then leaned in further and pressed her lips to his. His hands cupped her breasts again, gently massaging them. She moaned and kissed him firmly, the tip of her tongue touching the seam of his lips.

They parted their lips slightly and their tongues met at the juncture. She moaned again.

Then she began to slide down, breaking the kiss, her breasts falling from his hands, until she was kneeling and the hot water bubbled around her chin. She smiled slowly at him, giving Lawrence her best seductive grin, feeling wicked. Taking a deep breath, she slid beneath the water. Nic kept her eyes closed and used her hands to find his erection. She closed her lips over the tip, then slid half the length of his cock into her mouth and began to bob up and down. She kept her lips tightly closed to avoid taking in any water. After just a few motions, she felt Lawrence's hand in her hair, tugging her upward.

She broke the surface of the water with a gasp and wiped water from her eyes.

"You crazy lady, you'll drown down there."

Nic laughed. "Please. I do know to come up for air." She reached for his cock with both hands and stroked him, one hand over the other. "Please? I want to."

It was one of the biggest turn-ons for her, in a way that fellatio had never been with any of her other lovers. She felt as if she was making love to his cock and he was so grateful for her attentions, encouraging her to try different movements and techniques. Now, Nic anticipated with great eagerness the opportunity to take him, either to orgasm or as foreplay. If he came in her mouth, she would be thrilled.

Lawrence frowned. "You kinky girl. I'm not going to let you drown just so you can get your greedy little mouth on my cock." He took her by the wrists and removed her hands from him, then shifted over so he was sitting on the shallow top step. He leaned back on his elbows along the tile and lifted his hips slightly. "Come here, Nic."

She looked at his cock, hard, water dripping down it, a throbbing vein twining up it and a glistening bead of pre-cum balanced on the tip. Nic licked her lips and drifted through the water to him. She knelt again, the hot water swirling around her neck. She took his cock in her hand and brought her lips so they were just hovering over the tip. Then she delicately licked the drop of cream, closed her eyes, and savored the delicious taste of him.

"God, girl." She looked up to see Lawrence looking at her with something like wonder, shaking his head slowly from side to side. "I have never seen such a sensual creature as you."

Nic had never felt so sensual as when she brought her lips to his cock again and slid him as far into her mouth as she could. The tip of his cock tapped the back of her throat. She held him there and moaned. She heard Lawrence's gasp and the involuntary jerk of his hips upward pressed his cock slightly into her throat.

Nic pulled back. Lawrence stroked her hair and whispered "Sorry." She returned to work, using her tongue and lips, saliva and mouth, all of her concentration and devotion, to please him. She felt the heat rising within her, her heart thudding and her pussy throbbing.

She moaned and sucked and bathed his cock, massaged it with her tongue. Lawrence continued to stroke her hair. His breathing sounded harsh.

Suddenly he cupped her face in his hands and pulled her gently up. His cock left her mouth and she mewed with disappointment.

"I need to be in you," he said urgently. He reached for a cushion from the lounge chair nearby, placed it on the tiled rim of the hot tub, and pulled her to it. "Here. Now. From behind."

Nic eagerly knelt on the bench below the water and lowered her upper body on the cushion. She gripped the cushion with both hands as she felt Lawrence move behind her. Then he pushed firmly into her. She gasped at the penetrating sensation. He pulled back slightly and pushed in further.

"Oh, God, Nic." He began to rhythmically thrust into her and Nic groaned as she felt his entire length buried in her body, stroking all of her sensitive spots.

Her moans became louder as he picked up the pace. His hands gripped her hips and his balls began to slap against her clit with each thrust, so deeply was he embedded inside her. Nic cried out, digging her nails into the cushion beneath her. With a few more strokes, she exploded, sparks bursting and showering throughout her entire body. She trembled all over, grinding back against him.

Lawrence thrust again, another time, his fingers digging into her hips. He pounded into her one last time and held, with one final push. He gave a hoarse shout and she felt his cock pulsing inside of her. At the feel of his hot fluid flowing into her, Nic cried out loudly and a shudder of pleasure went through her. Her cries softened and turned to whimpers as Lawrence leaned against her, panting.

Finally, he slowly pulled out of her. Nic stayed where she was, resting on the lounge cushion. She took in deep lungfuls of the cold night air. Her body felt heated and tingly.

Lawrence ran his hands down her back and over her ass. "My beauty. You are one sexy bewitching woman. Look at you, bent over and having just been fucked by me. You make me feel like a king."

Nic looked over her shoulder at him and smiled. "You are a king."

Lawrence laughed. "King of the Jacuzzi, in any case. Come, let's get you inside."

After they dried off, Nic wrapped herself in her robe again while Lawrence tied his towel around his waist. Shivering, they made a dash for the house, bursting into the back hallway and almost running into Sasha.

"Oh!" Nic held her robe tight around her waist.

Sasha smiled and continued into the kitchen.

"I just can't get used to that," Nic whispered to Lawrence as they made their way up the back stairway.

"Used to having other people around? I know. It took me a while too. But you do. Having people to help makes life much easier."

Nic looked back over her shoulder. "But she knows we're naked!"

Lawrence looked her up and down in mock astonishment. "You are?"

"She knows we were just doing it out in the hot tub," Nic hissed in an exasperated whisper.

"Yes. She does. Get used to it," Lawrence hissed back.

When they reached Lawrence's bedroom, he went into the attached bathroom to start a hot shower. Nic, still shivering slightly from the nighttime chill, pulled her phone out of her bag and checked for messages. She saw that she had a voicemail and called in.

"Hi there, Nicole. Jack here. I was hoping I could ask you out again. An art gallery opening next Thursday. I would like to take you with me. It would be the perfect place to showcase those incredibly sexy heels of yours. You know the ones. We could have a few glasses of wine and talk about art and all the subliminal messages we might see in the pieces on display. How does that sound? Call me. I hope you are having a wonderful weekend."

The recording ended and Nic listened to the echo in her ear of that voice. So preoccupied was she with the thought of Jack's voice that she didn't hear Lawrence come up behind her.

"You aren't working, I hope," he said as his hands came around her waist and untied the belt of her robe.

Nic turned her phone off. "Oh! No. Just a message from an old friend."

Now why had she lied? she thought immediately. She didn't owe Lawrence any explanation at all.

The robe had already left her shoulders and was sliding down her arms.

"You have goose bumps." Lawrence kissed her pebbled skin. "Let's get you in the shower. And then bed."

Later that night, as Lawrence made gentle love to her in the bed, cupping her face in his hands as he came inside of her, she wondered again.

What did she owe him?

CHAPTER SIX

Nic glanced at Jack repeatedly from the corner of her eye as he drove them to Pioneer Square. He was dressed in casual pants with an open-collar shirt and leather jacket, and completely owned the look, at least in Nic's opinion. She ran her hands over her lap, smoothing her short black leather skirt. She wore a loose silvery tunic over a black Lycra body suit. As she shifted in her seat, she felt the thong of the body suit pull up tightly between her legs. She had picked this outfit specifically to coordinate with her black high heels with the silver chains.

She had worn the heels because Jack had requested them. Again.

"You have beautiful legs, Nicole," he said and she looked up at him, catching his eyes on her legs.

"Thank you and watch the road, please." She pointed ahead.

Jack laughed softly and turned his eyes back to the street unfolding before them. It had rained that day and the pavement glistened. While the wipers had cleared the front windshield, beads of water raced over the side windows.

"How's your parking karma?" Jack asked, peering through the windshield. His eyes scanned the street for empty spots.

"Parking karma?"

"Yeah, do you have good luck finding available parking spots?"

"Oh. No, not by a long shot. I rarely drive."

"Really?"

"Yes, really. I don't even have a car at the moment." Nic smiled.

"How do you get around?"

"I take the bus or I, uh, get a ride, um, from a taxi. But mostly I take the bus. It's easy to do in the downtown area. My work is downtown and most of my friends live within blocks. Don't you usually have good parking karma?"

"No, actually. I have lousy parking karma. I almost always end up paying too much for one of the parking garages."

"You had good parking karma last Monday."

He glanced at her from the side of his eye. "Last Monday?"

"At the meeting."

"Ah, that's right. I got a spot right by the door. Hey" —he turned to look at her fully— "were you watching me?"

"I might have found myself standing next to the window when a certain Jeep pulled in." Nic smirked.

"Yes, I had good parking karma that day, didn't I. It must have been fate. However, tonight, not so much."

Jack circled a couple of blocks twice and then gave up, heading into the "Sinking Ship" parking garage, so called for its slanted, triangular shape, and slid into a stall.

Nic put her hand on the door handle when she felt Jack's hand on her arm.

"There will be people at this opening party that I know. Also, there will be people I'm supposed to know. I can forget names pretty easily. If I seem to hesitate with an introduction, would you mind jumping in and introducing yourself?"

Nic laughed. "No problem. I doubt I'll know anyone at this party, so we don't need to worry about my introductions."

"Your friends aren't into art?"

"My friends aren't into buying original art." She smiled. "So they tend not to get invited to these types of parties."

She thought of Lawrence, who did buy art on occasion, but wasn't thc typc to go to gallery openings.

"Ah, okay then. Have you ever been to a gallery opening?"

"No, I haven't. Do they get pretty wild?"

Jack laughed. "Not anymore."

"They used to be?"

"Yes."

Nic noted that he didn't explain further. "Shall we?"

"Yes, Nicole. We shall."

They walked the few blocks to the gallery, making small talk and Nic realized that she felt unusually relaxed when talking with this man, only on their second date and already able to talk easily about nothing in particular.

The gallery was lit up. The wet sidewalk reflected the lights. Inside, Jack took her hand, placing it in the crook of his elbow. "Come," he said. She was struck by such an old-fashioned but gentlemanly gesture and curled her fingers around his arm. The leather of his jacket felt smooth and slightly damp. His arm felt hard beneath it.

A moment later, she was handed a glass of white wine. A sip told her it was very dry and very light and perfectly matched the austere wood floors and creamy walls of the gallery.

"So," Nic said, leaning in toward Jack, "as a novice to this whole gallery thing, I'm not sure what we are supposed to do. It looks to me like everyone is just socializing."

"Well, supposedly we are to admire the art, compliment the artist, then spend thousands, perhaps tens of thousands, on his masterpieces. So how about we take a look at the artwork?"

Jack turned toward the wall to their left but was immediately approached by a tall woman in a long red dress.

"Jack!" The woman leaned in and kissed Jack right on the mouth. Nic was shocked at how intimate the kiss was. No one had ever kissed her in a social situation like that. She waited for Jack to pull back or do something to show his surprise.

Instead, she watched as Jack comfortably returned the kiss, a few seconds too long to be called a peck. Nic raised her eyebrows.

"Sylvia," Jack returned the greeting, smiling as his lips finally left the garishly-painted—in Nic's opinion—lips of this woman.

"Darling, you've brought another one of your winsome little lasses!" The woman turned to Nic and laid a hand on her shoulder, eyeing her up and down. "She's lovely, just lovely."

Jack made a move, as if to introduce them, but Nic held out her hand, grabbing the woman's hand and giving it a firm shake. "Hi. I'm Nicole Simmons, with the Tyff Foundation."

"Oh! Really? I'm so pleased to meet you. How is Cedric?"

Nic's bravado withered as she realized that the woman was referring to Cedric Tyff, the founder and CEO of the Tyff Corporation and Board President of his company's foundation. A man she had met in person just once.

"Oh, Cedric? He's doing well. Thanks for asking."

"You tell him that Sylvia said hello, would you?"

"Of course."

"Yes, Nicole. This is Sylvia Diaz. Owner of the gallery."

Nic pasted on a smile, and told herself to relax and not feel so offended that this woman would plant such a kiss on her date. “I’m looking forward to viewing the works.”

“Well, naturally! We are so fortunate to have such a talented artist featured here tonight. You must let me introducc you.” Sylvia inclined her head toward Nic and her voice lowered to a loud whisper. “He’s Native American.”

“Right.” Nic glanced at Jack, a slight smile curving the corner of her lips.

“Come, come.” Sylvia beckoned to them and moved off into the crowd, expecting them to follow. Which, with Jack’s hand on the small of Nic’s back urging her forward, they did.

The crowd parted for Sylvia, as almost every person turned to smile or greet her. Nic noted with amazement and not a little admiration that the woman’s back was well-dcfincd, muscular and trim, and very much on display in the backless and almost bottomless dress that she wore. The opening dipped down to display a third of her upper buttocks. Nic could look directly down into the crack of her ass.

Nic herself had never worn, or even tried on, a dress as revealing as this. It was undeniably sexy. Sylvia must have been in her late thirties, perhaps forties. She certainly exercised and took good care of herself. Nic wondered how her own back would compare to the one leading her through the gallery. She wondered when was the last time that she had even looked at her own back.

Sylvia turned finally as she reached a stocky older man. His long hair was steely gray and gathered in a braid. His eyes were already turned on her. Nic caught her breath at the intensity of the gaze, her own eyes dropping before it. Her lowered sight took in Sylvia’s obviously hardened nipples in her clingy red dress. No bra. Nic decided she hated this woman. And she was very much okay with that.

"Jack and … Nicole. That was it, wasn't it? This is Rudy Roanhorse. He is the remarkably talented man who created these pieces."

Rudy and Jack shook hands and then Rudy turned to Nic, taking her hand in both of his. She wondered for a moment if he meant to kiss it. Instead he just held it between his own warm hands, massaging it, his palms pressed to her skin. Nic licked her lips and looked him in the eyes. His gaze was just as intense as she had thought. She had to fight the urge to look away again.

"Hello, Nicole. Such a lovely lady. How do you find yourself here tonight?"

"How do I find myself here?" Nic wasn't sure what he meant.

"Have you come of your own volition? Hm, no. I think you are a guest. You are not familiar with my work, are you?"

Her hand felt overly warm in his grip and she shifted her feet. She felt one of his fingers press along the middle of her palm, stroking it.

She pulled her hand away and wiped her palm on her skirt.

"No, I'm sorry. I'm not familiar with your work. In fact, we've just come in, Jack and I, and haven't yet had a chance at all to look at anything." Nic took a sip of her wine, the glass clinking against one tooth. A little wine sloshed over the rim of the glass, trickling down her wrist. If she had been by herself, she would have licked the trickle from her skin, but couldn't do anything about it here.

"Hm, I so rarely encounter anyone who truly has not yet been touched by my art. Please, Nicole. Let me be the first to touch you."

Nic looked at Jack, floundering for words. "Well, um, I guess." Jack just grinned at her and took her glass from her hand. Nic tried to give him a desperate look, asking for some kind of rescue, but Jack just grinned more, his amusement at her predicament all too obvious.

She gave him a mock glare.

"Hm, close your eyes." Rudy moved behind her, his hands coming to rest on her shoulders.

"Really?"

"Yes."

Nic's eyes fluttered closed. She lifted her hands, one hand touching Rudy's on her shoulder, the other not knowing what to touch, just raised and pressing against the air before her.

"A few steps straight ahead. I'll guide you," Rudy said. "Trust me," he whispered in her ear.

Nic giggled, high-pitched and trilling. "I don't even know you."

Rudy's hands propelled her forward.

"You will know me as much as you've ever known anyone in your life. You are about to meet my inner thoughts. The true me. The naked me."

She hoped not.

"When I tell you, open your eyes." Rudy's hands slipped from her shoulders and settled on her hips. Nic was feeling distinctly uncomfortable and wondered if all artists were this touchy-feely. She realized that the din of the party had muted somewhat. Rudy must have pushed her to a quieter area. How alone were they?

"Open your eyes, Nicole."

She opened her eyes and found herself face to face with a penis.

It's a portrait of a dick, Nic thought and had a fleeting fear that she might have said it out loud.

"It's a portrait of a dick," Rudy said. "A self-portrait, actually."

Nic swallowed. She tried to speak, but had no words. Finally, she exhaled with a "wow."

"Yes, I'm rather proud of it. See the flare? And the texture here. That is a rarity."

Nic's eyes swept over the painting. It was a swirl of colors, mainly reds and oranges. She wondered over his words. Was he describing the painting technique or his actual appendage? There was nothing else in the painting to compare the size of the object to, but the portrayal was impressive.

"It's … wow … really amazing." Nic gathered her thoughts. "You have an immense talent."

Rudy still stood behind her, his hands on her hips. Nic wondered where Jack was.

The man behind her leaned in closer, his lips tickling her ear. "I can guarantee you a private peek."

Nic knew her mouth had fallen open. When he came close, the obvious inspiration for his masterpiece was pressed firmly against her backside. She finally broke out of her shock and whirled around.

Just in time to see a large hand descend on Rudy's shoulder and pull him back.

Jack pressed his hand to Rudy's chest and pushed him firmly back, his eyes darting between her and the artist, a stiff smile on his face.

"Everything okay here?" Jack's voice sounded a little tight.

"Everything is fine now," Nic said, not missing the breathiness in her voice. She smoothed her hands over her skirt. Jack's eyes narrowed and she decided that he needed a little more reassurance. She put her hand on his arm, the flexed bicep holding Rudy away. "Really. Fine. Shall we walk around?"

Nic curled her hand around Jack's arm and took a step away. She looked at Rudy and gestured to the large painting.

"The painting. It's … nice. Really. You must take great pride in your" —she faltered as she gestured at the painting, once again confronted with the lurid image—"work."

They crossed the room, Nic's hand still tucked into Jack's arm. She leaned in toward him and whispered, "Thank you."

His jaw was still clenched. She felt the flex of his arm under her fingers. "He was pushed up against you. That hardly seemed appropriate."

"It wasn't. Neither was his painting, in my opinion. Hey, I could use a replacement one of those." She pointed to a waiter with a tray of wine. Jack scooped up two glasses and handed one to her. He clicked his glass to hers in salute and then took a deep drink. Nic took a grateful sip of her own.

"I take it you aren't going to become a fan of Rudy Roanhorse's?" he asked.

"I don't want a picture of his penis in my home, if that's what you mean."

"Good. This crap is garish anyway. Let's take a look around, say our goodbyes, and then I'll take you out for a real drink just down the block."

"A real drink? I better pace myself. I think I need my wits around me, considering the company you keep." Nic grinned at him.

"I would protest. On the other hand, Nicole, you are more right than you know."

"Oh really?"

He smirked and led her to another work of art, if it could be called that. Many of the paintings featured male body parts—shoulders, chests, chins, legs—that Nic assumed where Rudy's images of himself. They moved from one piece to another, sipping their wine and glancing at each other, smiling. When they reached what seemed to be a red-hued stark landscape, Jack paused.

"This one looks innocent enough."

Nic leaned close, peering at the painting.

"What are you searching for?" he asked, also leaning close, his arm against hers.

"I just don't think he's abandoned his self-infatuation." Her eyes examined every corner of the painting. "A-ha!" She pointed to the figure of a naked man entwined in the bare limbs of a dead bush.

"Well, well, well. I am impressed." Jack straightened up and grinned at her.

Nic grinned back, pleased with her find.

She watched Jack's eyes shift from her to someone over her right shoulder. She looked behind her to see the most beautiful woman she had ever laid eyes on approaching them with a smile on her full lips.

"Hello, Jack." The woman almost seemed to sigh the name, so gently did it drift from her mouth. She stood next to Nic, her hands clasped in front of her, her head slightly lowered.

"Erica." Jack nodded. "Nicole, this is Erica."

Nic noticed that he didn't explain the relationship. She took that to mean that she was meeting one of Jack's former lovers. For all she knew, perhaps current lover.

"Hi, Erica."

Erica turned soft brown eyes to her. "Nicole. Nice to meet you." She held out her hand and Nic shook it. There was no strength in the woman's hand. "Have you been viewing the art?"

Nic smiled and shot a glance at Jack. "Yes, I have. I feel a real intimacy in it. Don't you think?"

"Oh yes. Intimate. Provocative. Erotic."

"Are you in the market for this type of work?"

Erica smiled, her soft-pink lips curving perfectly. "I'm afraid not. My indulgences are less expensive."

Jack cleared his throat and slid his arm around Nic's waist. Nic watched Erica's eyes lower to the hand curved around Nic's side.

Definitely an ex-lover, and fairly recent to judge from the jealousy evident in the other woman's face. Nic leaned into Jack. She didn't really want to provoke the woman, but she had to admit that she liked showing which of them had the upper hand. At least for that night.

"Erica." Jack spoke softly. "Nicole and I are going to walk around some more. It's been nice seeing you here tonight. I hope you enjoy yourself."

The woman's eyes dropped to the floor. "Yes. Thank you."

As Jack led her away, Nic glanced back over her shoulder. Erica still stood there, with her hands clasped and her head bowed.

"Jack, is she okay?"

"She's fine," Jack muttered and then blew out a breath. "I'm ready to leave, if you are. Shall we say goodbye to Sylvia?"

Nic tilted her head to look Jack in the face. "Is everything all right?"

"Fine. I'm fine. Erica's fine." He did look back then, checking on the woman they had just walked away from. Nic felt a twinge of concern. There was something off, something strange, about this relationship between Jack and Erica. The woman was needy, not yet disconnected from Jack. Nic could sense that in the vulnerability the woman had displayed before him.

So strange. Nic knew that when a woman was forced to face an ex, she was more likely to display independence and bravado. Not wilt like a cut flower. She knew she had felt like that. Once. The forced smile, the lifted chin, the pleasant greeting. Shaking the other woman's hand and pretending that nothing was wrong.

That was the way a woman did it.

But this?

This was a recent breakup, maybe?

Jack took her hand and she realized he was looking carefully at her face, smiling. "A quick stroll through the room. We avoid the great artist and the adoring fans of his penis and the other riff-raff around here. Then we slip out and go for a drink at a little spot I know. What say you?"

"I say that sounds great. How quick of a stroller are you?" Nic returned his smile.

He jerked her arm playfully and they were off, walking as quickly as possible through the crowd. They skirted the room. The rest of the artwork was along the same lines, but perhaps more impressionistic. Garish color, phallic symbolism, and inelegant eroticism.

"Any final thoughts?" Jack asked as they reached the door.

Nic thought for a moment. "I think Rudy is caught idealizing his masculinity, summarizing it in these stark symbols."

"Wow." Jack raised his eyebrows and nodded. A smile hinted in the curve of his lips. "That's deep."

Nic shrugged and grinned. "I did take an art appreciation class once."

"It shows." He craned his head and caught Sylvia's eye not far away. "Let me just say goodbye to Sylvia and then we'll go."

He quickly stepped toward the woman in red, leaving Nic uncertain whether to follow. She stayed where she was, looking around and glancing at Jack every few seconds. Jack put his hand on Sylvia's shoulder, leaning in to mutter in her ear. Sylvia looked around and nodded.

Jack returned to Nic and gave a wave to Sylvia as they headed for the door. A few people who obviously knew Jack smiled and said hello, but Jack didn't stop. He took Nic's hand in his and pulled her along behind him. Nic just had time to set her wine glass on a waiter's tray before they were on the sidewalk.

The rain had started up again, a steady drizzle. Jack assured her that their destination was just two blocks away. They walked with no conversation, heads tucked against the flick of rain drops.

A few moments later, they were seated at a corner table, lit by the tremulous flame of a nautical style oil lamp. Jack asked her what she might like and then ordered a Mac & Jack's beer for each of them.

After the bartender returned with the two glasses, Nic and Jack leaned in toward each other. Their conversation was quiet.

"Well, that was an enlightening event," Nic started.

Jack laughed. "Enlightening? If you say so."

Nic laughed too. Jack took her hand on top of the table, pulling it up and surprising her by kissing the back of her knuckles. In all of her many dates, she had never had a man kiss her hand like that.

"Why, kind sir. How chivalrous you are," she teased.

"Indeed. I'm trying to impress you."

"Really. Why is that?"

"To convince you of my gallantry. My considerate nature. However," he grimaced comically, "I doubt that after that showing you will be much impressed with my artistic sentiments."

"Oh, I don't know about that. One penis painting does not convey all of your artistic sentiments, does it? If it does, I might have to rethink my choice in dates."

"Believe me, I had no idea about the nature of the gallery show until I saw that painting. I also had no idea about the nature of the artist until I saw his hands on you." He turned serious. "I'm sorry about that."

Nic waved a hand at him. "Don't be. It wasn't your fault. I've dealt with men like him before."

"But it is my fault that you were there in the first place. I thought he was just going to be a harmless pest."

She leaned toward him and put her hand on top of his. "I was the one who agreed to walk off with him. Please, forget about it."

He nodded.

"Besides, I rather enjoyed myself tonight. Rudy was definitely entertaining," she said.

Jack ran his fingers over her wrist. "Your hand was almost doused in wine earlier, wasn't it?"

"You saw my spill?"

"I saw the most graceful trickle of white wine dance down your thumb."

"I was tempted to lick it."

He raised his eyes to her. "So was I."

Jack seemed about to continue and Nic wanted to hear what he would say. Instead, a buzz came from Jack's coat pocket and he grimaced. He glanced at the screen of his phone and frowned.

"I'm sorry, Nicole. I need to make a phone call. I'll be right back." Jack got up and walked out of the bar to the sidewalk.

Man wants his privacy, I guess, Nic thought. She played with her beer glass and looked over her shoulder once or twice to check on Jack. She could see him through the big front window, talking animatedly on his phone, pacing up and down in front of the bar. She was just starting to get uncomfortably impatient when Jack strode back to their table.

"I've got to go," he said as he shrugged into his jacket. "Emergency."

"Oh no!" Nic got to her feet and grabbed her purse. "I hope it isn't too bad."

"Bad enough. Come on, I'll take you home."

"Please, I can get a cab. You need to take care of your emergency."

Jack hesitated, frowning.

"I've taken a cab before, you know."

He nodded. “Okay, but I’m paying for it.”

“Don’t be silly.”

“Don’t argue the issue just now. If you insist, you can make it up to me another time.”

Nic swallowed her arguments and sat back down as Jack approached the bartender. She knew that a cab was being called for her.

Jack had left his phone on the table and the screen was still brightly lit. Nic saw that when he hung up the phone call, the screen had returned to the text screen. She was looking at it upside down but still saw a few words. She quickly turned her head away.

Jack returned and took her by the shoulders, leaning down slightly to look her in the eye.

“I’m sorry, Nicole. I don’t want to leave you. I’ll call you and if you are willing, we’ll continue this date another time.” It was almost a question, so she nodded.

He leaned in closer and kissed her lightly on the corner of her mouth. His arm came around her shoulder and held her more tightly. “I wanted so much more tonight,” he whispered and then let her go.

He smiled at her, picked up his phone, then turned, disappearing out into the rain-flecked gloom.

Nic sat back down and rested her head on her hand. She hadn’t kissed him back. She hadn’t returned his hug. And she wasn’t sure there would be another date.

She really had tried to turn her head in time to not read the text, but she caught the name at the top of the screen. Sylvia. She of the slinky red dress and barely covered ass. Of the intimate kiss and the “winsome lass” comment. But the text was about someone else.

Come quick. Erica in a state. Needs you. She’s gone deep.

That other "winsome lass." The one with the soft brown eyes and full lips and quiet longing. Jack had gone to her.

CHAPTER SEVEN

"She's a dog."

"Hardly," Nic said.

"She's a whore."

"I have no idea."

"She smells like Grandma's panties."

"I doubt that. She probably smells like jasmine or something."

"Okay, so she's hot and sweet and Jack's ex-something. So what? She's still an ex, isn't she?" Evi lifted her eyebrows as she asked the question.

Nic didn't reply, just tore the corner off her paper napkin.

"You mean she might not be an ex?" Evi pulled off one of the other corners.

They were seated on high stools along a window counter, not eating their sandwiches and not sipping their lattes.

Nic shrugged at her friend's question. "No, I think she is an ex. Jack made the situation clear when he put his arm around me while we were talking with her. But it was something about her. She didn't act like an ex. She wasn't pissy or smarmy or regretful or any of those other things I would expect. She seemed, I don't know, desperate, maybe."

"Ugh. You don't want to acquire a boyfriend with a pre-made stalker in tow."

"Definitely not."

"Well, fuck him then. Adios, Jack-o."

Nic tore the third corner off her napkin. Evi unwrapped her sesame tofu club sandwich and bit in. As she chewed, she grabbed the napkin away from Nic and crumpled it in her hand.

Evi swallowed. “Right, okay. I knew it wouldn’t be that easy. He must be some kind of damn good kisser.”

“You know it’s not just that. I have this real attraction to him.”

“Sex. You’ve already got sex—good sex, so you tell me—with Lawrence.”

“Awesome.”

Evi leaned in close. “What makes him so awesome? The dude is in his fifties. Is he, like, hung or something ?”

Nic rolled her eyes. “Please. No. I mean he has a very impressive, um, anyway. It’s the”—she dropped her voice— “things he does.”

“Such as?”

Images flashed through Nic’s head, far too graphic to share explicitly with her friend. She tried for generalities.

“When I’m with him, he makes me feel like I’m the only person in the world he’s interested in. That this amazing, successful, handsome, clever man would rather spend time with me than do anything else. He gets so turned on by me, telling me about the way I move, the way I smell, the way I feel, what it does to him.”

Evi nodded. “That would be nice. But, all that and you’re not in love with him?”

“We don’t use the ‘L’ word.” Nic shrugged.

“You’ve told me that. Doesn’t mean you don’t feel it, though.”

“You know why.”

Evi took a slurp of her iced tea. “You’ve gotta get over that. It was so long ago. You were young and it was one fucked-up relationship with one fucked-up man. Love is good! Look at me.” She grinned.

Nic smiled. “You would be the proof of love being a good thing. But, in this situation, in this relationship, no, I don’t think this is what love is.”

"You might be wrong."

"I might be wrong." Nic nodded, then changed the subject. "Anyway, Lawrence has definitely acquired some, hm, skills." Nic lowered her voice again. "I've done things with him that I never even thought of before."

Evi eyed her. "I'm not sure I should ask, but like what?"

Nic chewed, trying to think of one thing she could relay. "He likes to look at me."

"What? Like how do you mean?"

Nic gave a little nod at her lap. "Look at me. Like up close."

Evi's eyes opened wide. "Wow. Wow. Okay. I'm not sure how I feel about that."

"I know, it sounds a little weird, but when he does it, it is so intimate and erotic. It really is incredible. Also, he's taken some photos."

"Of that?" Evi looked horrified.

"No! Pretty pictures, nude pictures, of me in his bed."

Evi resumed chewing her sandwich. "There goes your future political career."

Nic laughed. "I'm not sure of much, but I do know I'm never going into politics."

"Eat up. Your lunch hour is going by fast."

Nic unwrapped her turkey and avocado on whole wheat and took a big bite. It was good and she was hungry after all.

"Did Jack call this morning?"

"No," Nic mumbled around her food.

"He should have, you know."

"Yeah. I know."

Evi tossed the crumpled napkins and her sandwich wrapper into a nearby trash can. "Okay. The way I see it, this thing you got for him is making you hot and all, but creepy ex-girlfriends are a big turnoff. His not calling you to apologize? Another big turnoff. How much do you need to turn you off of him?"

Nic nodded and finished her sandwich. "It's over before it started, I guess."

Evi put her hand on Nic's arm. "You've got a good thing. Don't endanger it without thinking things through carefully. It sounds like Lawrence deserves that."

They pulled on their jackets and started the walk back to their respective offices. They had two blocks to walk together before their paths would diverge.

"When do I get to meet Lawrence, anyway? You've been dating him over six months."

"Gosh, we hardly ever go out. I'm going over there to spend the night tonight."

"Two Friday overnights in a row! Getting serious."

"Mmmmmm, it is so wonderful to wake up in his bed, with the sun coming in the big windows. His bedroom is so beautiful. And about as big as my whole condo."

"Come on, Nic. Can't I meet him? Does he have a brother? A cousin? A friend?"

"For you? You're happily hooked up with Saul!"

"Maybe I can arrange a Nicole Simmons style of multiple relationships. Where the sex is fantastic and all the men are understanding and they all want me."

"Well, it looks like I'm back down to one man now. One pretty wonderful man." They arrived at their parting point and gave each other a quick hug. "I'll call later tonight with some idea about introducing you. You'll be at home?"

"Me and Saul. Watching *Fast and Furious* for the fortieth time."

"You must really love him."

Evi smiled. "Yeah," she said. "It really sucks."

Nic strode up Westlake Avenue. Although it had rained earlier that morning, it had stopped for the time being. But she still had to dodge the rivulets running off the overhangs and awnings of the buildings.

She thought about Evi and Saul and their obvious love for each other. She had only experienced that once, that kind of romantic love at that level. She had been young, in college. But it was doomed from the get-go and she had known it. Had she loved since? She did love Lawrence, she supposed, but not like Evi and Saul loved each other. Ever since that first experience, all of her many relationships had been casual, no strings attached, companionship and fun and caring and sex. Lots of sex. She knew that arrangement was what she preferred. It was healthy and respectful not to put conditions or expectations on each other.

Wasn't it?

Just steps before opening the main door to her office building, she felt her phone vibrate in her purse and faintly heard the chirp of the ring tone.

When she got to her desk, she pulled out her phone. As she halfway suspected, the caller ID said it was Jack. She hadn't attached a photo to his number yet. It was too early for that.

Nic waited as the voicemail connected and Jack's voice came on the recording.

"Hi, Nicole. I owe you an apology. You were very gracious last night, understanding my need to leave suddenly. I didn't want to leave, I was having a great time with you. I called back just as soon as I could. It has been a state of emergency around here since I left you. I'm hoping against hope that you'll grant me another opportunity to take you out. I could say some things about how I understand if you don't want to pursue this any further, but I really hope that isn't true. You can give me a call back if you are so inclined, but in any case I will try you later. Again, I'm sorry."

Nic erased Jack's message and quickly texted Evi.

He left a message and apology.

The response was almost immediate.

What's the grade on the apology?

Decent. I'll give it a B.

And?

I'll let him call me again.

The response took longer this time.

Enjoy L. this weekend. Don't think of J. Take care of it Mon.

Good idea. Thx.

NP. Go back to work. Call me tonite.

Nic put her phone away and picked up her office phone to listen for messages there. As she listened, she took notes, then added to her to-do list, selected a file folder from a pile on the right side of her desk, flipped it open and bent over it, clicking her pen.

And thought of Jack.

CHAPTER EIGHT

Nic held Lawrence's hand in her lap and smiled at him. "You're so nice to do this. I know going out on a rainy Friday night wouldn't be your first pick of things to do."

Lawrence grinned. His enthusiasm and easy attitude belied the scattering of fine wrinkles around his eyes. Nic thought the fan of lines in fact highlighted the sparkle and vitality in his blue eyes.

"Well, it's not my first pick. You're right. But I have to admit that I'm flattered you would like to introduce me to your friend."

"You are?"

"Yes. You haven't suggested it before and I thought perhaps you wanted to keep the old man a secret." He sniffed playfully and then regained his smile.

"Oh no! Not at all! I thought you didn't like to go out."

"Well, here we are."

With his easy knowledge of the east side of Lake Washington, Lawrence had suggested that they meet Saul and Evi in the relative quiet of a small bar off Main Street. Golden lamp light washed over the wood table and chairs and glinted in the patrons' hair, sparking auburn, ash, chestnut, and silver highlights everywhere. Nic thought this kind of lighting should be installed everywhere, the way it dramatically shadowed and showed off everyone's best features.

She pulled her favorite blue-green shawl around her, nestling her chin in the soft warmth. Her long silver earrings caught in the fuzz of the garment and tugged slightly on her earlobes before releasing again. It was cozy in the bar. Nic and Lawrence sat close together, their knees touching and their arms grazing against each other. She almost regretted that Evi and Saul would be joining them.

Just as she thought that, they showed up.

Saul was a hulk at six and a half feet tall. His personality matched his size. He swooped Nic into a hug as soon as she was on her feet. There was the slightly awkward shuffle of shaking of hands between Saul and Lawrence while Nic and Evi traded hugs.

"Lawrence, this is my best friend, Evi," Nic said.

"So nice to finally meet you." Evi smiled and shook Lawrence's hand. "I have heard a lot about you."

Nic blushed and grimaced at her friend.

"Have you?" Lawrence replied. To Nic's ears, his voice sounded so smooth, deep and sexy.

"Oh, indeed." Evi smirked and then relented into a natural smile. "All good.

"Good."

The conversation flowed during the first round of drinks. It grew a bit more animated during the second round. Nic sipped her Tuaca and soda and beamed at her friends and Lawrence.

"So where does the name Evi come from? Is it a nickname for Eve?" Lawrence asked.

Evi rolled her eyes. "Nope. It's short for Evelyn. It's such an old-fashioned name. I can't stand it." Just as the words were out of Evi's mouth, she stammered and brought her hand to her lips. "I mean … not that there's anything wrong with old-fashioned … I mean, I'm sure Evelyn was a very popular name back when … not that you'd know of course, because …well … it was before your time?" Evi finally gave up trying to rescue that line of talk and let her hands drop to her lap.

Lawrence smiled at her. "I had a great-aunt named Evelyn. Yes, the name is a little old-fashioned, but beautiful, nonetheless." Nic took his hand again and smiled at him.

"So, Evi, what do you do?" Lawrence asked.

"I'm an engineer. Structural engineer."

"Really! I like that."

"I know. There aren't a lot of female structural engineers, but I love it."

Nic was proud of her friend's career choice and flagrant refusal to give in to stereotypes. Plus, Evi made at least twice as much money as Nic did, with more regular hours to boot. Nic had often wished she had an engineer's brain, but hers was definitely set in the liberal arts.

Evi and Lawrence chatted about some of the iconic Seattle structures and their construction history, while Saul and Nic talked about the Mariner's chances, however slight, this coming spring and Saul's job as a Starbuck's trainer. The new store in which he trained employees was in a small trendy condo development on Queen Anne. Nic wondered momentarily about Jack's condo on Queen Anne, but quickly put all thoughts of him out of her mind.

Jack didn't belong here tonight.

Evi and Nic went to the ladies' room together later in the evening. Nic grinned at her as soon as the door closed behind them.

"Well?"

"Well … I like him! A lot!" Evi returned the grin. "I mean, yeah. There's the age thing, but he's good-looking, smart and I have to admit there is a sexy vibe to him. Oh, and he adores you."

Nic turned to the mirror and applied some lip gloss in her favorite pale peach color. "I'm lucky, Evi."

"Yeah, you are. But" —Evi held up her finger— "there's that other … complication."

"He's not a complication. He was just a temporary distraction." Nic didn't look away from the mirror.

"I don't think so," Evi sang teasingly. "But seriously, as casual as Lawrence has always wanted to keep your relationship, he deserves to be treated well."

"I know that." Nic put away her lip gloss and washed her hands. "I'm just not sure what being 'treated well' would include. Or not include."

Evi nodded. "I don't know why you don't just get some normal-aged boyfriend, like Saul. The expectations are easier."

Nic smiled. "I seem to have a thing for older men."

"Yes, you do. That could have some consequences down the road, you know."

Nic rolled her eyes. "I'm just dating them, not marrying them."

"Kissing in the tree … first comes love … then comes …" Evi sang the childhood tune.

"Yeah, yeah, yeah. We better get back to the table."

*   *   *   *   *

It was after eleven when Lawrence gave her the signal that he was ready to go. Nic began to make their excuses. Evi gave her another hug and Saul did the one-armed shoulder squeeze. Lawrence adjusted her shawl around her shoulders and then pulled it up slightly around her head, almost like a hood.

"Fetching," he murmured.

She smiled at him, proud and grateful at how well the evening went. She had to admit that she had held some reservations. Would Lawrence appreciate her friends? Would Evi understand why she was dating him? Would Saul refrain from making any old-timer jokes? She thought it had all gone very well indeed.

"Let's go home," she said with a smile, knowing that her use of the term *home* would please him.

Nic linked her arm through Lawrence's as they walked back to the car. The steady rain had given way to a mist that shimmered in the streetlights and dampened her face. They didn't speak until Lawrence pulled out his key fob and turned off the car alarm on the Lexus with a subtle beep. He opened the passenger side door for her and then stepped in front of it, preventing her from sliding into the seat. Without a word, he pulled her into his arms and kissed her deeply, taking her pleasantly by surprise. His tongue touched her lips and she parted them. His arms tightened, his tongue playing with hers. Nic moaned and slid her hands up his arms and around his back.

Lawrence pulled back to look at her after several moments. "I want you, Nicole Simmons. You are bright, beautiful, and vivacious. And you make me horny as hell. I haven't felt like this in years." He stopped talking but his eyes still studied hers.

Nic smiled at him, still breathing a little too hard. "I thought we were going home."

Lawrence released her then and handed her into the seat. He was silent on the drive back to his house and she wondered if he was disappointed in her noncommittal response. She wanted him, too. She thought he was incredibly intelligent, charming, easy to be with, and also incredibly sexy.

But somehow, she just hadn't found the words to tell him that.

He pressed the button to open the entry gates and coasted up the long drive into one of the garages of his home. With a push of a button, the garage door closed behind them and they sat in the dim lighting.

He smiled at her and took her hand.

"It's okay, Nic. I wasn't asking for anything in return. I just wanted to let you know how I felt."

He pulled her in for another kiss and Nic gratefully leaned into him, relieved yet again that nothing else was expected of her but her companionship.

And her body it seemed, for Lawrence's hands were now pushing beneath the layers of her shawl and cupping her bottom through the suede skirt she wore. Nic turned her hip so she was pressed against his groin, immediately feeling his hardened bulge. Lawrence moaned at her contact and his hands gave her a firm squeeze.

Nic slid her hands down his chest and cupped his erection through his pants, stroking a finger and thumb up and down his length. She never did get over her amazement at the development of the male erection, or the magic of that thrilling organ. Her response now was immediate. Her nipples tingled, her legs tightening to try to suppress the building ache between them.

They moaned and moved together. His hands massaged her ass and she caressed him over and over, up and down, his erection filling her hand. When she finally moved to unfasten his pants, Lawrence didn't try to stop her. She broke the kiss and lowered to her knees, descending with the zipper. The cement floor was shockingly cold on her knees, so she pulled the shawl from her shoulders and dropped it in a thick fluffy bunch on the spotless floor.

Nic paused, as she always did at this point with Lawrence, just to admire his member. Stiff and solid in her hand, warm and smooth, like silk over wood. She stroked his length a few more times before she closed her eyes and leaned in to lick the slippery, salty tip, her tongue gliding over the head of his cock.

She sensed Lawrence leaning back against the hood of the car. His fingers threaded into her hair, combing it, letting the strands fall through his fingers back to her shoulders, over and over again. She delicately licked and kissed him from base to crown. Then she closed her lips around his cock tip and began the steady rhythm of caress of lip, stroke of tongue, and slight sucking that she knew he loved.

She was encouraged by his groan and by his hands gathering her hair back from her face. She knew that he wanted to watch her. She opened her eyes and gazed up at him as she sucked, holding his eyes with her own. As his groans continued, and his hips pulsed forward, she increased her rhythm and matched her hand strokes with her mouth.

"So good," he panted.

A few moments later he moaned and his fingers tightened in her hair.

His warm cream flooded her mouth. She kept her lips closed around the head as she swallowed his fluids. The taste of him was familiar, welcome and as salty as the ocean.

Nic finally eased back, sliding her lips from him and taking the last few drops with her tongue.

"Woman, you are going to kill me," Lawrence said with a laugh as he tucked himself away. He slid his fingers into her hair again and tilted her face up to him.

"Don't say that or I'll never do this again." Nic smiled and wiped her mouth with her fingers.

"Okay! I take it back," Lawrence reassured her as he helped her to her feet and then picked up and shook out her shawl. "I always knew this thing wasn't just beautiful, but handy too." He took her hand in his and pulled her to the door leading into the house. "Come on."

Just a few lights shone in the darkness. Tiptoeing up the stairs and into his rooms at the end of the hallway, Nic smothered a giggle. She felt like she was sneaking back into her parents' house after illicitly meeting her boyfriend outside.

"What are you laughing about?" Lawrence asked as he closed the door behind them.

"Oh, I just can't get used to there being other people in the house. You know that."

"Sasha is at the other end of the house. She can't hear us. We could be bouncing off the walls up here."

"Let's not get that rambunctious."

Lawrence took her into his arms and tilted her head up toward him. "I would never be harsh with you. I could never risk hurting you."

"I appreciate that, but I'm not going to break, just so you know." Nic really did appreciate his sentiment, but sometimes he seemed to handle her as if afraid of imparting lasting damage. Not that she wanted anything rough. She just didn't want him to be timid.

"Come. I'm going to show you just how precious you are to me."

Lawrence surprised her by taking her gently by the shoulders and turning her around to face the full-length mirror on the door leading to his dressing room.

He leaned down and kissed her ear, nuzzling her hair and causing her long earrings to jingle quietly. His fingers curled around her shoulders. Nic admired his elegant figure as he did so.

"Let me show you just how beautiful you are, Nic," he murmured as he reached around her to unbutton her blouse. His fingers deftly worked the buttons loose, and he parted her blouse and pulled it back over her shoulders and down her arms. Then he drew down the side zipper of her skirt and let that fall to the ground. When she moved to step out of it, he whispered, "Shh. Don't. Not yet."

He looked at her in the mirror, his eyes traveling from hers down her length. At first, she avoided looking at herself, keeping her eyes on him instead. If she contemplated her own figure, she'd start analyzing: the shadows beneath her eyes, the full breasts, the hips and thighs and waist that were never as tiny as the actresses in the magazines, her pale skin.

Then she did look at herself, her even features and blue eyes. She critiqued her makeup, thinking perhaps a slightly heavier eyeliner might have worked better. Thank God for mascara to lengthen her brown lashes. However, the wine moistened her generous lips nicely. That wasn't bad.

"Watch my hands," Lawrence whispered.

She looked from her own lips to his hands, as they skimmed over her shoulders and curled beneath her breasts. She was wearing a matching bra and panty set, in a soft charcoal color with lighter gray lace. She always wore matching panties and bras, having been impressed with the well-turned-out girls in the sorority in college who always had matched lingerie.

And back then, her lover had wanted her in matching lingerie.

Lawrence's hands cupped her breasts, slightly lifting them. Then his hands skimmed over her soft flat tummy and turned out to curve over her full hips.

Nic was alternately critical and appreciative of her curves. She didn't have to fight her weight; she was never underweight or overweight but at a healthy balance. The distribution naturally went to hips and breasts, however, giving her a lush figure that men seemed to love, she had to admit.

Lawrence slid his thumbs into the sides of her bikini panties and played with them, kissing her shoulder and nibbling her neck as he did so. He pulled the panties up slightly, then dragged the fabric down over her hips to the top of her thighs, then up again and seesawed them back and forth a bit. Nic felt the satin skimming over her sensitive mound. When he pulled them up, she could see the fabric pressing against her, outlining her contours.

Her breathing picked up pace.

Lawrence left her panties and unhooked her bra, letting it fall down her arms and to the floor. His hands again cupped her breasts, lifting and cradling them, as if they were treasures of great value. He lifted his head and looked at her in the mirror.

"Perfect. Gorgeous. Every man's fantasy."

"You boys and your tit fixation." Nic smiled.

"You better believe it, sweetheart." He went back to kissing her neck, more ardently, his fingers squeezing her breasts ever so gently, pushing them together, his fingers grazing her suddenly pert nipples. Nic moaned and her hands fluttered by her sides, wanting to touch but sensing that he wanted her to hold still. Her hands felt so restless, it was almost a distraction.

Lawrence lowered himself to first one knee, then the other, kissing down her spine. His fingers slid again into her panties, and this time didn't hesitate to pull them down over her hips. They landed on her skirt, still around Nic's feet.

She was completely naked.

Her hair hung in waves around her shoulders. Her silver earrings, the only jewelry she wore, twinkled in the soft lighting. Lawrence knelt behind her, just to one side, and looked at her again in the mirror.

"Again … perfect."

Together, they looked over her figure, from brunette mane of long hair, gentle oval face with a small nose and classic cheekbones, just visible collarbone above her teardrop-shaped, full breasts, rosy nipples, soft rounded torso, lithe legs of slightly longer than average length. Looking at herself through Lawrence's eyes and ignoring her overly critical analysis, she knew that she was pretty, sexy, a figure to induce lust in a man. The knowledge gave her a sense of quiet power, confidence, and an intense arousal.

She could feel the proof of the arousal between her thighs.

Lawrence leaned in and kissed and licked along the top of her buttocks, cupping them the way he had her breasts. Nic's hands splayed over her stomach, tempted to travel down to her wetness, but she let him take the lead. He did, his hands coming around her hips to stroke the front of her, still kissing and licking wherever he wanted. His fingers slid around her thighs and gently parted them. Nic widened her stance just a little.

One hand returned to cup a buttock, while the other stroked her slit. Then two fingers settled over her clit and pressed.

Nic moaned again and felt a tremor course through her. Lawrence didn't stop. He circled his fingers over her clit steadily.

The hand that was covering her buttocks began to slide between her thighs. Nic widened her stance a little more and Lawrence slid his index finger along her slit from front to back. Nic could sense the wetness gathered on his finger. As he stroked back and forth, her flesh became slick.

"Your wetness is so sexy, Nic," Lawrence said, his voice still hushed. "You are so amazingly fuckable."

She met his eyes in the mirror, silently imploring him to do more with his finger, rocking her hips back to him.

He smiled and used his index finger to gently part her flesh and slide deep inside of her.

Nic opened her mouth and gave a little cry, tilting her head back. Her legs began to tremble.

He worked his finger in and out of her several times. In the dim light of the room, watching in the mirror, Nic was able to see the evidence of her arousal on his glistening finger. She rocked back on his finger as he pushed into her, beginning a rhythm that intensified her need. She felt her body clenching around him. He obviously felt it too, for he wiggled his finger inside of her. She almost lost it at that moment, gasping and shuddering.

Then he deliberately removed his single finger and replaced it with two. At the same time, he steadily rubbed her clit.

She let herself ride him then, pressing down on those filling fingers as he pushed them into her, faster and faster. His other hand flew over her clit, frigging her relentlessly. Her eyes met his in the mirror again and he licked his lips. She could see his chest rise and fall with his fast breathing.

"Don't look at me. Look at yourself."

She brought her eyes again to her figure in the mirror and moaned at what she saw. A woman in the throes of sexual ecstasy, panting, a fine sheen of perspiration gleaming on her skin, her breasts bouncing with her exertions, and a handsome man's fingers buried inside of her. Fucking her there in the middle of the room. She cupped her breasts, watching his hand moving between her legs, his other fingers wetly frigging her blazing clit. Nic brought her hands up over the tops of her breasts, up the sides of her neck, and into her hair. She shuddered again, moaned, went up on her tiptoes and lifted her hands, fingers threaded with her long strands. She never took her eyes off herself as she came.

A wild cry burst from her throat as her body shuddered in spasms. She felt her pussy clenching his fingers over and over and over and her cries filled the room, over and over and over, for what felt like long moments. She thought she might never stop coming. Then the fingers withdrew. His hands caught her as she came down off of her toes and her knees sagged.

She clutched at him, helpless to stand up, reliant on his strength. Next she knew, Lawrence was laying her softly on his plush bed and smoothing the hair off her damp face.

"My God, Nicole. Do you know what you are?" His voice was hoarse, his face serious.

"I'm beautiful," she whispered.

And then she added, "Thank you," and held out her arms to her lover.

CHAPTER NINE

"In the end, we had progressed from a rudimentary internship program for a handful of gifted high school students already following a STEM pathway, to a multi-layered, multi-faceted internship system for students of all STEM levels and abilities. Our hope is to find and nurture those young people, who have not had the opportunity to discover their science-related talents or the encouragement to consider careers in these types of fields."

Nic pressed the button on her tablet to switch to the next slide on the screen behind her. She lifted her head to look out over the audience of technology business leaders and potential internship hosts and took a deep breath. "Especially in our populations of underserved communities, science and technology careers are not often considered to be a realistic pathway. And yet there is so much hidden talent here. The artistic and white-collar industries have aggressively recruited from minority and economically-disadvantaged communities. The stats show the results."

Nic gestured to the screen behind her. "You can see the change in demographics in these industries. Significant, aren't they?" She leveled her eyes over the men and woman focused on her. "The science and technology industries, your businesses and professions, are missing out if you don't also attract, recruit, and train these young people. Often the first significant exposure that high school students have to a profession is the opportunity of internship."

She had them. She knew it.

She could see it in the thoughtful expressions on their faces. Nic tucked a stray strand of her hair behind her ear and ran a finger down the side of her tablet as she let the information displayed sink in for a moment.

And now for the "ask."

"You have an opportunity to not only make a difference in the future of your own industry, but also in the future of a young person who has the talent, the drive, and the intellect to become a significant asset to your company. What they don't have is the connection. That is what I am offering today: the connection. The introduction. The"— Nic lifted her hand toward the audience— "hand that will bring you and your intern together."

Nic let her hand waver in the air for a split second before she brought it back to her side. "Thank you for inviting me to speak with you today. I am happy to entertain any questions or thoughts you might have for me." Nic flicked off her tablet and picked it up, turning to greet the luncheon host as he crossed the stage to shake her hand.

She wouldn't have any time to check her phone until she returned to her office.

Nic rushed back to work, hopping onto the trolley to return to the South Lake Union area.

She had never bought the S.L.U.T. shirt herself, but Evi's boyfriend, Saul, had been one of the first to snag one. The city of Seattle, in an extraordinary moment of short-sightedness, had blithely named the city's new streetcar, between the downtown core and the burgeoning South Lake Union area, the South Lake Union Trolley. Within twenty-four hours, enterprising local businesses had printed up t-shirts, proclaiming I RODE THE S.L.U.T. Nic would be the first to admit that it was clever, although she didn't find a need to display it over her chest.

Nic took out her phone as she entered her office. She knew there was a voicemail from Jack. She had seen the notice of it when she was walking to work in the morning, but hadn't listened to it then. She decided to do so now.

He had called and left the voicemail message on Sunday evening.

"Hi, Nicole. Jack here." He paused before continuing. "I hope you had a great weekend. Would you give me a call? I would definitely like to hear from you. Definitely. Bye."

Well, that was short and to the point.

She touched the return call button and listened as it rang twice before Jack's smooth voice came on. "Hello. This is Jack LaTour. Please leave a message for me after the tone."

"Hi, Jack. This is Nicole. Thanks for your messages. I had a pleasant weekend." A sudden image of kneeling over Lawrence, while he thrust up into her, flashed through her mind. "And I hope you did too. You can give me a call back." Nic hesitated before adding, "I'd like to hear from you as well."

She hoped that came off sounding friendly and carefree.

Nic's intercom rang. It was Frances wanting to know how the presentation went. Nic picked up the proofs of the new marketing materials for next year's education summit and hurried down the hall to Frances's office.

Frances called her in after Nic knocked on the door jamb. The door was usually open, but Nic liked to make sure her boss wasn't on the phone.

Frances stood up from behind her enormous desk, which was placed before a wall of windows that looked out over Lake Union. One of the charter floatplanes raced over the water at that moment, ready to lift up and clear Queen Anne Hill on its way to Vancouver.

Frances sat on the edge of her desk and motioned Nic to one of the chairs in front of her. Even semi-seated,

Nic's boss was still inches over her own height. Nic filled her in on the luncheon and the reaction to her presentation. Recruiting internship hosts was one of the most difficult parts of the program, but Nic had made an enormous difference since she became program director just two years before. Frances was pleased.

Then Nic shared the marketing proofs with her, which Frances critiqued with her natural eye toward style and symmetry. She made several suggestions, as they went over the message and tone that they hoped to convey with these materials.

Nic gathered up the proofs and her notes twenty minutes later when the conversation seemed to be wrapping up. Steph came into the office with some papers for her boss.

"Hey, Nic, how was your weekend?" Steph asked.

"Awesome! Thanks for asking. Yours?"

"Eh, okay. Nothing special. You still seeing that guy Jack?"

Nic didn't miss Frances's raised eyebrows and her sudden interest in the casual chitchat.

"No. Well, not this weekend. Not sure. Maybe." That about summed it up.

"God, he's cute. Like, really cute." Steph grinned.

Nic knew she was blushing bright red. Frances cleared her throat. "Thank you, Stephanie."

Steph retreated back to the reception area and Nic turned to follow.

"Nic, would you close the door and sit for a moment?" Frances asked.

She did so, perching on the edge of her chair. Frances had her head cocked and Nic could tell that her boss was considering her words. She wondered if she would get in trouble for going out with a man who she met through work. She didn't think that there could possibly be a policy against dating someone in a related business. After all, Frances had never seemed to have an issue with her dating Lawrence.

She decided to take the first step.

"You have something to say about Jack, don't you?"

"Maybe. It's not my intent to pry into your personal affairs, nor am I in a position to do so. There is nothing wrong with you dating Jack LaTour, at least from a professional standpoint. However, I would not be pleased if any fallout between you two were to affect the workings of the community center committee."

Nic sighed. "We went out twice. We may go out again. It isn't serious, at this point. I fully intend to keep it out of our professional lives."

Frances smirked. "You know that is rarely possible, once something becomes serious."

"We are a long way from serious."

Her boss swung one leg back and forth and seemed to be studying her shoes.

"You know that I know Jack."

"Yes."

"We run in somewhat of the same … I guess you could say social circles. Has he mentioned that to you?"

"No, but I assumed it was something like that. Or you knew each other from professional organizations."

"Has he talked about his past relationships?" Frances asked.

"We've only been out together twice, hardly the moment to talk about our past." Nic thought of Erica. "Although he did take me to an art gallery opening. I met someone there that I think he used to date."

Frances's leg stopped swinging. "Who?"

Nic studied her, wondering at Frances's sudden intensity. "A woman named Erica."

Frances's mouth fell open. "Seriously? Erica showed up there? I hadn't realized—"

"Realized what?"

Frances stood and walked around the corner of her desk to look out the window, her back to Nic. She was silent for several long moments before speaking again.

"This is something that Jack should speak to you about and I'm disappointed he hasn't already. I'm not sure what he is intending here." Frances looked over her shoulder at Nic. "He has always been forthcoming since I've known him. As for Erica, she is an ex of Jack's, I suppose you could say. I met the girl a few times at some of our social functions. It was well-known that she had a difficult time with the breakup."

Nic was alarmed by the vague information that Frances seemed to be trying to give her. "Is she dangerous?"

"No. Not to anyone but herself. But she did make a nuisance of herself and Jack felt responsible for ensuring that she was okay." Frances shook her head. "The girl should have handled it better. It took us all by surprise."

"Frances, I have to admit, I don't get what you are saying. Is there anything dangerous about Jack that I should know about? Because otherwise, having an unhappy ex-girlfriend isn't really all that shocking."

Frances turned to face her again, her arms crossed. "Jack isn't dangerous, no. And I probably shouldn't have said anything. Please forget that I said anything at all. It's not my business and Jack is a fine, charming, and attractive man. There is absolutely no reason you shouldn't see him."

Nic tried out a guess. "Are you attracted to him?" she asked softly.

Frances laughed. "I can see how you might ask that. No, definitely not. Jack and I wouldn't be suited."

"Suited?"

"You know how in a relationship between two people, there is usually a yin-yang element to it that is necessary for it to work?"

"Um, okay, yes."

"Well, Jack and I are both yins."

Nic had no clue what her boss was talking about, but she nodded anyway, wanting to end this conversation. Take her papers. Go back to her office. And check her phone for messages.

CHAPTER TEN

The wine was fabulous, the flowers were elegant, and the scent of saffron wafting from Jack's paella pan was making Nic drool. She nodded when Jack offered to refill her glass.

He refilled his own glass and then lifted it in her direction in a silent toast. Nic did the same in return.

They had finally talked in person on Monday evening and Jack asked her over to his condo for dinner on Wednesday night.

What a condo it was! Nic was still glancing around in delight. Jack had half of the top floor of one of the historic Queen Anne buildings, but his home wasn't stuffy and old. He had completely refurbished it to consist of one large room the length of the building that housed the living room area, kitchen, and his workspace at the far end from the entry door, underneath the sloping roofline. His bedroom with connecting bath, and another bedroom with a guest bath, opened off the inner wall. He invited her to look around when she first walked in, and Nic found herself drawn into the large space, floored in blond wood, walls painted a soft white, wood furniture with white cushions. The ceiling was beamed and spotlights along the beams showcased the art on his walls. A large skylight centered the room. His kitchen was aligned between the wall and a brushed steel counter that ran for an impressive twelve feet.

This wasn't any dark dingy man-cave. This was the home of a man who lived in the light and collected objects of beauty and intrigue around him. Nic spent several moments looking over his art pieces, pen and ink drawings, watercolors. All were abstract, emotive pieces of lines and shadows.

She returned to him after her perusal, where he was opening the bottle of wine in the kitchen. A ceramic vase held a variety of white flowers and green foliage. Jack said that he had selected the flowers earlier in the day, thinking of her as he did so.

Jack took a sip of wine. "Thank you for coming tonight. I know we didn't part under the best of circumstances last Thursday."

Nic shook her head. "Thanks for the apology, but it sounds like you had something you needed to take care of. Something important?"

Jack nodded. "Yes, important. I'm glad you understand."

"It's resolved now?" She had to know more. After all the hints that Frances dropped, and Jack's own mysterious lack of details, she knew that she wouldn't be able to let it rest until she knew a little more about what happened on Thursday night.

Jack looked at her over the rim of his glass as he took another sip. "Let's eat and then we can talk a little."

He asked her to tear up some arugula and maché for a light salad, which he dressed with a mustard vinaigrette after he had spooned the paella in a big bowl.

"I hope you don't think you and I will be able to eat this entire thing tonight," Nic said, gesturing to the enormous bowl.

"Nope. I like leftovers." He grinned. "I'm a bachelor, remember? I freeze things like this to eat on those nights that I'm sitting lonely in front of the TV, with only a beer and a baseball game to keep me company."

"Oh, poor guy!" she said. "I get the feeling that this doesn't happen often."

"No, it doesn't." Jack held out a chair for her at the small table for two by the floor to ceiling windows. "I tend to work in the evenings."

"One of those types who can't leave the work at the office." Nic took a seat. Jack placed a generous serving of paella, including shrimp, chicken, sausage, rice, and a variety of savory vegetables, all tinted warm yellow with the saffron. He added a mound of salad next to it.

"Well, not exactly. I do my work at the office. I do my scheming and creating at home."

"Scheming?"

Jack smiled as he lifted a forkful of paella. "I'll show you after dinner."

"Hmmm, we seem to have a lot to cover after dinner." Nic took a forkful and was quick to compliment him on the results, with a few appreciative noises added.

They ended up chatting more than they ate, quickly finding the easy repartee that first characterized their exchanges. They sipped their wine and laughed as they cleaned up together.

He closed the freezer door and turned to Nic. "So which first, schemes or explanations?"

Nic had to think about that question, but sensed that the explanation might be the deeper conversation. "Schemes first."

Jack led her to his workspace, where an architect's drafting table was set against the wall. He flipped through some of his drawings as he talked.

"So when I'm at the office, I'm working on current projects and developing upcoming projects. But when I'm at home, I create the designs I dream of and scheme on how to bring them to reality someday."

"So nights are your time to daydream."

"Yeah, you could say that."

"What kind of things do you design in your dreams?"

"My dream house. Where I can bring together all of the design challenges and elements that fascinate me."

"Your dream house? This place here seems like a dream to me. It's so perfect."

"It's perfect for one person. Just as I designed it to be. But someday, I hope to have a home for more than one person."

Nic smiled to herself and leaned over to look at some of his drawings. Each sheet seemed to show a different facet of a residence: a bay window, the corner of a porch, a tower.

"Is this a turret?" she asked, pointing to the tower.

"Yeah. So I want a turret! From there I can shoot flaming arrows at my enemies and protect what is mine."

"Do you know what this house will look like as a whole?"

"Yes, I do." Jack leaned against his table.

"Do I get to see the design?" Nic held her glass of wine against her cheek as she smiled at him.

"Nope."

"No?"

"Nope. I've never shown anyone my dream house."

"Maybe someday you'll show me?"

Jack took her hand and pulled her slightly toward him. He took the glass from her and set it down on a side table, then twirled a lock of her hair around his fingers, watching the silk as it slid over the palm of his hand. "I want material that feels just like this, looks just like this, dark and fine and as smooth as satin. I want this in my bedroom. Someday." He looked at her.

Nic couldn't find a thing to say. The meaning of his words was clear to her. His bedroom.

He urged her toward him, pulling gently with his hand on hers, giving her every chance to pull away.

She didn't.

Their lips met softly, hesitantly. Nic put a hand on his chest, to create just that much of a barrier to getting any closer. Their tongues touched, just the tips meeting. He didn't pull her to him. He didn't crush his mouth against hers. He let her tell him how intense she wanted to be.

She wanted to be much more intense. Her pulse was racing from the first touch of his lips and she had to suppress the moan that threatened when he parted her lips with his tongue.

But not yet. Not yet. There was more to talk about first.

She pulled back and looked down at her hand on his chest. Jack covered her hand with his own. She could feel his heart beating.

"Let's go have a seat on the couch," he said.

He went to the kitchen to retrieve the bottle of wine and met her on the couch, where they sat facing each other, one leg drawn up. He refilled each of their glasses and looked out the tall windows to the city, golden lights twinkling across the sightline. Nic took another sip of her wine, then decided that she probably needed a clear head. She cradled her glass in her lap.

She could see that Jack was contemplating his words. Her mind raced on what he could possibly have to tell her. He was still with Erica? Erica was dangerous? He had run away and married her last weekend?

She looked around the condo. Definitely not much of a feminine touch here. If Erica was in residence, she hadn't made much of an impact. Yet.

"When we were at the art gallery the other night," he began, running one hand up and down his thigh, "you asked if Erica was all right."

"Yes."

"Why did you ask that?"

Nic thought back on what she had seen in Erica's face. "She looked so bereft. Stunned. Almost hopeless. As if she didn't know in what direction to turn."

Jack nodded. "Accurate."

"Jack." Nic was suddenly a bit irritated by everyone's circumspection around this issue. "Would you please just tell me what is what?"

He looked at her for a long moment. Then nodded. Took a long drink of his wine and put the glass on the table, then leaned toward Nic.

"Erica and I were in a relationship."

Nic rolled her eyes. "Duh."

Jack smiled, but continued. "Our relationship was very intense. When it came time to end it, I was ready to move on. She wasn't. I was careful, very gentle with her. I did everything right, or the best way that I knew how. At least I thought so."

He frowned. "She seemed fine for a while, but then she seemed to really have a breakdown. While I'm not denying my responsibility in it, I can't help but wonder if there might have been something else going on in her life, or at least in her mind. Something besides me. I was really baffled at her response."

"Well, breaking up with a girlfriend can go so many ways. I know that," Nic said.

"She was a little more than my girlfriend."

Nic drew back, stunned. "Your fiancé?"

"No. Not like that, but we were in a committed relationship, of a sort."

Nic stood up, set down her own glass, and paced to the window before turning to face him. "I don't understand what you're talking about. You're hedging around this issue and I don't know what you are trying to tell me. Or not tell me. You want me to understand what happened. I can sense that, but you want to do that without actually explaining some important facts." She kept her voice level and quiet, not wanting to sound upset.

She saw Jack's jaw clench. He didn't respond, just seemed to be thinking.

Nic stared at him for a second. “What the hell is going on? Is this some club? Some closed group of friends?” They watched each other in silence then.

Finally Nic walked toward the door. “You know, it really isn’t any of my business. You guys act like this is all some dire secret. That there is some lofty idea that I wouldn’t understand. I don’t want to pry. I will just say this.” She pulled her coat from the closet by the door and slung it over her arm, picking up her purse as well. “It’s not my business. Perhaps it should stay that way.”

She turned to the door, but Jack’s hand was already pressed to it, holding it shut. He stood just behind her, his breath hot on her shoulder.

“Don’t go,” he whispered.

She held still and listened to the sounds of their breathing. They were still in sync. Breathing together.

“I’ll tell you,” he said and took his hand from the door.

CHAPTER ELEVEN

"First of all, I want to get to know you better," Jack said. They were back on the couch, but not touching. Nic decided that was the right move, for the moment. "For whatever reasons, I feel drawn to you. I can already see so many things between us. How easy we are with each other, how much we laugh together. I can see the spark in your eye when we're close."

Nic bit her lip but didn't deny this, for she felt the same rapport with him.

He continued."There's something between us that I want to explore further. One of the reasons I'm so attracted to you is because I feel differently with you than I have with other women."

Jack fidgeted a little and then took Nic's hand in his, playing their fingers together. "For the last few years, I have only been with a certain type of woman."

Nic rolled her eyes and pulled her hand back. "There it is again. Those confusing and vague terms."

"No. Listen. I'm going to explain." Jack swept his fingers through his hair. "Okay. The women I've always been with have been very demure."

Nic lifted an eyebrow.

"Very … ah … receptive."

Nic just looked at him flatly.

"Okay, I know. I'm getting to it." Jack sighed. "The women I've been with have all been very submissive."

Nic waited for the big reveal. "Yeah? All right."

"Well, you aren't quite the same."

"Is that bad?"

"Not at all. It's what has me in a quandary."

"Seriously? Am I that difficult to date?" He still wasn't being forthcoming.

Jack exhaled in frustration. Then he seemed to reach a conclusion, took her hand in his again, and went on.

"I belong to a type of private sexual subculture. Where the women I've been with have all been submissive and abided by certain rules. Where my relationship with them was dictated by the terms of what was accepted by the culture."

Nic tried to process this information. "Is this a club?"

"Kind of. It is an understanding among a group of people."

"Is Frances part of this group?" she asked.

Jack grimaced. "Yes, but I would have liked to have avoided that complication."

"And the girl at the art show? Erica?"

"Yes. She's part of it too."

"Part?" Nic thought that girl was more to Jack than just a member of his sex club.

He hesitated. "She was a regular partner of mine."

"Do I know anyone else in this group?"

"I don't know. I doubt it."

"I feel like I'm playing Twenty Questions here. Is this a small group of people?"

"No, it is quite large, but still a relative minority."

"Does this group have a name?"

Jack bit his lip. "Here in the Seattle area, we refer to our group as the Lush Life. It's a sex network, I suppose you could say. Fetishes, swingers, BDSM. That kind of thing."

"Ah." Nic sat back. "Like tying people up and stuff."

"Yeah. And stuff." Jack nodded.

She had seen photos of such things. She had seen the movies *The Secretary* and *9 1/2 Weeks*. She had even caught sight of listings for BDSM sites during internet searches. She wasn't completely innocent about internet porn and even liked to read the occasional erotic short story on the Erotica Readers website. There was a whole category of bondage stories on there, and she had read, and enjoyed, several of them.

But she had never participated in tying up or gags or spanking.

Nic stared at Jack, at a loss for words. She finally stated what she thought was the obvious.

"So what's the big deal with that?"

His eyebrows almost disappeared beneath his hair and his mouth fell open. "Big deal?" he stuttered. "Well, I … I … you … so, you …" He didn't seem to be able to put two words together. Nic laughed and pressed his hand between her fingers, trying to reassure him.

"I'm not opposed, I guess. I mean, it seems harmless enough. Just some fantasies."

He grimaced. "It's a little more involved than that."

"Okay, so you have been involved in this type of thing and you are attracted to submissive women. That kinda fits. Where does that leave me? And you?" Nic was suddenly struck by a thought. "Wait, do you like me because you think I'm submissive?"

"Nicole, I'm attracted to you because you are you. You might think that sounds trite, but I met you in a neutral setting at that meeting. I wasn't thinking in those terms at all. You have such spark, such energy, such confidence. You have characteristics that I didn't even know I was attracted to, but I now find I'm completely fascinated with." He leaned toward her. "I'm completely fascinated with you."

She again found herself at a loss for words. She was flattered. No, she was elated. Yes, that was it, she was elated that he was seemingly enthralled with her, because she felt the same about him. His banter, his wit, his magnetism. His authentic laugh. His physical grace. She looked at his hands, layered with hers on the couch cushion between them. For just a moment, she imagined those hands in her hair, around her wrists. A flash of an image of his hands tightening a scarf around her wrist.

Would she let him do that? She didn't know.

"I'm glad," she said softly.

"I think I know that. I can sense your attraction as well." He didn't say this boastfully, but just as a statement. Nic nodded.

"Well." He reached over, took his wine glass and lifted it in her direction. "Here's to us."

Nic lifted her own wineglass and clinked it against his. "Here's to us," she repeated. They drank and then looked at each other silently.

Then Nic broke out in a giggle. "Well, that was a heavy conversation for a third date. What's next? Inner urban decay? Nuclear disarmament?"

"How about" —Jack took her wineglass from her hand and set both of the glasses on the table— "we just sit back, relax, and think of other things." He leaned back against the couch cushions and drew her toward him, so she was resting on her side. His finger ran along her cheekbone and down her chin. He watched her as he did this. When she didn't pull back, he continued to explore the lines of her face, tracing her chin, her other cheek with the back of his finger, her hairline over her forehead, playfully down the bridge of her nose, and then rested his fingertip on her upper lip. She felt her lips soften into the slightest of smiles.

Very deliberately, very slowly, she parted her lips to gently lick his finger.

He watched her intently, his eyes boring into hers. She stroked his finger with her tongue, at first her smile suggesting playfulness. Then she let her smile fade as she sensed his quickened breathing, saw his lowered eyelids, felt the signs of his arousal. She had a feeling that this was a test of sorts. But she wasn't afraid of failing. She would just do what instinct instructed and see what came of it.

She was fully aware of the first signs of her own arousal.

She tilted her head a little and languidly slid her tongue along his finger.

"Dear God," he breathed and then the dynamic shifted as he slid his hands down her sides and pulled her to him. He brought his lips to hers, crushing her in his tight arms. He raised up, looming over her, pressing her back to the couch cushions. She gasped just before his lips were on hers again, her breath becoming a moan as his tongue pressed into her mouth and captured her tongue. Her hands clutched at his shoulders as he laid over her, his weight not fully on her but enough to pin her to the couch. His thigh pressed between her legs. Her moans continued, his tongue relentless as it explored her mouth as much as he wanted.

Nic had never felt this kind of urgent, frantic sense of *needing* someone so much. Needing him as if he were suddenly and confusingly essential. She pulled mindlessly at his shirt. She arched her body up to him. The physical yearning overwhelmed any conscious thought or decision.

Jack's hand swept over her hair and down her body, his touch searing her through the fabric of her clothing. He held her hip as he pressed his leg more firmly between her thighs. Then he brought his hand up to cup beneath her breast. Nic moaned again and pressed against his hand. He seemed to read her wordless signals perfectly, for he closed his fingers around her.

Nic inhaled deeply as he broke their kiss. He lifted his head to look at her, his leg and hand continuing to work their magic on the most sensitive areas of her body. He studied her and she let him, returning his steady gaze with her more unfocused one.

Then he pushed himself back and settled on the other side of the couch, still watching her.

Nic laid there, wondering what had just happened, wondering if there was something wrong, and still trying to catch her breath.

"Jack?" she asked, pushing up on her elbows. She didn't even know what to ask about. Or for.

He smiled slowly. "If you let me, Nicole, I think we could do some amazing things together."

She shivered and nodded her head. "I think so too."

"I won't rush you, but I hope you can trust me enough, even this early on, to lead you."

"Lead me?" Nic pressed her legs together and drew them up to her chest, sitting up and wrapping her arms around her knees. The burning need for him still clutched at her stomach, making her feel tense and restless. But her mind, clearing of its lusty fog, began to ask questions.

"Jack, I don't know if I can be the kind of woman, do the kind of things, that you are used to."

Jack shook his head slowly, still smiling at her. "I want you to be exactly the way you are."

"Can't we have a, like, a normal type of relationship?"

He laughed and moved back over to sit next to her. "I doubt it. Does this feel normal, what just happened between us?"

"You felt it too?" she asked quietly.

"I was desperate to have you."

"I was desperate for you to have me. But why did you stop?"

He ran his fingers through his hair and frowned. "I don't want this to go too far tonight. Tonight I wanted to explain some things to you, talk with you, and see what your reaction was. But next time" —he smiled— "I won't hold back. As much."

She smiled and tried to hide the tremor that coursed through her from head to toe. "Should I be afraid?"

"No, not afraid. Uncertain? Nervous? Curious? Definitely."

"How about hot?"

"Oh, yes, I certainly hope so."

Nic nodded. "I should go home then. It's late. I'm feeling uncertain, nervous, and curious. We better save all that for next time."

Jack stood and pulled her to her feet. "Nicole, thank you so much for coming here tonight. For your open mind and your patience." His hand held hers as they walked past the kitchen, toward the entry door. She swallowed audibly, still a bit shaken at her strong reaction to him.

"Thank you for that incredible dinner. For showing me your drawings of your dreams. For talking with me," she managed, but just barely.

He called a cab for her and they walked to the door. He picked up her coat and purse where she had dropped them to the floor earlier. She had been about to leave then, planned on leaving for good. She was so thankful that he had stopped her.

She shrugged into her coat and took her purse from him. He took her chin in his hand and leaned in to kiss her goodnight.

And like a match to gasoline, their fiery passion burst back to life. He pushed her back against the door. His hands grasped hers and brought them up on either side of her face as he devoured her mouth, seizing her lips. Her breasts, aching, pressed against his chest as he leaned in. He wouldn't let her go this time, she could tell. She could feel the swell of his arousal pressed against her hip, feel the hunger in him as his fingers tightened around her wrists and he secured her beneath him. His power seemed to rise around them both, enveloping her as well as him. She whimpered with her need for him. Her knees began to give way, but it didn't matter. He had her.

There was a honking from the street outside and Jack jerked his head back from her. "Damn cab!"

Nic panted and he looked back at her. "You okay?"

"No." She shook her head. "I'm not okay. You are amazing."

He smiled as he released her hands and put his arms around her. He led her from the condo and cradled her against his chest in the elevator. "It's you who are amazing, Nicole. You aren't the only one who is affected." He took her hand and brushed it against the front of him, so she could feel his erection through his pants. He then brought her fingers to his lips for a light kiss over her knuckles.

"When can I see you again?" he asked.

"When do you want to see me again?"

"Tomorrow night."

"Yes."

He helped her into the cab, and she twisted around to look back at him through the rear window until the cab turned the corner and he disappeared.

She sat back with a groan. *What the hell was she getting herself into?*

CHAPTER TWELVE

"Hi."

"Hi there. How are you feeling this morning?" Jack's voice flowed into her ear from her phone like an intoxicant.

"I feel decidedly … I don't know." Nic laughed.

"A lot happened between us last night."

"Yes, it did."

"Would you still like to come over to my place tonight?" She could sense him holding his breath, waiting for her answer.

Her mind was saying *Oh, yes!* But she took her time with her response. "Let me check my schedule."

"Well, if you're too busy," he said and she could hear his grin.

"My evening seems to be clear."

"Good." Now she could almost see that grin. "How about I pick you up after work, when I'm on my way home?"

Nic bit her lip, thinking it over. "Let's make it my apartment. I would like to go home and get changed and such."

"Okay, I'll pick you up at your apartment." She gave him the address and asked him to call her when he was in front of the building and she would run downstairs. That way he didn't have to deal with the truly abysmal parking in her neighborhood.

"Since you are going home before coming to my place, could I make a request or two?" he asked.

Was that a teasing tone she detected? "You can make them. We'll see if I accept them," she said.

He laughed. "Okay. First, I would like you to wear a skirt. A short skirt. I know you must have a few."

"Hmm, okay, I can probably do that."

"Second, I would really like to see you in some high heels. They don't have to be the ones with chains or anything fancy, but at least three inches in the heel."

"Well, we'll see about that. I don't often wear really high heels. So I will wear the skirt and contemplate the heels. Is that okay, or were these orders?"

"No, no, no. Just requests. No orders. Not yet."

She noted the *not yet*. In fact, she thought of little else the rest of the day.

* * * * *

She heard her phone buzz, just as she was slipping her feet into some plain black pumps, simple but the requested height. They wouldn't be too hard on her feet. Her legs were bare from shoe to mid-thigh, where the flirty, flared black skirt brushed against her. She was very conscious of her naked legs. She wore a loose red blouse and underneath it all, a matching black lace thong and bra.

You never know, she thought. Although she had an idea that Jack might be seeing at least some of what was beneath her clothes that night.

"Hi, yeah, I'm coming right down," she said into the phone as she picked up her purse and a black leather biker jacket and headed for the elevator.

She pushed through the street door to find his Jeep idling directly in front of her. He turned to look at her and his mouth fell open.

Nic's heart skipped a beat. She had half a thought to run back upstairs and change into something less revealing.

Then she thought, *No, own it. You want him to want you.*

She sauntered toward the car and slid into the passenger seat, drawing her legs up slowly and smoothing her skirt over the little bit of her thighs that it did cover. Since she was wearing a thong, she could feel the tops of her thighs, even the slightest bit of her buttocks, against the black leather of the seat.

"Wow, Nicole." He was still gaping at her.

She smiled back. "Did I fulfill your requests?" she asked teasingly.

"Definitely. You're like a fantasy come true." He turned back to face the street. "I better get you back to my place before I make a scene right here."

She knew he was teasing, but Nic still curled her toes inside her shoes, or at least clenched them since there was little room to curl them.

He swung into the parking garage beneath his building and led her up to his condo. Nic smiled as he held the door open for her. She walked in, again admiring his home—the lights of Seattle laid out beyond the windows, the high ceilings and big open space, the sense of being able to breathe, move, twirl around if she wanted to.

Jack had picked up some Thai take-out. He set the big bag on the kitchen counter and she moved to help him unpack it.

"No. Wait." He took her hands, kissed her knuckles, and looked her in the eye. "We'll talk some more tonight, after dinner. I've got to keep my hands off you until then. But I just want you to know how pleased I am you are here again. How pleased I am that you didn't brush me off after last week. And how damn pleased I am that you are just as you are. So don't worry about being anything other than that."

Nic blushed, smiled, and shrugged. "I'm glad you want me to be here." But she didn't feel as casual inside as she tried to sound. In fact, her stomach was jumping and her pulse felt a little flighty. She hoped the Thai food wasn't too spicy.

She also hoped he had wine.

He did. He brought out a bottle of slightly chilled Array Cellars Chardonnay.

Jack served up the Thai food, asking her what she might want out of the six different dishes he had selected. She asked for some of the green chicken curry with plain rice. Thankfully, he hadn't ordered it too spicy. Jack piled his plate with rice, nine-flavored beef, and pad Thai. He would have a lot left over.

They ate at the small table near the window, chatting a bit about the community center. Jack asked for her thoughts on what needed to be included and listened carefully as she described what she thought a community center should be.

He asked her to take a seat on the couch while he brought the plates back to the kitchen. Then he came back to sit beside her, taking her hand in his.

"Now, last night I told you a bit about the kind of relationships that I've been involved in. It's only fair, and will help me get to know you better, if you tell me a bit about your relationships. No details, but just" —he shrugged— "the nature of them."

Nic thought of Lawrence and immediately pushed the thought away. Not now, not here.

"I haven't had a lot of long-term relationships. Usually they fizzle after a few months. A year, maybe."

"Fizzle?"

Nic frowned, trying to explain. "They lose their spark."

"You get bored."

"No, not really. I've never had a relationship end badly, but they just tend to trail off. I'm still on good terms with everyone I've ever dated. Although not in touch with all of them." She laughed. "I make it sound like there have been scads of men. That isn't true at all."

"Older? Younger?"

"Well, I have rarely dated someone in my own age range. Almost always older."

He smiled. "Good news for me. How many relationships have lasted over six months?"

Nic hesitated. "Two," she finally replied.

He raised his eyebrows and nodded. "You should know I've had only one very intense, long-term relationship. That happened quite a few years ago. I spoke last night about the other type of intense relationships I've had in the last ten years or so."

Nic felt a pang at the thought of the women he had been involved with and what he meant by *intense.*

"Jack," she began, and then faltered. She took a breath. "What kind of relationship do you want with me?"

"I just want to see what develops between us. As I told you last night, you fascinate me."

She didn't hold back her bright smile, but his next words caught her by surprise.

"I mentioned submissive women. Do you want to see what submission is?"

She knew she must have looked wary, for he immediately held a hand up to her. "Okay, I'll tell you what it isn't. It isn't whips and chains and abuse. It isn't taking advantage of someone or putting them in danger. In fact, it's just the opposite. It's when the person submitting gives of herself to the other person. The other person takes that gift as something valuable and is very protective and caring of it.

"It's a journey, a developing of a relationship, a growing of trust, a melding of personalities, each meeting the needs of the other."

"Isn't that the way all relationships should be?"

"I think so, yes, but I have tended to take it a bit more formally, and further, than most people." He stroked a hand down her hair. "I want to discover you, Nicole, in a way that I think no one has ever done before."

"How do you plan to do that?"

He smiled. "How about I start here?" He leaned in, his hand sliding behind her neck, and kissed her softly on the lips. Her heart trotted to a faster pace. He kissed her, pulled back a little, then kissed her lips again. She leaned toward him and brought a hand up to touch his shoulder.

"Yes, touch me," he murmured as he continued to lay light soft kisses on her lips.

She stroked his arm, encouraging him.

"Come here. I want to kiss you more deeply." He took hold of her hands and pulled her to her feet, so she was standing before him. He tugged downward, gently, almost asking, looking up at her. His eyes were warm and his breathing was slow and steady. "Please."

She knelt between his legs and turned her face up to his. His hands cradled her face as he started to kiss her again. But this time he took her lips, his own mouth slanted across hers, harder and hungrier. She sank against him with her arms folding around his thighs.

His hands strayed into her hair, caught it and pulled her head back slightly, angling her face up to his. Her lips parted and he seized the advantage, his tongue invading her mouth with the same urgency as the previous night.

She felt caught, but not trapped. Held, but not a prisoner. She felt his desire for her and she responded in kind. Her moans were caught between their mouths, muffled.

She let him. He kissed her, he held her, he directed the tempo and rhythm. She gave all that control to him and it felt amazing.

When he was ready, he broke the kiss and sat back slightly, her face again cradled in his hands. He studied her, locking eyes.

Nic licked her lips. They tingled and felt swollen.

"Strip for me, Nicole. I want so much to see you."

She inhaled. *Could she?* The lights were on and he had not seen her naked yet. It would be so blatant, so exposing. So fucking sexy.

She stood up and his hands dropped to skim over her bare legs. He kept his eyes on her face as he caressed her knees, her calves, her lower thighs.

"Start with your blouse."

Nic took the edge of her blouse and pulled it up, past her breasts, over her face, and over her head. She dropped it onto the floor next to her.

"Fuck me," he whispered as he took in her breasts. They were barely concealed behind the lace of her demi-cup bra.

She half suspected that his exclamation was an order, but said nothing.

Jack swallowed. Nic was elated at the effect her body seemed to be having on him.

"Your skirt," he said softly.

She unzipped the skirt in back and then pushed it over her hips. Once past her curves, it dropped around her feet.

His eyes were fastened to her tiny thong.

His hands came up the back of her legs and cupped her buttocks. He licked his lips, leaning forward, just inches from her pussy. She wondered if he could smell her arousal. His nostrils flared as he inhaled and she suspected he could.

There were men in Nic's life who had admired her, lusted after her, and made her feel incredibly sexy, but standing before Jack LaTour and seeing the naked lust in his eyes along with his carefully controlled touches, she felt exalted. She felt worshipped.

"Would you walk to the table and back? So I may view you fully?"

Nic took a few steps back and then pirouetted, presenting her ass for his view. The ass with nothing hiding it, only a single string between her cheeks. She sashayed to the dining table, letting her hips sway with each step. The string of her panties slid between her ass cheeks and nestled against her damp pussy lips, tantalizing her with every step.

She was having too much fun. Submission? She could feel her power as she tempted him.

So much fun that when she reached the table, she placed her hands on it and leaned forward, her ass tilted back in his direction. She looked out the floor-to-ceiling windows framing her city.

Then she looked back over his shoulder at the man sitting on the couch, with his legs spread and his eyes locked on her. *Was he looking at her ass or her face?* From this distance she couldn't tell. His breathing had definitely picked up. His dark hair had fallen over his forehead.

He was stroking his obvious erection through his pants. He didn't seem to care if she noticed.

Her own breathing picked up, knowing that he was hard because of her. She actually had to suppress a moan as she turned to him. The thong was tormenting her now, the way it rubbed against her.

In for an inch, in for a mile, she thought. While he thankfully wasn't showing a mile, the bulge in his pants was definitely more than an inch.

She made the most of her return. She ran her hands over her stomach and then skimmed them over her breasts, along her neck, and into her hair. Her hips swayed and her thighs brushed against each other with every step.

She stopped before him. He didn't stop stroking himself.

"You vamp," he growled.

"You didn't like it? I could do it again." She smiled sweetly.

"No! You're not going anywhere." He hissed in a breath, his lips thin and his eyes narrowed. "Are you ready for Phase Two, Nicole?"

"Phase Two?"

"Trust me. If you are at all hesitant, we can stop now."

Nic shook her head. "I don't want to stop." She sounded more than a little breathless.

He widened his legs. "Kneel, please?" It was a request.

She did.

"Unzip me?" Another request. She sensed she could refuse. She didn't want to.

She ran her hands up his legs from his knees to his hips. She worked the button through the hole and then carefully unzipped his pants. She began to slip her hand into the opening. He grabbed her wrist.

"Not yet, sexy. Aren't you eager?" His thumb caressed over the pulse on her inner wrist. She could feel it throbbing under his touch. He sat quietly for a few moments, as she watched him. His eyes flicked over her, from hair to eyes, to lips, to breasts and she could feel a spark of heat at each place in turn. Her nipples hardened and pushed against the lace of her bra.

"Straddle me." It didn't sound as much like a request this time, but she wasn't at all reluctant to comply. Nic stood and placed a knee on either side of him, lowering herself onto his lap. Her breasts hovered inches from his mouth. Her barely clad pussy grazed his trouser-covered erection.

He kissed her shoulder, kissed the swell of one breast, licked up her cleavage, from her bra to the dip at the base of her neck. Nic pressed down slightly against him, feeling her inner heat growing. Her hunger grew with it.

His hands came behind her and unclasped her bra.

She briefly noted that he didn't fumble with it at all. *Of course not*, some inner voice griped. *he must have years of experience at this*.

Then all thought left her head, as he slid the straps down her arms and bared her breasts.

His mouth touched lightly on the tip of one nipple, then the other. He looked up at her when she moaned.

"You have sensitive nipples," he said, as he cupped her breasts and flicked his thumbs against them.

"Very," she whispered, shivering. She felt a rush inside of her.

"You are gorgeous, Nicole. Your mind and your radiance, combined with this mysterious, reactive body. I feel like an explorer just beginning a journey."

"Indiana Jones and the Lusty Lady." She smiled through her audible breathing.

He chuckled. "A real wit," he said and closed his lips around one nipple, sucking softly.

Nic gripped his shoulders and arced toward him, exclaiming in a soft sigh. He suckled her, alternating between one nipple and the other, until the peaks were rosy and hard. Within minutes, she was pressing down on him and undulating her hips against his bulge. With every circle, she could feel the brush against her clit. The fragile lace of the front of her thong suddenly felt coarse against her.

When she was ready to ask him to lay her down and remove her last remaining garment, he instead let go of her nipple and in a level voice said, "Kneel again. Suck me as I have just sucked you."

She knelt. Her thighs pressed together and she could feel the slick moisture between them. The string of her thong pressed up between her slit, against her clit, with frustrating friction.

That frustration was more than cancelled by the eagerness with which she parted his pants and closed her fingers around him, drawing his cock toward her.

Her lips parted. He was beautiful. Straight and strong, hard as a steel pole. He was fully erect and easily long enough for her to need to use both fists to cover his length, although she could close her fingers around his girth.

She had never seen a cock so awe-inspiring. Not personally, not in photos (thank you, *Playgirl* magazine!), and not in any work of art.

She licked her lips.

"Thank you," she breathed as she lowered her mouth to kiss the tip of him. "Thank you," she whispered again, just before she slid her lips around his cockhead and took him into her mouth. She found she wanted more. She wanted him inside of her, not just in terms of fucking, but *inside* of her.

She wanted to please him, to give him the same pleasure he had just given her.

She languidly suckled him the way he had her, pressing her lips down him, sucking as she drew them back up. She laid her tongue beneath his cock, pressing, massaging his length.

His fingers curled into her hair, caressing the back of her neck.

"God, Nicole, you have a magic mouth," he said gruffly and pressed up into her mouth a little more. She moaned and met him, pressing down at the same time, so that the tip of his cock came dangerously close to the back of her throat. He didn't press further, letting her judge the depth. She came back up and then down again. Up and down, faster.

Fucking him with her mouth. But so much more.

It felt like making love. It wasn't just her mouth with which she was pleasuring him. It was her entire body. Her entire mind. Her hand held him at the base, while her saliva dripped down his length. Her breasts rubbed against the edge of the sofa cushion with each bob. The string of her thong was practically masturbating her, the way it rubbed between her legs.

His breathing was harsh, as his fingers gripped her hair and pulled it back so he could watch her. She moaned, he cursed, she brought a hand between her legs and stroked her clit.

"Yes!" he exclaimed. "Rub yourself! Let me feel your orgasm!"

He was rhythmically thrusting into her mouth. The taste of him, the sense of being filled with him … within minutes she came. Her cries were muffled by his cock but shc shook all ovcr, lightning racing up and down her spine.

Lights burst behind her closed eyelids as she trembled in one last release.

Just as the last lightning bolt raced down her spine, he pulled from her mouth.

"Lay back!" His voice was harsh. It was an order this time. She dropped back onto her hands, her back arched and her legs parted, still on her knees. He came with a growl, pumping himself with his hand. His glistening white semen spurting onto her breasts. Again and again, he shot onto her and she gazed in wonder as the creamy fluids landed on a nipple, her cleavage, her stomach.

At last, he groaned and fell back on the sofa. Nic tried to control her breathing. Jack wiped a hand over his face. She thought she saw the faintest tremor in that hand.

He looked at her from between his fingers. "Wow."

She smiled, feeling as ragged as he looked. "That was incredible."

He slid from the couch and leaned over to kiss her wet lips.

A moment later, he gently cleaned her breasts and stomach with a towel. Then he pulled her into his arms and rocked her there, on the floor. He stroked her hair, while murmuring something she couldn't make out. It was comforting, soothing, and quiet. Just what she needed to steady and center herself.

She thought she must be in a half stupor, for she thought she heard him murmur, "Mine."

She lifted her head to look at him.

"Um, no," she said. A wave of alarm drove all blissful dreaminess out of her head.

CHAPTER THIRTEEN

Jack frowned at her after her whispered denial. "I'm sorry. That was premature of me. Of course you couldn't feel that way, yet."

Nic smiled, but it was just to hide the flurry of confused thoughts spinning through her head. Her smile felt tense, as if the corners of her lips were pushing up against a forceful weight.

Mine? Where did that come from and what did he mean? Was it all part of his weird feelings toward women? How could she possibly be his when she was still seeing someone else?

Lawrence. Dismay swept through her, leaving her cold. What she and Jack had just done was way beyond what she had done with any other man since she began to see Lawrence. He said she could, and should, see other people. She suspected he didn't mean giving groveling blowjobs to some man who comes on her tits. *What did he mean then? Why had she never asked?* Of course she had never asked.

Questions crashed through her brain, each one demanding an answer that she didn't have.

"Nicole?" Jack brushed the hair out of her eyes. "Are you okay?"

She took a deep, shaky breath. "Just a little overwhelmed, I think." Oh, yes. Just a little.

"Was that too much? Too soon? Just tell me."

Images flashed before her eyes. Jack's lips surrounding her nipple. Jack's cock rising before her eyes. Her fingers wrapped around him. Jack standing over her as his semen rained onto her breasts. Looking down and seeing his glistening drops on her skin. Heat crept through her at the memory.

Nic turned to him and touched his cheek, then his lips. "Not too much, but more than I expected. Not just what we did, but what I felt."

"Tell me. What did you feel?"

She searched for the right words. "Giving. Open. Daring. Naughty." She looked at him, feeling uncertain. "A little dirty and loving it. And at the end, a hazy euphoria."

He nodded. "I hoped you would feel all that. Your feelings will grow even deeper, as we explore further."

"You seem to be an expert," she said, with a twinge of jealousy.

"I am." He was matter-of-fact. "I've been around a long time, remember? I'm much older than you."

Nic smiled, bemused. "You aren't that much older than me and I don't consider age to be much of a factor. It is all about the dynamic, isn't it?" To which she silently added, *You have no idea how much age is not a factor to me.*

"It is. You're a mature lady to believe so." He seemed about to ask something else, but left it at that.

His arms tightened around her and he got to his feet, easily lifting her with him. She wrapped her arms around his neck and nuzzled her cheek against his shoulder as he carried her the few steps to the couch. He laid her down and gazed over her. She noticed that he had zipped up his pants and looked relatively pulled together, compared to her mostly nude body and tousled hair. She touched her lips, which still felt swollen and sensitive, but in a pleasant way.

He sat on the floor next to the couch and stroked her hair.

"We have a few practical matters to discuss, I'm afraid."

"Yes? Should I be worried?" She touched him too, drawing her fingers up and down his arm.

"No, no. It's just that at this moment I want to hold you and caress you, but I know I need to get you home and there are a few things to go over before I do that."

"Mmmmm, go ahead."

"Nicole, I want to go further. I want to make love to you. Completely. Fully. In order for that to happen, we should know that we are both safe. Safe sex."

"Condoms?"

"If you prefer." He made a bit of a face.

"I don't prefer. I get checked annually and am on birth control, if that's what you need to know."

"I also get checked annually and I always use condoms, if I'm uncertain of a partner's situation. If they're safe or not." He hesitated, then continued. "I would be happy to share the results of my last check up with you. Everything is clear."

"I've always been clear too."

"What kind of birth control do you use?" He wrapped a wisp of her hair around his finger.

"The pill."

"And that works for you? No side effects?"

"I've been on it since I was in high school, no problems."

He nodded. "Good. A responsible girl. I like that." He blew out a breath. "Well, that clinical part of the conversation is over."

"Thank goodness. Not very sexy."

"But very important." He leaned in close. "Because when I say I want to make love to you, I mean I want to be inside of you, to experience you as deeply as I can. To breathe you in as I push into you. To lie with you joined together. I want to spill my seed into you, so that you possess a part of me the way I intend to possess a part of you. For those moments, we will be as close as two people can be. No walls, no barrier between us. We will do anything and everything together."

Nic had forgotten to breathe, lost in his description of love making. As the silence stretched out between them, her held breath began to burn in her chest and she was startled out of her trance.

"Ohhhhh," she breathed out. Then, "Oh, yes."

She thought of that word again. *Mine*.

"And now, my girl, I need to get you home."

As he helped her dress, she thought of telling him about Lawrence. She felt she ought to, but tonight felt like a dream, like a frontier newly explored, and the words died on her lips. Those words didn't fit here. Not now, not tonight. That resolution felt familiar and she realized she had thought the same thing the last time she was with Lawrence and thinking about Jack.

They were quiet as he drove her back to her apartment. He found parking, amazingly enough, and walked her up. His hand rested on the small of her back. She felt drowsy and a little foggy. He took her key and opened the door for her, then led her to her bedroom, which was just off the main room and not hard to find. He helped her undress without touching her overtly, wrapped her fluffy thick robe around her, and kissed her fully on the lips.

"Bolt the door after me," he said. "I won't go to the elevator till I hear that."

She followed him to the door where he kissed her again. He smiled and pulled the collar of her robe tighter around her.

"Do you know how close you just came to being ravished again? I'm capable of great self-control, as you can see. That will be important for you to know."

With that, he kissed her a last time and left, closing the door behind him. She flipped the bolt and chained the door. Then rested her forehead on the white-painted wood.

"Good night, Nicole," he said. The sound of his footsteps faded as he walked away.

CHAPTER FOURTEEN

Nic leaned her head back, resting it on the edge of the hot tub, and stared up at the night sky. Clouds skated across the expanse, refusing to let the light of a single star through. The waning moon glowed feebly off in the distance. She imagined that it shone much more brightly over Seattle than it did here across the lake in Bellevue.

Lawrence wasn't home yet, but he had sent the taxi for her at the same time as usual. However, it was Saturday night instead of Friday night.

Today she had spent quietly, reading and cleaning her apartment. Taking an extra long, extra hot shower. Shaving her legs, lotioning all over, and towel-drying her hair into soft waves. Just the way Lawrence liked it.

Yesterday at work she had been a jittery, distracted mess. Jack wasn't just on her mind, he seemed to have gotten *into* her mind. Thoughts of him crowded out all other thoughts, including her internship project and returning a call to Evi.

Including, for the most part, Lawrence.

When Lawrence had called her mid-morning, she begged off coming over that night, saying that she was feeling rundown, headachy, and couldn't wait to go home. He tried to talk her into taking the afternoon off and going home to bed, but she insisted she could last the afternoon. She promised to call him that night and anticipated coming over on Saturday, if that was okay. He said it was definitely okay, although he wouldn't be home from dinner with his son until after eight. He confirmed that he would arrange a taxi for her at 5 p.m. and urged her to come and relax in the hot tub, or watch a movie in the media room. Sasha would cook dinner for her. She almost argued that she could fix herself a sandwich, but then she thought of Sasha's incredible cooking. It was too good to miss out on a chance to indulge.

Another call had come right after Lawrence's. It was Jack.

"Hi, Nicole," he said in a low voice.

"Hi," she breathed.

"How are you? Everything okay?"

"Everything's very okay. You?"

He chuckled. "I've been hard all morning, thinking of you. I can't get a thing done."

Nic shifted in her chair, uncrossed and crossed her legs. "Me too. Oh, not the hard part! The thinking. And the not doing."

He laughed openly. She hoped no one was nearby on his end.

"When can I see you next?"

Nic hesitated, tapping her nails on the desk. "How about Monday after work? I've got some things to do this weekend."

There was a significant pause, before he replied. "Sure. That works for me. How about we meet near your apartment for dinner?"

Nic gave him the name of a little bistro.

"I'll let you get back to work, baby, but I'm going to think about you all weekend."

She choked on the obvious reply of "I'll be thinking of you." Instead, she made an approving sound and said a warm goodbye.

Frances shot inquiring glances at her all day yesterday, every time she had to be brought out of a reverie or prompted for an answer. She finally pulled Nic aside.

"You look tired and preoccupied," Frances said. "Anything keeping you up at night?"

"Yes, but I'm fine. Just something on my mind."

"Nic." Frances pushed aside a file folder and sat forward, clasping her hands on her desk. "If you have anything you would like to ask me, I will do all I can to answer. That's all I'll say on the subject." She twisted her lips in what could have been a smile or a grimace. Perhaps a little of both. "Seems that I may have spoken out of turn the other day. At least that's what I've been told."

Nic didn't pursue that hint, just excused herself and did her best to finish her work.

She had called Evi Friday night and asked her friend to join her for Sunday afternoon coffee.

"You at Lawrence's?" Evi asked.

"No, not tonight. Tomorrow night."

"'K. Call me Sunday when you get home. I think the eggnog lattes are starting up for the season this weekend and I'm craaaaaaaaving one."

Nic sighed now and sank down further in the steaming water. There really was nothing more soothing than a hot tub on a cold November night. Except for Jack's hands stroking her hair and his whispered words in her ear.

She groaned, climbed out of the tub, and wrapped herself in her white robe. Sasha was busy cleaning up the kitchen when she ambled in and plopped down on a stool by the counter.

"Cookie, Miss?" The matronly woman pushed a plate of crimped butter cookies toward her.

"Oh, yeah." Nic bit happily. These things really did melt on the tongue, probably because of the enormous amount of butter contained in each cookie. She would have one.

No, two. She reached for another.

"Dinner was so good, Sasha. Thank you so much for feeding me."

"My pleasure. You are so appreciative."

"I don't even usually like fish that much. What kind was it?"

"Well, in Russia we might use what is called sudak, but I substituted cod here. It worked quite well, I think. My mother used to prepare it in cream like that. I have simply tried to duplicate her recipe."

"Soooooooo good. Cream, butter cookies. You are going to make me fat."

Sasha smiled. "When you marry, you are supposed to get fat. It means you are being provided for. At least that was the way it was when I grew up."

"I don't know if you've noticed, but it's not true so much with the married ladies around here. They seem to just keep getting skinnier and skinnier."

"I have noticed."

They both laughed. Then Nic heard the garage door opening.

"Ah, he is home. Go greet him." Sasha shooed her away. Nic grabbed another cookie and went down the hall to open the door to the garage. Lawrence was just getting out of the car.

For a half second, the image of her on her knees there in front of the car, with Lawrence leaning on the hood, flitted through her mind. She mentally brushed it away.

"Here. For you," she said and fed the cookie into Lawrence's mouth. He smiled and quickly swallowed it to give her a firm buttery kiss.

"Mmmm. You taste sweet," he said.

"It's the cookie."

Lawrence dropped his coat on a chair in the hall, took her hand, and led her upstairs. She curled up on the chair in the wardrobe area and watched him shower through the opaque glass, his lean body just a shadow. He came out, wrapped in a towel, and knelt before her. He swept his fingers through her hair.

"How has your weekend been so far?"

Nic shrugged one shoulder and smiled. "The best part was luxuriating in your hot tub. So far." She tucked his silver hair behind one ear.

He grinned at her. "Let's see if we can perk up your activities." He parted her robe with his hands and leaned in to nuzzle her breasts. She cradled his head in her arms as he kissed and licked the swell of her breasts.

Then his lips closed around one nipple, flicking it with his tongue.

She jumped and pulled back with a soft cry.

"Hey! What's up? You okay?" He looked shocked and concerned, but she had no words with which to explain.

"No. Sorry. Yes, I'm okay. I just … I guess I'm still not myself." No, she wasn't herself. What was the matter with her?

Lawrence sat back, then got to his feet. He put his hand on her forehead, checking for temperature, she could tell. She smiled ruefully.

"I'll go make you some tea. Be right back."

"Oh, Lawrence, you don't have to."

"No problem. Just relax, sweetheart." He threw on a robe.

Once he had disappeared through the door and his footsteps could be heard on the stairs, Nic sighed and slumped in the chair, dropping her face into her hands.

She knew what was wrong with her.

Mine.

Lawrence had touched her intimately and it felt wrong. So wrong that without thinking, she had recoiled from him.

She felt terrible. Confused. She felt in some way, she had betrayed Lawrence, while at the same time also betraying Jack. Neither knew about the other. She had gone too far with both to make that fair.

She had to do something. She didn't know what. Lawrence was back with the mug of steaming tea before she had come up with any plan, before she had even lifted her face from her hands.

"Nic, what's wrong?" His voice was low and level. He set the mug on the table next to her.

"Oh, Lawrence," she said and caught her breath.

He knelt on one knee and took her hands away from her face.

"Has there been some bad news?" he asked.

She laid her head on his shoulder. It would be the last time she would do that for a while.

She inhaled his scent. He was clean and soapy from the shower, but his natural smell was there too. It would be the last time she would do that too.

She sat up, blinked and licked her lips.

"I'm seeing someone else."

* * * * *

Lawrence looked stunned. A piece of Nic's heart seemed to break off. She almost took the words back, she felt so awful hurting him, but they were out there now and couldn't be withdrawn.

"I'm so sorry," she added.

He held up his hand. She sat there, silent, until he gathered his thoughts.

"Don't be sorry," he said huskily. "It's for the best."

"No, don't say that!"

"Nic, I'm happy for you. I'm happy for me, too. It's time." His voice sounded so calm and final. That was her undoing. She choked and then let the sob out. Tears quickly overflowed her eyes and ran down her face.

"Oh God, Lawrence. I don't want to be like this. I was so happy with you. I wish nothing had ever happened to change that," she managed to say, between cries.

"Shhhhhhh." He drew her into his arms, cradling her. "It was inevitable. I always knew it. You should have known it too."

She sobbed, wetting his robe with tears. He stroked her hair, her back, and gave her a few moments.

He finally straightened her up and clasped her hands in his.

"We can't see each other anymore. Not romantically. You know that."

She nodded. She didn't think she had ever been this miserable.

"I have always told you to see other people, but I knew that if anything ever became serious, you would let me know. That is the kind of woman you are. You've done the right thing in telling me tonight."

She nodded again, not feeling the least less guilty.

"Now I want to tell you something else. I want to say thank you."

She frowned and started to speak, but he shushed her so he could continue. "You, my beautiful girl, brought me back to life after Ingrid died. My world was so gray and you lit it up like a kaleidoscope. You are one of the most significant people I've ever had in my life. You should know that I love you."

She groaned with despair, but he shook his head with a half-smile.

"No, darling. Don't feel bad about that. I know that you have a love for me too. I know that I have been significant in your life. I know that I have brought something very special to you. So don't feel bad about anything. It was worthwhile, it was amazing, and it was good."

"I do love you," she said, so quietly that he ducked his head to hear her. Then he kissed her forehead and caressed her lip with his thumb.

"I will miss you, Nic. I will miss you so much. But" —his voice became a little sterner— "this was inevitable. I love you, but I could never have had children with you. I would never have asked you to marry me. So this wasn't sustainable."

"We could have gone on as we were."

"No. We couldn't have, not forever. You need more. I don't know if this man will give you that, but it's time for you to look about you and see." He brushed her hair back from her face and then asked, in a voice that was purposefully casual, "Should I know who this man is?"

"Jack LaTour."

"The architect?" Lawrence's hand stilled on her hair.

"Yes." She looked up at him. "Why?"

"The one working on the community center?"

"Yes. I—" She opened her mouth, suddenly frightened. "This won't affect his work on the community center, will it? I know you are one of the donors, but I never thought …"

"No, no. It won't affect anything from my end. But does he know about me?"

She dropped her head again. "No."

"Good. I think it best that he doesn't."

She wanted to ask why, but at the moment didn't have the energy.

He tilted her chin up with his finger and gave her a gentle lingering kiss on the lips. "You should get ready to go home."

Pushing herself to her feet, separating from him, brought a physical pain to her. She felt a little shaky as she walked across the room to where her bag sat on the end of his bed.

"I guess it's a good thing you never took me up on that offer to leave some of your things here permanently," he said behind her.

Another bolt of pain shot through her. She wrapped an arm around her middle.

His hands came up to her shoulders. "You get dressed and pack up. I'll go downstairs and call you a cab."

Nic let the tears flow freely as she changed into her clothes and packed her bag. She folded the robe she had always worn at Lawrence's home over the back of the chair that she had just sat in. The chair where she had taken apart their relationship.

Lawrence waited for her at the bottom of the stairs, his cell phone in hand. "They'll be here in a moment."

She looked toward the kitchen and wiped her cheeks with one hand. "Say goodbye to Sasha for me."

"I will."

He wrapped his arms around her shoulders and held her against his chest. They didn't say anything until the lights of the cab swept past the windows by the front door.

He walked her out and handed her bag to the driver. The back door of the cab stood open for her.

She turned to him and he grabbed her, holding her as tight as he ever had, burying his face in her hair. She wrapped her arms around his waist and held him just as tight.

"My head knows you must leave. My heart doesn't really want to let you go quite yet," he choked out.

She started to cry again.

He pushed her gently away from him. "No tears, Nic. Call me if you need me. Always." He pulled himself away from her and she climbed into the cab. He shut the door and turned back to his house. She thought she saw him swipe at his eyes.

"Where to, Miss?" the cab driver asked in a heavy accent.

"Seattle," she said. She would give him a more accurate address when they had crossed the lake. The one word was all she could manage before she dissolved into sobs.

CHAPTER FIFTEEN

"I broke up with Lawrence."

Evi froze with the first seasonal sip of her eggnog latte halfway to her mouth. She settled the paper cup back on the table. "No," she moaned.

"Yes. It was time. It was—" and then Nic choked and had to wipe her eyes with the back of her hands. "It was practical, you know. We couldn't ever have … it would never have … it's a good thing …"

"It's Jack," Evi said with a glower.

"Yeah." Nic nodded. "It's Jack."

Evi finally managed that sip of her first eggnog latte of the year, but it didn't look like it brought her much joy. "Well, I'm disappointed."

"Good God, don't make me apologize to you too."

"I hope you know what you are doing."

"I have no idea what I'm doing."

Evi leaned across the table. "Then why the hell did you break up with him? He was awesome!"

Nic fidgeted in her seat and then looked steadily at her friend. "Because I had to."

"You had to." Evi nodded. "Yeah, right. What the fuck is going on, Nic?"

Nic bit her lower lip and played with her coffee cup, also filled with eggnog latte. "Look, Evi. All I know is that I had to do it. Lawrence has always told me to see other people. Other men, you know?"

"Yeah, and you did. As I know very well." Evi arched one eyebrow. "I remember the guy who took you to a Sounders game. You made out with him in his car, in the parking garage on Royal. I remember the guy who took you to the opera. That, as I remember, didn't warrant more than a kiss. I remember the guy who took you to see Witchburn at the Comet Tavern. Let's see, did he maul you in the hallway to the bathrooms, or in the alley behind?"

"Okay, right. I got it." Nic sipped her coffee, but didn't enjoy it as she usually would. "I saw a few guys, but it never went as far as it did with Jack. With him, things just felt different."

Evi narrowed her eyes. "How far have you gone with Jack?"

She rolled her eyes. "Evi …"

"Come on, you've always told me."

Nic shrugged. "Pretty far, but not totally far."

"So what does that mean? Third base?"

"Really? Bases?" Nic lifted her eyebrows. "I've never known what the different bases related to."

"'K. First base is a kiss." Evi ticked off one finger.

"Yeah, first base is rounded."

"Second base is a bit of nudity and a French kiss."

"What? Are we in high school?"

"Got it. We breezed over second base. Now third base is feeling you up." Evi touched her third finger and looked at Nic.

Nic sighed in exasperation. "I gave him a blowjob. What base is that?"

"Whoa! Seriously? A blowjob?"

Nic noticed the two guys at the next table giving them interested glances. She leaned in across the table.

"Quiet," she hissed, but couldn't help giggling along with the frown.

Evi shifted her eyes to the guys and then looked back at her friend. "How was it?" Her voice was quieter.

"How was it? Well, you know what happens."

"Did he cry?"

"Cry?" Nic wrinkled her nose. "What are you talking about? Do men cry during blowjobs?"

Evi sat back in her chair, her mouth open. "What? No! Oh my God." She started to laugh. "I was talking about the breakup."

"God, Evi." Nic shook her head. "I've got no idea what you're talking about."

Evi wiped her hands on the paper napkin and leaned close. "What is Jack about?"

Nic looked toward the big front window of the coffee shop. It was just a local place, called Milo's, with great coffee and a relaxed attitude. People could sit here all morning, tapping at their laptops or writing in their moleskin notebooks, while sipping at cups of coffee that lasted them over two hours, without anyone trying to shoo them out. Life here was low-key and relaxed. Not at all like the atmosphere in Jack's condo.

"I've never felt the kinds of things that I felt with Jack."

"And you've seen him, what, three times?"

"Four."

"Four. And you're blowing him. Not that there's anything wrong with that." Evi put up her hands in answer to Nic's glare. "I'm just saying that you had more to lose than the average girl."

"Yeah, a much older man who wanted to fuck me on the weekends and cuddle me at night."

"That's not fair, Nic." Evi frowned at her.

Nic sighed. "No, it isn't. Lawrence deserved so much more than that, but that was all our relationship could ever really be. He told me that. He seemed kind of relieved, actually." Another pang of grief hit her stomach, making her regret the coffee.

"What will you get with Jack?"

Nic tapped her fingers on the table before she answered. "What will I get with Jack? I don't know. But I know that it's the most exciting prospect I've ever had. I feel like I'm traveling to a foreign country and I've barely read the Rick Steves guidebook."

"Does he make you happy?"

What a basic question and one that should be easily answered. With Lawrence, she was happy. Content. Comfortable. She could have answered Evi's question quickly. With Jack?

"I feel intrigued. It's almost better than happy."

Evi nodded. "I think I know that. The most intrigued I am by Saul is what Nicolas Cage movie he'll download for us to enjoy Friday night. But you know what?" Evi took a big sip of her coffee. "I'm totally down with that. Saul makes me happy. I guess we have to define our own terms."

Nic nodded and tore a piece off the rim of her paper cup.

"Will you keep me informed?" her best friend asked.

"Yeah. I will." But Nic knew that there might be some experiences with Jack that could be too complicated to explain to someone who was still captivated by Nicolas Cage.

CHAPTER SIXTEEN

Nic shivered over her roast chicken. She tried to eat another bite, but Jack's hand brushed over her knee again. Her fork clinked loudly against her plate when she jumped.

"If you don't stop, I can't eat," she hissed at him with an exasperated smile.

"If you're hungry, you'll eat." He slid his hand higher.

She glanced around the small bistro and brought a bite to her lips. She managed to get it into her mouth without dropping it, although some of the delicious sauce caught on her lip. She used her napkin to pat her mouth.

She did need to eat, because lunch had been beyond her. She had packed a salad that looked spectacularly unappetizing when she opened the container. She had sat there at her desk, torn between daydreaming of her meeting with Jack later that night and ruing the crash of her relationship with Lawrence two nights before. No wonder that a few torn pieces of lettuce, some chopped cucumber, and a toss of limp ham slices splashed with balsamic failed to hold her attention.

The dinner was fantastic. This bistro, two blocks from her apartment building in the Belltown neighborhood, was one of her favorites, but usually too expensive for her.

The simple roast chicken breast was pan-fried and then the pan juices deglazed with wine, mushrooms, and thyme. Haricots verts, with a sprinkle of nuts and lemon zest, finished the plate. Someday, she would cook like this. Someday when she had a kitchen larger than a twin-size bed.

Jack sipped his red wine and watched her over the rim of the glass as his other hand, hidden under the tablecloth, squeezed her lower thigh. She pressed her legs together, wanting to keep him from progressing any further. But she knew she was also trapping his hand there.

He smiled.

Sipped his wine.

Watched her.

She finished most of her chicken and green beans and the waiter arrived promptly to remove their plates. Jack stroked her inner thigh, while the waiter took his time clearing the table. If he noticed Nic's trembling hands around the stem of her glass, he was too discreet to smirk. She concentrated on her glass of wine, a white wine that had well complimented the dish, and squeezed her thighs, wondering how even through her pants, his hand could make her skin tingle.

They stared at each other over their wine glasses. Then Jack slid his hand from between her thighs and brought it up to hold her hand openly on the table.

His fingers were graceful but strong, with short clipped nails. She stroked her thumb along a whitened scar on his index finger.

"What's this from?"

"From a broken beer bottle in college."

She glanced up at him. "You should make up a better story than that. Hand-to-hand combat with a martial artist, maybe?"

"It was a fight with broken beer bottles over a woman."

"Really?" Her thumb froze on his hand.

"Yes. I got this cut and another on the back of my shoulder."

"The back of your shoulder?"

"Yeah. By that point, I'd realized that the woman wasn't worth fighting her two-hundred-pound boyfriend. I was trying to make a quick exit. He got me on my way out the door."

"You didn't know she had a boyfriend?"

"I knew." He shrugged, grinned, and took another sip of his wine.

"Cad." She laughed.

"I definitely was then. I floundered around and didn't have much respect for relationships. I was more interested in getting laid, in new and numerous ways."

"Oh." She touched his scar again.

"Are you disappointed in me? I'm a different person now. I like to think I've matured a little."

"I'm not disappointed. I didn't always have respect for relationships either."

"You were busy in college too?"

"No. I had one boyfriend through most of college. He was my professor and advisor." She took a breath and then continued. "He was also married."

"Ah." Jack took another sip of his wine. "Was it a good experience overall?"

"The four years with him were amazing. Yes, it was good. The ending was … difficult."

"Did his wife find out?"

"She knew pretty much the whole time, but I finally matured enough to realize that for him, it wasn't love. I was his fetish, I guess. His guilty pleasure. He cared for me very much. But he loved his wife."

"He told you that? That you were just his guilty indulgence?"

"No. I knew. It took me four years, but I finally knew." She didn't feel a pang of bitterness anymore, when she thought of Tom. A certain wistfulness, yes, but mostly just gratitude for all he had taught her and all the support he had given her. And gratitude that she finally had the good sense to realize how he felt about her.

But at the time, she was certain that breaking up with Tom would be the worst thing she would ever go through. So far, she had been right.

"You broke up with him."

"Yes."

Jack nodded. "Good for you. It was time for you to move on. And now" —he leaned in close— "here you are. I'm very glad I met you at this point in your life."

Nic smiled. "You are?"

"Yes. Lovely and mature for your age. Open to new experiences. And unencumbered by a jealous two-hundred-pound boyfriend."

She fought off a pang at the thought of Lawrence. *It's okay, it's okay*, she thought to herself.

"I'm glad you found me too," she said.

"Do you have family you are close to?"

She shook her head. "No, not really. My parents live in California and I visit them about twice a year, but I can't say we are exceptionally close. No siblings. I've always relied on my friends as my family."

Jack laced his fingers with hers, playing with their intertwined hands. "My parents live up in Anchorage. I grew up there."

"Wow, a real frontiersman. You came to Seattle for college?"

"Yes. Proud graduate of the University of Washington."

"I've only lived in Seattle for about five years."

"Why did you come here?"

"The jobs. There is so much more opportunity here than in California, it seemed. And it is the hip place to be." She laughed.

"Why do you laugh?"

"Because I'm so not hip."

"No, you aren't. You are classy. It's much better than hip."

"Oh, I hope so. Because being hip is beyond me." Nic liked that thought of being classy.

"I've never been hip either, believe me."

"Classy also?"

Jack guffawed. "I just try for dependable and leave it at that."

"And mysterious. And sexy."

"Oh? Do go on."

Nic leaned in over the small table. Their heads were almost touching, their hands linked.

"Sensual. Confident." She licked her lips. "Ardent. Virile. The scent of sex seems to surround you." She took a gulp of her wine. "I can't believe I just said that."

"I can. I've been thinking of little else all day."

"Sex?"

"Yes. Specifically involving you."

She inhaled sharply and felt her heart trip and then speed up. "Want to ditch this hot dog stand and go back to my place?"

"I thought you'd never ask."

Jack settled the bill and then wrapped her coat around her shoulders. The walk back was short, but the wind was brisk. Nic opened the door to her apartment gratefully.

"I didn't show you around when you were last here. How about I give you the grand tour?" She hung up their coats.

"Yes, I'd like that."

She stood in the middle of the small room and pointed at the kitchenette along one wall. "Gourmet kitchen." She waved her hand toward a door on one side of the room. "Three-quarter bath." She gestured to the one other door on the other side of the room. "Master bedroom. Or Mistress bedroom in this case." She pointed to the coat rack on the entry door and the plastic mat on the floor nearby which held a pair of boots and a pair of slippers. "And of course, the mudroom."

"Like a featured residence in *Pacific Northwest* magazine," he said, looking around.

"Yes! They get so tiresome, asking to feature my place all the time."

Jack took her hand and led her to the small slipcovered sofa. "Actually, it is a historically significant building."

"Seriously?"

"Yes. Built in the 1930s. The man who built it dedicated it to his wife, who died of flu the year before it was completed. The architecture is representative of its time."

"But what a sad legacy." Nic drew one leg up beneath her as she sat, facing him.

"I like to think that this building has housed many happy moments since then."

He brushed her hair behind her ear and then laid his hand against her cheek. She leaned into his hand and then turned to kiss his palm.

"Before we start tonight," he said softly, "I would like to give you something."

"Oh. Okay." Nic wondered what it could be. A present? She really hoped not. She felt a little flustered just at the thought.

Jack got up and stepped over to his coat and removed something from a pocket. He dropped a folded piece of paper into her hand.

She unfolded it. It was his doctor's report. She glanced at him, then scanned it.

"I should give you mine," she said.

"In your own time."

"No, let me get it." She got up and went into her bedroom. Kneeling on the floor, she pulled a file box from beneath her full-sized bed and flipped through the folders.

She held the piece of paper up. It was like a license to make love freely. Clearance to feel him move inside of her.

He took it, looked it over, then handed it back. “All good?” he asked.

She smiled, infused with a rising warmth throughout her body. “Very good.”

He drew her to him, took her in his arms, and looked at her steadily. “I intend to make you feel incredible,” he said and then lowered his lips to hers. His hands caressed her back, his fingers trailed down her spine from neck to bottom. His mouth was firm on hers. His tongue stroked her lips, demanding entry. She parted her lips and he entered her. She welcomed him, her tongue twining with his.

His hand swept up beneath her shirt, touching the bare skin of her back.

She moaned. Their kiss didn’t break as he laid her down on the sofa.

The sofa was too short for them.

He lifted his head and looked back at where his feet laid over the arm of the sofa. “Damn thing,” he muttered.

“I apologize for my child-size furniture,” she said as she kissed the underside of his chin. She licked his neck as he fidgeted, trying to get comfortable. He finally sat up, exasperated.

“Okay, this sofa is as efficient as a chastity belt,” he said.

Nic thought she had an excellent alternative. She knelt between his legs and laid her hand on the front of his pants, meaning to unzip him and perform the act that she had demonstrated the other night at his condo.

His hand came down on hers. “No.”

“No?” she echoed, startled.

“No. Stand up, Nicole.”

“I was just going to—”

“Stand up, please.” He smiled, but his eyes blazed with a fevered intent. She found that she couldn’t refuse his command.

She didn’t want to refuse. She realized this with a sudden startled clarity.

She stood and he took her hands in his. He kissed her fingers, each in turn.

Then he stripped her. He lifted her shirt up over her head without getting to his feet. He lifted each foot and slipped off her heels. He unzipped her pants and pushed them over her hips and down her legs. As each inch of skin was exposed, he kissed it. His lips burned against her skin. He licked her. His tongue set her tingling. Her arms, her shoulders. Her stomach, which quivered beneath his mouth. Her hipbone, her thighs. He brought her legs up, one at a time, to kiss her knees, her calves, lick circles around her ankles. She felt blanketed in the heat of him. No one had ever kissed her from head to toe before.

When she stood in nothing but her bikini panties and bra, he sat back and admired her. She clasped her hands in front of her and tried not to fidget under the heat of his gaze.

“You’re having trouble keeping still,” he said.

“Well, I’m standing here half-naked in front of you. The lights are all on and everything.”

“You are a work of art, Nicole. A masterpiece of creation.”

She rolled her eyes. “Oh, please.”

He took one of her hands and pulled it away from her body, her arm held out to the side.

“The face of a lady. Eyes that express your candor. Hair like a Pre-Raphaelite beauty. The graceful lines of your neck flowing into your strong shoulders. Breasts, full and abundant. Nipples, beautifully rosy and oh-so sensitive.” He touched her nipple through her bra and she shivered from the coursing tingle that ran through her. “A toned torso that quivers when touched by my lips. Hips that curve perfectly, hinting at the wonders that they cradle within you. Lithe legs, muscular thighs, fine ankles, and elegantly arched feet."

She knew this could be a load of bullshit, but in some way, she believed that perhaps he did see all of this in her. That her parts made up the whole that he was attracted to.

"In your face and body, I can see your history. Scandinavian ancestry in your cheekbones. True blue eyes that can't hide feelings. A lush figure that speaks of sensual fertility. Strength in your frame and muscles." He breathed in, as if inhaling her scent. "A work of art, like I said. As expressive and interpretive as any creation by a great artist."

At that moment, she felt as beautiful and unique as one of the famous muses of those great artists.

"Jack," she breathed.

He reached behind her to unclasp her bra, drawing it down her arms. He looked up at her as he traced his tongue around each nipple, first one then the other. She bit her lip. The sensation was exquisite and almost too much to bear.

He pulled her panties down and dropped them with the rest of her clothes on the carpet.

She was completely nude. He held her hands out to the side when she tried to bring them in front of herself. "Don't try to hide yourself from me."

It wasn't easy, but she fought the instinct to modestly shield herself from him, and won. It really wasn't easy.

"Good girl," he said. "Now spread your legs slightly."

She did, and felt a ripple of excited anticipation go through her.

He cupped his hand beneath her pussy, his fingers touching her buttocks. The pad of his thumb pressed against that sensitive nub.

Then he just held there.

"Do you feel my hand on you?" His voice was so low that she had to concentrate to hear his words.

She nodded.

"Yes?" he asked.

"Yes."

He flexed his hand, squeezing her. Nic took a deep breath at the feel of him.

He pulled his hand back to him, sliding his middle finger along her slit. "Already wet," he noted.

She blushed and felt some shame at how wantonly her body responded to him.

"So ripe and ready." He almost seemed to be talking to himself.

His finger stroked her again. Again. Again. Slowly. Teasingly. She felt her wetness on his finger.

"I—" she started but he shushed her.

"No words. Not unless there is an emergency or you need to stop me from doing something. Otherwise, just feel me."

She shuddered and stayed silent.

He pressed his middle finger and parted her lips. His finger touched her opening. She moaned. She wanted that finger inside of her. Any part of him inside of her. Now. She needed to be filled, penetrated. Her body cried out for his. Now.

He complied.

His middle finger slid smoothly and fully inside her. She moaned again and closed her eyes and felt her pussy clench around him.

"Good. You are doing so well," he said.

He slid his finger several times into her. She felt her lubricating juices coating her lips, wetting her, as he drew them from her. She heard the increasingly wet sound of his finger-fucking.

She bent her knees just slightly, without even really thinking about it, and pressed down on his finger, just the tiniest bit.

It was gone.

Her eyes flew open. He had withdrawn his hand from her. He smiled.

"Don't move, Nicole, or I stop. I just want you to feel. No work on your part. Let me give you this."

She almost replied, but remembered his earlier dictate and just nodded. Swallowed and nodded. It was arousing to not speak, to not move, to rely on his actions completely.

He cupped her again, squeezed, stroked, teased, and finally inserted his finger deep into her again. She trembled and moaned, but held still.

He withdrew his finger and then stretched her around two of his digits. She began to pant.

Three fingers and she was whimpering, as he fucked her slowly, languidly, fully out, fully in. Her legs trembled and she gritted her teeth, steeling herself.

He thrust again, almost bringing her onto her toes. She brought her hands behind her back to clench them together.

It was too much. She began to tremble and moan.

Then he curled his fingers inside of her, stroking her sensitive area, on the front wall of her pussy.

Nic fell into orgasm with little warning, unprepared. Her cries filled her apartment and she danced on her toes, barely able to keep her balance. Her hands flew forward to grip his arm. She was flying and he still stroked her. And again. Not stopping, not slowing. She was caught between ecstasy and panic.

She was falling, but his arm was around her waist, steadying her.

Slowly, gradually, she came back to her senses. He was standing beside her, his arm wrapped around her, his other hand cupping her pussy but no long embedded inside of her.

"Oh my God," she cried.

"You did well." He kissed her hair. "For your first orgasm of the night."

His words penetrated her foggy brain and she realized the significance after several moments. "First?"

"First," he said.

She moaned and sagged against him. "I can't."

"Yes you can." He maneuvered her so she was lying on the sofa. He knelt on the floor and parted her legs, pushing one leg over the back of the sofa, the other foot so it rested on the floor. He leaned toward her and stroked her pussy lips.

"God, you are beautiful," he breathed.

She closed her eyes with a groan, feeling exhausted. "You are deluded. Pussies aren't beautiful."

"Nicole." His stern voice made her open her eyes and look at him, paying attention. "Your pussy is beautiful." He was gazing between her legs, his eyes soft. He stroked the contours of her. "How does it make you feel, knowing that I am looking at you like this? Looking at your opening where my three fingers just were. Seeing you glistening." He licked his lips and she caught her breath.

"It makes me feel … vulnerable," she said.

"Yes."

She swallowed. "Admired."

"Yes." One of his fingers circled her opening and she felt a resulting shiver in her thighs.

"Examined."

"Yes." He purposefully wiped his wet fingers on that thigh, showing her how reactive she was. "You are so ready to have me, aren't you?"

She caught her breath. "Oh yes."

Jack smiled. "You will, but not tonight."

She was about to protest when he slid three fingers into her again. She arched her back, crying out.

He stroked, he sparked, he caressed her. He spread his fingers slightly, stretching her. His thumb came down on her clit.

She whimpered. She moaned. She finally wailed as another strong orgasm washed through her. Her body shuddered under his ministrations. Before she could come to her senses, she came again.

She was barely aware of her surroundings as she laid on the sofa. She was spent, her legs splayed. She didn't have any regard for her nudity or modesty or vanity. He played her like an instrument and she responded.

After a brief rest, he did it again.

This time, as she came again, he whispered, "I will have you. You will be mine." She screamed and arced up, out of her mind, out of control, only aware of him, his presence inside of her.

"Yes," she cried. That was her last coherent thought for a while.

CHAPTER SEVENTEEN

"Nic!"

Nic jerked her head up at the sound of her name, breaking out of her reverie. "Huh?"

"I need you to do something." Frances frowned at her. "Still not sleeping well? I can tell." Her long red nails tapped on the door frame.

"What? Oh, uh, no. I'm sorry I was just daydreaming." *About multiple orgasms*, she added in her head.

"Well, would you be able to take a break and deliver these docs for me? I would send a messenger, but I need you to explain them."

"Yeah, sure. The fresh air will do me good."

"Okay. Steph has the docs. They need to go to Jack, at his office."

Nic froze. Jack's office. Jack. The man with the magic fingers.

He had made her orgasm with those fingers, more times in one night than she ever had. He didn't even have to fuck her or go down on her. Just his fingers. After the last time, when she had laid on the sofa almost senseless, he brought his fingers to her mouth and told her to lick them clean.

Which she did. She licked her own essence from his fingers, her tongue flicking over and between them. She even licked his palm and his wrists, where her wetness had dripped over him.

In the four days since, he had called and texted every day. Every night they murmured to each other on the phone, sharing history, opinions, and feelings. He would give her some dirty suggestions, things he was remembering about his times with her. Her mouth, her breasts, her tongue, her pussy. Then he would verbally tuck her into bed and she would drift away for a night of sex-filled dreams about him.

"Nic?" Frances's voice broke through her daydreams again. "Seriously, girl, you need some coffee. You are in a daze!"

"Sorry. Yes. I'll get going." She stood and collected her coat and purse.

"I've finalized the report on the demands—" Frances stopped herself. "No. Rephrase. 'Requests' of the board members for amenities to the community center. You know what needs to be explained. Let me know if Jack has any additional comments."

"I will."

Nic strode down to the street to catch first the trolley to the city center and then the bus that would take her to Jack's office in Pioneer Square.

It was a brisk day outside and the cold air did much to wipe her mind clean. Refreshed, she took out her phone while on the bus and sent a text to Jack.

I'm on my way to see you.

The reply came back within three minutes.

Really? To what do I owe the pleasure?

Bringing some docs from Frances.

K. I'll be ready to molest you in my office.

Nic smiled.

Tsk. Behave. We are adults.

I promise. We will only engage in adult behavior.

I'm not dropping my panties for you.

In my office? Or in the next twenty-four hours?

I can only commit to modesty for the next hour or so.

There was a brief pause.

We will see.

She shivered.

His architectural office was in one of the old brick buildings on Cherry Street. Outside, it looked typical of the style of the buildings built there in the 1890's. Nic pushed open the door and entered the lobby. Inside, it was airy and modern, with an atrium that rose the full four stories, and an open staircase that wound up from the lobby.

And an intensely hot blonde at the front desk.

"Hi," Nic said. "I'm delivering these to Jack LaTour."

The blonde smiled brilliantly and held out her hand. "You can leave them with me and I'll make sure they get to him."

"Actually, I need to discuss these with them. He's expecting me." Nic smiled back. "Nicole Simmons."

"Of course. Let me dial him." The blonde gracefully picked up a headset and pressed a button on the console in front of her. "Jack?"

A casual workplace, Nic thought, noting the use of the first name. *That's to be expected from Jack.*

As the blonde spoke, the sleeve of her form-fitting dress slipped down her arm. On the inside of her wrist was a circular tattoo but she dropped her arm before Nic could figure out what it was.

The stunning woman smiled. “Jack will be here in a—” she broke off as a voice was heard above them.

“Nicole!” Jack jogged down the stairs from the top floor. “Come on up!”

Nic met him halfway. He kissed her on the cheek and then led her back up the stairs, with his hand on her lower back. Nic hoped that the blonde down below noticed this.

Although the office was four stories, each floor only seemed to have two or three rooms off of a short hallway. The top floor was all Jack’s.

Well, Jack’s and the luminous, sultry woman who greeted her at the top of the stairs.

“Nicole. Hello. Jack has told me about you.” The woman offered her hand to Nic.

She was exquisite and exotic, of some kind of Middle Eastern descent, with eyes that naturally looked as if lined in perfect eyeliner. Full lips. Full tits too, from what Nic could tell from beneath the blouse. Form-fitting pants and heels. She looked very professional, classy, and very sensual.

Is this an architect’s firm or a modeling agency, Nic wondered to herself. The gorgeous women couldn’t be an accident.

Jack had an eye.

Nic shook herself from her thoughts, just in time to keep from looking awkward.

“Has he?” She added a laugh for good measure, as she took the woman’s hand and shook it lightly.

“Nicole, this is my assistant, Shada. She would have had to hear me talk about you, as she would wonder why I was cutting out of work at a reasonable time at night.”

Shada laughed charmingly. “It’s so nice to meet you. I did note when Jack started having reasonable hours.

Of course, that has reverted this week with all of his late nights."

"Yes, it's been a few days." Shada had several inches in height on her. Nic was still entranced by her breasts, which were beautifully displayed in the open V-neck of her blouse. She had a mole at the top of the swell of her left breast.

Nic turned her eyes away and looked at Jack.

Who was grinning wickedly at her.

"I've missed you," he said, but his grin hinted that he might have been aware of what she was staring at. "Come on, let's go in my office."

"Can I get you something to drink? Coffee? Tea? A soda pop?" Shada offered.

"Oh, no thanks," Nic said.

Jack closed the door behind them. His office was flooded with the minimal daylight that marked the end of October in Seattle. There was a large desk covered with papers, as well as a large drafting table against the windows, and a circular table and four chairs in the corner. A working office.

Her eyes swept over the interior and then she was in Jack's arms. He pulled her to him and smothered her with his kiss. The need and savagery of the kiss thrilled her. His arms encircled her, his tongue invaded her mouth. The envelope with the documents was smashed between them.

He growled.

She moaned.

He broke the kiss and studied her face.

"Glad to see me?" he asked, a little breathlessly.

"Oh yeah." She was also breathless.

He looked at her a moment more, then released her. She smoothed a hand over her hair.

"What do you have for me?" He took a seat at the table, holding out his hand for the envelope.

They went over the documents, discussing the relative merits of the requested amenities and the politics of meeting the demands of big donors. After about fifteen minutes, Jack nodded and tossed the report on his desk.

"I'll show you around."

He led her out of the office. Shada looked up from her spacious desk.

"It was so nice to meet you, Nicole. I hope to see you again." She had a slight lilting accent that hinted at a foreign birth, but many years in America since then.

"I hope so too. Thanks, Shada." Nic waved as she and Jack descended the stairs.

The third floor held the offices of Jack's two assistant designers. One was an average-looking man, she was relieved to see. The other was a petite wholesome blonde, who smiled broadly at her and greeted her warmly.

The second floor held the accounting and marketing offices. Another two exceptionally pretty girls filled those two positions.

Hm, Nic thought to herself. *It's like the Playboy Mansion around here.*

Once they reached the lobby, he introduced her to the receptionist. Veronica smiled, offered a hello, and coolly went back to flipping through some kind of directory. Jack walked her to the front door.

"I'm sorry about this week. I've been crushed with work."

"I know, but you still called every night and kept in steady touch with me. I appreciate it."

"Tomorrow night?"

"Yes, I'd like that."

"Dinner at my place?"

"I would like that as well." She smiled.

"I'll call tonight." He leaned in closer and whispered, "Have you enjoyed my nightly phone calls?"

"Mmmhmmm," she murmured.

"Tomorrow night, I would like to make love to you, Nicole," he breathed into her ear.

"Yes." Her voice was barely audible, just a sigh. She twitched and pressed her legs together, to suppress the sudden flicker of heat there.

He slid his hand into her hair, cupping her head, and brought his lips to hers. A kiss that started as something proper, began to blaze when his tongue touched the seam of her lips. She made a muffled noise in her throat and he pulled back, glancing at Veronica.

Nic looked over and saw with some satisfaction that the woman had to quickly drop her eyes back to her obviously faux task.

"Bye for now." He drew his hand from her face. "God, you make me hot."

The same could be said for her, but she didn't need to tell him that. She was sure her flushed face and parted lips gave her away.

"I'll talk with you soon." She smiled and touched her lip. Then gave a jaunty wave to Veronica and was out the door.

* * * * *

"Did you see Jack?" Frances asked, as Nic arrived back at the office.

"Yes I did. Nice offices!" She grinned hugely, in a great mood after that public kiss from Jack.

"Yes, indeed." She smirked. "What did you think of his staff? Rather gender-specific, don't you think?"

Nic shrugged. "I did notice. He likes pretty girls. I'm sure they are all proficient at their jobs."

"Oh, they are."

"He only has girls at his office?" Steph asked, looking incredulous.

"No, he does have male employees," Nic said.

"Oh, really? That's new," Frances said.

"Mark. One of his assistant designers."

Her boss nodded, still smirking. "Maybe Jack needed to balance out all that estrogen."

Nic resented Frances's obvious digs at the man she was seeing. Especially in front of Steph. "Anyway, back to work," she said and strode down the hall to her own office.

Frances followed her in and closed the door behind her.

"My apologies, Nic. That was unprofessional of me."

Nic sighed. "Thanks for the apology. I was getting uncomfortable."

"I've just never seen Jack actually dating someone, the way he is seeing you. I really didn't think it would go anywhere."

"It's only been three weeks. You don't have to beat around the bush. Jack told me about the kind of 'dating' he did before me."

Frances gaped at her. "Seriously? Wow. He really is taking this in a new direction."

Nic smiled wanly, suddenly feeling a little drained by the conversation. "Yeah, well, we'll see where it goes."

"He certainly is being open with you. Telling you about his girls at the office and all."

She froze. "His girls?" she finally managed to ask.

"Yeah. For whatever you can say about Jack, he really took care of his girls after he ended those relationships. They were all, more or less, especially important to him, but Shada was with him for several years."

Nic didn't know what to say. Her confusion was so complete, she couldn't even think of a question to ask.

Swallowing hard, she straightened up and smiled at her boss, hoping her smile looked more authentic than it felt.

"Jack's quite the guy," she said.

CHAPTER EIGHTEEN

"Hi, Nicole." His voice, on the phone, was a smooth as honey.

She didn't have much of a craving for honey at the moment.

"Hi, Jack."

He seemed to hesitate and she knew that he had detected the chilly tone in her voice.

"Is everything okay?"

Nic sat down on the edge of her bed and rubbed her forehead. She wished she could pretend that Frances hadn't said what she said, but Nic had heard the words. She had to ask.

"Can I ask you a question?"

"Of course."

"All those women that work at your office, are they all your ex-girlfriends?"

"No." He seemed about to go on, but didn't.

"I think they were." She wouldn't mention Frances, but she wasn't going to let him off easy.

He sighed. "Yes. Kinda."

Now it was her turn to swear.

"Okay, let's talk about this. Would that be all right? I can explain some things that might put this in a different light," he said

"Fine. Shoot. I'll listen." She swung her legs up on the bed and reached for her glass of wine. "Go on. This should be interesting."

"Every one of the girls in my office was a former sexual partner of mine. I know that sounds bad."

She guffawed. "Oh, really?"

"It doesn't mean what you think it means. I've been involved in this kind of thing for ten years. The vast majority of women I've been with are players in the club and take on many sexual partners. I am with them only once or twice and all it involves is sexual play. No feelings between us. There have been a few exceptions"

"Like Shada." She could tell that he and Shada had some kind of special connection.

"Okay, yes, Shada was with me for several years, but it wasn't love. I care about her as a person and she makes an excellent assistant. She is extremely loyal. She was not my girlfriend. Now she is happily married to a very nice man."

"Really?"

"Yes. Not only that, but she liked meeting you today and wants me to be happy with you."

"But … why? Why do you keep an office full of your women?" So far Nic was keeping it together, her voice level and steady.

He sighed. "The women you met today, I had exceptional relationships with. They were some of my longer-term relationships. When we parted ways, we were on good terms, but these relationships can be very intense. They feel dependent on me to some extent. In turn, I feel responsible for them to a limited extent. This solution has worked out well with this group of women. They have secure jobs at good salaries, we understand the motivations and habits of the other, and I have excellent help. This isn't charity. I only hired the women who would excel at their job."

She shook her head, her mind whirling. "It's weird."

"What's weird?"

"I can't fathom a guy surrounding himself with a half dozen of his ex-girlfriends and getting anything done at work."

"Nicole, baby. This was not love. There was no love. No dating. I never took them to dinner, or art galleries, or anywhere but the club or my home. Concern and compatibility. That's all I feel for them. They are in no way ex-girlfriends. In fact, my last ex-girlfriend was from twelve years ago. I haven't had a girlfriend since."

"That's weird too."

"It really isn't. I didn't need one. I didn't want one. I was fulfilled with what I was doing." He blew his breath out in an exasperated sigh. "Until I met you."

Her heart stilled. "What do you mean?"

"I want you in more ways, deeper ways, than I've wanted any woman in the last dozen years. Including the ones you met today."

Nic reviewed what she saw earlier that day at Jack's office. "Veronica still has feelings for you."

He was quiet for a moment. "It's possible," he admitted. "If she became a problem, I would have to let her go."

"Do you still have sex with them? Even casually?"

"No. That's one of the conditions of employment. We are completely platonic. Most of them are involved with other people."

"Boyfriends?"

"Boyfriends. Play partners. Doms. Other women, even."

"Oh."

"Nicole" —he broke off, then continued, fumbling over his words— "I don't want to screw this up with you. I know this is weird and maybe my lifestyle makes you uncomfortable. The truth is, I'm about the most unattached man in Seattle. I haven't cared for a woman, as other than a plaything and friend for so long. If you are nervous about dating me, I'm at least as nervous about dating you."

She had not heard him sound vulnerable until that moment. He was always so confident and in charge. Yet here he admitted that he was worried about a relationship between them not working out.

"I have another question," she said.

"Okay."

"You say you had a girlfriend. A real girlfriend, ten years or so ago."

"Twelve years."

"Why were you ready to have a girlfriend then? And what happened?"

He was quiet for several seconds. She didn't say anything either, letting him decide what to say.

"It was complicated. At least it was at the end."

"Breakups often are, but I'm curious why you've never had a real girlfriend since then, as you say."

"You mentioned that you thought it was weird."

"It kinda is."

"Then you'll probably think my reasons are weird too."

"I still want to know. Just in general."

"We started off as your average boyfriend-girlfriend, during the college years. We were nineteen or twenty, around there. But by the time I was twenty-two, I had graduated and was working at an architecture firm. I, uh, found that I wanted to branch out a little."

"Branch out?"

He made an exasperated sound. "I wanted to explore some sexual fantasies. Things that she wasn't interested in. I started going to this club, but just to watch, to experience things. Anyway, she ended up freaking out when she found out, which I don't really blame her for. She wouldn't talk about it, she wouldn't talk with me. She just ended it and never talked to me again."

"She might have been hurt."

"I'm sure she was, but I wish she had attempted a conversation with me. I don't even know what she thought in the end."

"So you thought you were done with girlfriends."

"I never met anyone that I was interested in, outside of sex. Until you."

She chewed on her lower lip. "I feel a little overwhelmed. It's a lot to take in."

"Take a chance. We'll both take a chance. We'll figure this out together."

She was silent, blinking up at the ceiling. Was there any way that this could work out? Was she nuts? Who wants to date a man who lives like Hugh Hefner?

She stopped thinking and let the feelings flow through her. His breathing sounded in her ear. She thought of the smell of him. Him standing over her. His fingers inside of her. His grin from four floors above today when he saw her. His heated kiss in front of anyone and everyone at his office.

She had given up Lawrence in order to pursue this.

"I want to love you, Nicole. In a real way. Not just have some superficial sex relationship. I want to know you. For us to know each other."

She believed he was sincere. She knew her desire for him was real and incredibly intense. She knew that they had a unique connection that she had never experienced to this degree before.

She nodded and then added a "yes."

She heard his sigh of relief over the phone. "Tomorrow night?"

"Yes."

"Will you spend the night?"

"Yes. I will. If you would like me to."

"I would really like you to."

"Then I will." She turned to look at her bedside clock. It was getting late. "I like orange juice in the morning."

She could visualize his slow smile. "I'll make sure of it."

She smiled too, tiredly. "I should get some sleep."

"Can you get under the covers now?"

She shrugged off her robe, lifted the blanket, and slid her feet beneath the covers.

"What are you wearing?" His voice again was as smooth and rich and mellow as honey. She might develop a taste for honey again after all.

"Panties."

"And?"

"And nothing. Just panties."

"Bad girl." He laughed. "I am tempted to verbally molest you. Instead, I'll let you sleep. Tomorrow night, we will get little sleep."

"Mmmmm," she murmured, "good night, Jack."

"Good night, Nicole. And thank you."

She ended the call and placed the phone on her nightstand. She turned off her light, rolled onto her back, and stared at the ceiling.

He was exciting. Different. A risk.

This could all go incredibly wrong.

CHAPTER NINETEEN

Jack let her into the condo and took her coat. Then his eyebrows rose with obvious delight.

"Wow."

Nic spun around. "You like?"

She wore a form-fitting knit sheath dress in a midnight blue shade. Half of her hair was gathered up in a clip at the back of her head, to let the soft dark waves fall down her back. Minimal jewelry.

With matching midnight blue panties and bra underneath. But he didn't know that yet.

"I like!" He pulled her to him and kissed her fully, but not hard. A sensual kiss, as if he were stroking her all over. But without using his hands. Yet.

She felt that jittery heat flare inside of her. It had been flickering on and off all day, keeping her agitated. She wasn't sure she wanted to bother with dinner, as her anticipation for what would come later was too demanding.

He pulled back, offered her a glass of Prosecco, and led her into the kitchen.

He gave a few more mixes to something in a bowl and then spooned it into a crystal glass surrounded by crackers.

"Caviar dip." He pushed it toward her.

"Really?" She wrinkled her nose. She had never tried caviar before.

He smiled, and she knew that he could tell. "Taste it. You'll like it."

She dipped a cracker into the creamy white mixture and took a bite. "Mmmmm, it is good," she said, surprised.

"I always thought caviar was supposed to be so salty and weird."

"Wait a minute."

He watched her as she continued to chew. Suddenly her teeth met a caviar egg, which burst into a salty earthy wonder in her mouth.

"Wow!" She brought her hand to her lips. "It's like bubble tea, but better!"

"Sour cream, lemon juice, minced green onion, and good caviar. Plus a few other secret ingredients. Caviar by itself can be strong, although many people love it. This is a nice halfway point."

"For caviar novices."

"Such as you." He smiled. "I prefer it to the 'hard stuff.'"

He took a bite himself and she helped herself to another one. He leaned in close and touched a finger to the corner of her mouth. "You've got a spot of it here." He wiped his finger against her lip. She turned her head just enough to lick the tip of his finger. His gaze grew instantly heavier and hotter.

"You did that on purpose. The dip on your mouth."

Nic smiled at him. She might be a caviar novice, but she was very familiar with sexual foreplay.

"I am tempted to ask you to do that again. I know what a spectacular mouth you have."

"Yes, you do know that," she responded.

He shook his head from side to side, slowly. "Not tonight. I have other plans for tonight."

"You do?" She almost took a step back as he came close. His approach had all the tension of an incoming thunderstorm, of pent-up energy and unknown course, that crackle in the air that forewarned of something potentially dangerous.

He placed a hand on the counter on either side of her, pinning her there. He leaned in, skimming his lips over her shoulder and inhaling the scent of her against her neck.

"I do," he whispered. His breath tickled her skin.

"Do you always plan everything ahead of time?" She rested her hands on his chest.

"Yes." He touched his forehead to hers. "I plan on making love to you."

She nodded.

And gasped as he swept her up in his arms. She held tightly to his neck as he made his way to his bedroom.

The room seemed to shimmer as the draft set the lit candles fluttering.

"Oh, wow." She stared about in wonder.

It was the first time she had seen his bedroom and she doubted that she would ever forget it. This was no sterile bachelor bedroom. No futon on a wooden frame or a flat bed in Swedish modern.

This was a decadent bedroom fit for a pasha.

Heavy deep-red drapes hung from the walls and swayed along each side of a massive bed. Darkly carved wood posts marked the four corners of the bed, covered with a satin spread of maroon and dark brown. A huge carved armoire stood to one side, with a high dresser to the other.

Candle flames danced everywhere: on the dresser, on each side table next to the beds, on tall lighted pillars in the corners of the room. Four individual wall sconces cast a soft electric glow along the walls.

Above the headboard of the bed was a work of art. The brush strokes wove into waves of lines. Although abstract, Nic could feel the sensuality of the work. It must represent human movement, specifically a woman's body.

Jack let her absorb the atmosphere for several seconds. Then he laid her on the cool soft covering of the bed.

He looked at her, then knelt to take off her shoes. He rubbed his thumbs in circles around her ankles as he did. She moved up onto her elbows to watch his next move.

To her surprise, he didn't instruct her to remove her clothes.

Instead, he began to remove his.

She parted her lips as he gripped his shirt in his hands and tore it off over his head, dropping it to the floor.

It was the first time she had seen his naked chest. Well-muscled and toned, tapered only slightly to his waist. He was built solidly, with more muscle than many men. She could tell he got it from genetics, not just working out. The scattering of brown hair on his chest narrowed down to a distinct line that traversed his stomach and disappeared into his jeans.

He unbuttoned his jeans.

She licked her lips and flicked her eyes up to his. He stared at her intently again, his gaze sending an instant hot spark shooting through her to glow deep inside.

She sensed the motion of his hands and dropped her eyes again.

He unzipped his jeans and pushed them over his hips, easily kicking them off. His legs were proportional to his body, his torso flowing directly into the muscular line of his thighs.

He stood before her in tight boxer briefs, tight enough to conform to the ridge it hid.

Another spark shot through her. She began to sit up, reaching for him. A moan slipped from her lips.

Before she could reach him, he placed one knee on the bed next to her and knelt. His lips met hers and matched her sudden urgency. She slid her fingers into his hair, along the back of his neck, over his bare warm shoulders, across the contours of his back. His fingers were just as busy, running down her neck, boldly over her breasts and down her stomach, coming to a stop directly over where that ember burned inside of her. He seemed to sense the heat there, for his kiss deepened and he pressed toward her. His hardness pushed against her thigh. She wanted so much to turn to him, opening her legs for him.

Instead he moved down her body, kneeling between her legs, which hung off the end of the bed. Without pause, he pushed her fitted dress up over her hips, around her waist. He hooked his thumbs into the strings of her bikini panties and pulled them down. She lifted her hips and then her feet as he promptly discarded them, gripped the inside of her thighs in his hands, and opened her legs.

She could feel the weight of his eyes and shifted in response. She wondered if she looked as wet as she felt.

At her movement, his eyes came up to meet hers again. “May I?”

She almost smiled at his formal tone, but the seriousness of his gaze stopped her. “Yes,” she breathed.

And he was on her.

He pushed her thighs up and out, spreading her wider, as his mouth came down to her pussy lips. His tongue made a commanding pass along the entire seam of her, with no hesitation or tentativeness.

His tongue did amazing things to her, exploring her, wandering over her. He didn’t miss a spot and where his tongue touched, a burning warmth crept up to join that heat inside of her.

She was soon moaning and clutching the covers in her fists, writhing beneath him. He used his thumbs to part her, opening her for him. Then his tongue was inside of her, thrusting, flicking, curling, tasting. He moaned too and his fingers tightened on her thighs. He was so hungry for her, she could feel it in his mouth, hear it in his moans, sense it in his ardent attentions.

She arched up in a sudden spasm and he pulled his mouth from her, bringing his lips to her swollen bud. His tongue flicked there, hard, several times, and then she was off, her back arched. The heat exploded through her pussy, her clit, raced up her spine, and broke from her mouth in a cry as she spasmed. His fingers tightened hard on her, holding her in place as his tongue continued to relentlessly move on her.

Her orgasm seemed to go on and on, rolling through her, wave after wave. When she finally began to come down and her cries softened, he lifted his head and delivered a light kiss to her overly sensitive clit.

She blinked, staring at the darkly painted ceiling. He moved up to lie next to her, stroking her hair, letting her return to him.

Nic turned her head slowly to him. He was so close, she could smell her own juices on his mouth. The glistening of his chin and lips gave away how wet she had been.

She lifted her head and kissed his mouth, dragging her tongue over his lips, tasting herself just as she had the other night when she had licked his fingers. He moaned and drew her tongue into his mouth and she could taste herself there too. His tongue, which had just made her come extravagantly, locked with her own.

It was so sensual to be kissing him with the taste of sex shared between them.

And then he left her mouth and pulled her dress up and over her head. Her bra immediately followed.

He kissed his way back down her body and spent his time enjoying her breasts, kissing, sucking, licking and lightly biting the tender nipples until she wrapped her fingers in his hair, torn between keeping him there and pushing him further south for more magic.

He seemed to understand, for he did move down, again on his knees between her legs. Again, he pushed her thighs apart. She cried, startled at the sharp reaction, when his mouth came onto her again. Her pussy throbbed still with her orgasm and his touch was almost too much to bear, making her teeter between begging for mercy and begging for more.

He licked her again and murmured something against her skin that she didn't catch. His tongue was stronger this time on her, more aggressive, and he pushed her legs up higher, curving her hips, so he could fully cover her with his tongue.

She felt her body tightening, that fire inside of her threatening to consume her again.

Higher, he brought her. She could feel her juices running from her, wetting the covering beneath her hips.

Still higher, holding her like a kite on a string, playing her out a little at a time. His own moans increased.

So close. She was so close.

Then his mouth was gone. He stood between her legs at the foot of the bed, gazing darkly as he pulled his underwear down. He knelt again between her legs, his erection upright and aligned to enter her.

He held the base of his cock in his fist.

Her eyes traveled over him. That cock that she had held in her hand and in her mouth but not yet where she wanted it. Oh, yes, she wanted him, deep inside her. Him. Inside of her.

Her gaze traveled down the length of him, to where his fingers wrapped around himself. Just to the side of his fingers, on his left hipbone, was a dark tattoo, her dazed mind seeing some kind of a chain forming a circle.

"Nicole."

Her eyes flew to his face.

"Will you have me?"

She moaned, squirming. "Please, Jack, please. Yes. Take me."

He leaned forward, the tip of his cock just at her slick heated entrance.

Then he pushed in.

She cried out as he pushed deep into her, not holding back. She could feel the stretch of her body trying to accommodate him.

"God!" he groaned as he pushed in even more. "Oh, Nicole. Oh, my Nicole." He gritted his teeth, rearing above her, with his hands on either side of her body as he settled closer to her.

Then he pulled out halfway. Drove back in.

She cried out at the shocking pleasure, spreading her legs wider.

He grunted. Pulled out a little. She could see the tension in his clenched jaw.

He plunged back into her and went even deeper this time. She cried out again.

This time her cry included "Yes!"

"My darling. My Nicole. I can't hold back," he panted over her.

"Don't, please don't hold back. Take me, take me!" she whimpered, meaning every word. She didn't care what he did, she only knew that she needed him in some primordial way that she couldn't have explained. Every part of her, every thought, every sensation. It was all Jack, all Jack's.

At her words, he reared back and then thrust in, coming into her again and again, like a desperate man. His fingers clenched her hair. He took her lips as he took her body, wildly and with abandon, kissing, his tongue plunging into her mouth, their cries mingled in the air between them.

She wrapped her legs around his waist and he bucked against her. She felt that tightness returning and she ran her fingers hard down his back. He cursed, sweat dripping from his brow to splash on her breasts. He reached behind himself to grab her wrists and then held them over her head as he took her.

She felt herself clench around his cock in orgasmic need. His repeated roars announced his own orgasm. At the first heated rush of his release, she came with him.

Bright flashes of light burst before her eyes as she screamed her own release, driving her hips up to meet his again and again and again.

He pumped himself into her, emptying, and she absorbed every bit of it. She could feel his cum pooling deep inside of her.

He collapsed on top of her, gasping, sweaty, and semi-conscious. He released her wrists and she brought her hands to his back, stroking him, feeling him trembling as much as she.

He moaned and nuzzled her breasts, his head on her shoulder. Her legs had fallen away from him and now she let them join her hands in stroking, her feet stroking his lower legs. She rubbed her cheek against his hair, mesmerized by the soft flickering of the candles.

She had never felt anything like it. A joining. For those amazing moments, they were one, moving together to achieve bliss as one. It was something she felt deeper than just her body, more intensely than in just her pleasure points. When she came with him inside of her, especially with his seed pouring into her, it was as if she was elevated to another plane of consciousness.

She wanted that again.

He brought his head up slowly to smile at her. “Did you feel it too?”

She nodded. “I was just thinking about it.”

“I’ve never experienced anything like it.” He shook his head in seeming wonder as he gazed at her.

“I had that same thought.”

“You will undo me, Nicole Simmons.” He propped himself on his elbows and stroked the hair off of her forehead.

She laughed. "Let's do it again!" she said, feeling a little giddy.

"See? You really will undo me. I won't be able to walk by morning." He chuckled.

"You? What about me? I'm already feeling the effect of that cock of yours."

He pulled back, frowning.

"Are you okay? Was I too rough?"

"No! Oh no! You were rough, but—" She caught herself, blushing a little.

He smiled. "Just rough enough?"

She joined in the smile. "Yeah."

"You liked it?"

She stretched a bit, feeling all the delicious achiness inside her. "Mmmmm, yes."

He shook his head, his smile now bemused. "I meant to hold back. To give it to you slow. I couldn't."

"I didn't want you to. I think our need was pretty high."

"I know mine was. Give me a kiss and then I'll go get the rest of the Prosecco."

The kiss didn't break for many minutes. He didn't manage to get the Prosecco before they made love again. This time, he went much more slowly, the way he said he had intended. She winced and caught her breath as he entered her again. He watched her face as he sheathed himself inside of her tender passage. He murmured to her, seeking reassurance, listening to her sighs of pleasure and encouragement. Soon came her pleas for more and harder and more and more and more. He rocked with her, holding her tightly, caressing her breasts, kissing and tonguing her nipples, wrapping his fingers in her hair, reaching down to cup her bottom in his large hands as he moved deeper still. This lovemaking went on many times longer than their first urgent bout, communicating more than the animal lust and initial wonder of the first time. She felt his restraint in every slow stroke he gave her. She felt his skill in each sleek lick on her swollen nipples. She felt his growing desire for her. Not just need, but ardent desire for her. Once he began thrusting again into her, she buried her face against his neck, clinging to him. He growled and groaned and spilled into her once more.

He rolled onto his back and took her with him, holding her against his chest. She took in the sound of his heart beating beneath her ear and the shine of the candlelight over the tattoo on his hip. Her eyes followed the circle once around and then she slept.

* * * * *

She awoke in the semi-dark, confused. She was on her side, her hands tucked beneath her cheek, with a dark pillow cushioning her head. A lamp on the table before her was turned on very low, barely illuminating the top of the table, where stood an empty bottle of Prosecco and the now-gutted candles.

The candles. She remembered the flicker of them, the shadows on the walls, and the glow of the candlelight in Jack's hair.

Jack.

She moved to turn over, but his arm came around her waist, stilling her.

"You awake?" He barely whispered from behind her.

She nodded, not at all sure if she really was awake.

Then she moved to turn toward him again. His arm tightened around her waist, holding her.

"Shhh, baby. Stay like this."

His other hand slid down over her buttock and then her thigh. The hand on her stomach slid lower, grazing over her mound.

She shivered.

"Mmmmmm," he murmured into her hair. "Feel me?"

He pressed his hips against her and she felt his rigid form nestled along her backside.

She moaned and pressed back against him without thinking about it, still feeling half-asleep.

He curled his fingers around her thigh and pulled her leg up to rest on top of his, parting her.

Then his fingers gently danced over her tender pussy lips, softly stroking until the evidence of her growing arousal was slick on him. She held perfectly still, besides the slight twitching of her hips.

He didn't say anything else, just played her with his hand, taking his time. When she was abundantly lubricated, he slid his finger between her lips and inside of her. Just the one finger to pet her inside, tenderly feeling her out. She could feel the residual soreness from his fierce fucking, but it was just a slight discomfort that was almost completely blocked by the pleasure he delivered.

He withdrew his finger and bent his knee up, raising her leg up and over his hip. He brought the head of his cock to her, holding it in his hand, as he stroked the tip along her seam. She tilted her hips back to him, he parted her, and then he slid smoothly inside of her tight chasm.

She closed her eyes.

She could feel her pussy tightening around him, welcoming his cock back inside of her. He brought his hand back to the front of her stomach and began to undulate his hips, holding her with him. Gently, he moved with her, a low tide of movement. Behind her eyelids, she could imagine a crescent of sea, the waves lapping at the shore, trickling between grains of sand.

The fingers of his other hand splayed over her abdomen. "I can feel myself moving in you," he whispered, never stopping the motion of his hips.

She could feel him moving in her too. From this angle, his cock slid in along the inside front wall of her, sliding easily over that erotic spot. Over and over, he moved into her, as relentless and rhythmic as the ocean waves. She began to moan continuously as he increased his tempo, the tide pulling in.

They rocked together, ebbing and flowing, for an unknown amount of time. His whispers, his broad hand on her, holding her against his hips, his deft movements keeping her on the brink, lent an air of hypnotic sensuality. Orgasms were no longer the goal. Their lovemaking was the journey they wished to prolong.

Inevitably, his breathing became quietly ragged and his tempo increased. She ground her hips back against him, yearning for him somewhere deeper inside of her.

With one last hard push, she felt his cock swell inside of her, then felt the pulsing of him as he pumped his semen into her. He made no noise, but for his harsh breathing against her neck.

She bent her head, moaning deeply. She wondered if this was another form of orgasm, one she had never experienced. No fireworks, more like the moon breaking from behind the clouds, to bathe her in its radiance. She bowed her head in gratitude, trembling.

He pulled out of her and wrapped her tightly in his arms.

"It's magic," he said so softly, she almost didn't hear him.

She was already drifting away. She slept.

CHAPTER TWENTY

He did in fact remember the orange juice. It was on the table before the window, along with fresh bagels, cream cheese, smoked salmon, minced red onion, and capers, and orange sections in a bowl. Hot lattes from his espresso maker rounded out the meal.

Nic crossed her legs beneath her satin robe, then uncrossed them at the feeling of being swollen and sensitive. She shifted in her chair.

Jack looked at her over the rim of his coffee cup. He wore nothing but gray cotton sweatpants. She knew there was nothing on underneath, because she had watched him pull them up his legs and over that sexy bare butt of his. This was after they had awoken, in the late morning, and made love yet again.

No wonder she was sore. Four times in twelve hours.

After that last bout of lovemaking, he had asked her to stay with him until Sunday.

"How about a shower after breakfast? Then I'd like to take you on an excursion. If you didn't have anything else planned for today."

"I'd like that."

Nic went into the bathroom and studied the shower stall. There were six round knobs on one wall. Two faucet heads on opposite walls. One rain shower faucet head hung from the ceiling.

And six intimidating-looking spouts on all three walls. These walls were tiled in a black tile shot through with veins of a silvery substance. Mica maybe?

Clear glass made up the fourth wall, which also held the entry door.

The entire thing was enormous. At least six feet square. *Really? A thirty-six-square-foot shower?*

The thing could hold ten people.

Maybe it had.

Nic shrugged and turned one of the knobs. A jet of water spurted from one of the wall faucets. She tried another. Yep, the other wall faucet came on. Temperature seemed to be controlled by how far she turned each knob. She tried another knob. The ceiling faucet rained down thick hot drops of water.

She couldn't wait.

Nic dropped her robe and stepped in. Hit front and back by a forceful heated spray and from above by a warm waterfall, she first turned down the faucet she faced, and then she groaned and slumped her shoulders, lifting her face into the overhead spray.

How long she stood there, she didn't know. Hot water ran over every inch of her skin and the spray on her back was strong enough to ease her tight shoulder muscles.

Finally, she roused herself enough to borrow some of Jack's shampoo and conditioner. Of which, she noticed, there were several containers and varieties.

Guests? She wondered how long ago another female had showered in here.

She winced as she brought her soapy fingers between her legs, washing gently. Then she spent about two minutes figuring out how to turn off the various faucets. She discovered that another set of knobs sent steam out of several spouts.

She finally managed to turn everything off and opened the shower door, to find Jack lounging against the counter. He had a towel slung over his shoulder.

"I should deny you the towel," he said with a grin. "You are too sexy to cover up."

"I better cover up quick then, before you have your way with me yet again." She laughed and grabbed the towel from him. He made a move for it, but she was quicker.

She wrapped herself in the towel. He came behind her and wrapped his arms around her shoulders, kissing her wet hair and looking at her in the mirror. The muscles in his forearms corded as he tightened them.

"I've got something for you," he said.

Then he reached into a cabinet and handed her a small glass bottle.

"Tea tree oil," he said. "It will ease the soreness. Just apply a small amount to the outer area. Not inside."

"What? You mean down there?"

He smirked. "Yes. Down there."

She removed the lid of the bottle and took a sniff. It smelled like a calming herbal concoction.

"Tea tree oil?"

"Yes. It will help. I'll let you get ready while I dress in the bedroom."

She had no problem getting ready, including the tea tree oil, until she got to her makeup. As dark, masculine, and dramatic as the bathroom was, it was crap for applying makeup. The lighting was inadequate.

She came out of the bathroom. "Do you have another mirror? The light in there is terrible for makeup."

Jack stood in jeans and bare feet. "You're so pretty. You don't" —and Nic mouthed the ending line— "need makeup."

He looked puzzled. "You've heard that before?"

"It's what every guy says, the morning after first sex."

"Oh really?" He lifted an eyebrow.

She lifted an eyebrow in reply, along with a smile.

He considered for a moment, then suggested the guest bathroom.

This bathroom she had visited before. The guest bedroom was pleasant and welcoming, without any of the luxurious plushness of Jack's quarters. Creams and greens dominated and the bathroom was well lit with large mirrors.

Nic checked her face over. *Was that a patch of slight whisker burn on her cheek?* She applied some mascara and a brightening cream. She opened the cabinet under the sink, looking for tissues to wipe her fingers.

Feminine sanitary supplies. Enough to stock a small-town pharmacy. Tampons of every size and pads of every thickness. Panty liners. Midol.

She sat back on her heels.

Well, she knew that there had been others. Many others, it seemed.

She and Jack were new. She had no right to be jealous of the women that came before her.

She was the one here now.

She shut the cabinet door with a snap. *Fuck it*. She knew where to go if she suddenly got her period. He had more supplies here than she did at home.

* * * * *

He drove over Queen Anne Hill and down the north side to Nickerson Street. Nic twisted in her seat to watch him drive.

His hands rested lightly on the wheel and he let the Jeep drive until it needed correction. She was fascinated with his fingers, the length of them, the trimmed nails (thank God, considering where they had been!), and the way they flexed and curled.

"Where are we going?" she asked to get her mind off his body.

He gave her a quick smile. "You'll see."

They continued up Nickerson, to the west side of the Ballard Bridge, before he pulled into Fisherman's Terminal.

"We aren't going fishing, are we?" she asked worriedly.

"Get seasick, do you?"

"Very."

"No. No boats for us today. Come on, I'll show you."

He came around the Jeep and took her hand. They had both dressed warmly. Besides her coat, she brought mittens and he pulled a knit cap down to cover her ears. She was grateful for that, as the wind whipped off the salt water.

Dozens of fishing vessels bobbed along the docks. The screech of seagulls and the clink of boat lines blowing against masts resounded over the area.

Jack led her to a small white clapboard building with a bright blue carved wooden fish serving as the center ridge beam. It gave the entire building a feeling of whimsy. Surrounding the building on all sides were shrubs, flowers, and succulents in planting containers, the plants muted at this time of year.

Jack quickly ducked to the side of the building, pulling her out of the wind and unlocked a door. He pulled her inside.

"Whew! It's freezing out there," she said as she looked about her.

It looked like a bait and tackle shop. She looked at one wall, festooned with hooks, weights, and lures.

"Wait. I thought you said we weren't going fishing."

"We aren't." He leaned his hip against the counter and grinned, crossing his arms.

"Why are we here?"

"I wanted to show you my first architectural design."

She looked around at the single room, with a closed sales window along one wall. "This is it?"

"Yes. What do you think?"

She scrambled for a comment, trying to think of something to say. "The fish on top, is that part of your design?"

"Ah, you noticed that. That's what I am most proud of about this build. I was assigned this project by a professor when I studied architecture at the UW. He said to make something useful out of such a simple build. So while it is a fully functioning supply and bait stand, that fish on top functions as a rainwater director. The different carvings in the scales of the fish channel rainwater and condensation off the roof and directly into a rain barrel that supplies water to the landscape plantings around the building."

She smiled. "Impressive. I bet the managers of the Fisherman's Terminal didn't think of that themselves."

"Nope, it was all me. I was only nineteen at the time."

"Wow, the building still looks great!" She caught her breath, struck by what she had just said. "I mean, for being here for …" She trailed off.

"So many years," he finished for her, smiling. "Fifteen years to be exact. A solidly built building like this should have four times that lifetime. I however, should easily live five times that."

She came up to him and slid her hands over the front of his coat. "Good. I like to think of you sticking around for a while."

He took her hands in his gloved ones and leaned down to kiss her. His arms came around her and he leaned back on the counter again, so she was forced to lean against him. His lips explored over hers, boldly but not aggressively.

She hadn't planned on making out in a bait shop on this Saturday.

"Come on," he said finally. "I'll show you my favorite boats, if you can withstand the cold for a while."

They walked along the bobbing docks, admiring the pleasure boats, those floating pampered vacation homes. Tidy dinghies held on, roped to the sterns. In contrast, the professional fishing vessels had a look of military precision, with each item stacked and stored and roped into place.

Jack called out a name at one of the fishing boats. Within seconds, a bearded behemoth of a guy appeared, halloing to them. Jack walked with her along the dock to the side of the boat.

"Hey there, Carlos! This is my friend, Nicole."

Carlos held out his mammoth hand to her, shook it, and then pulled her aboard. Nic climbed up clumsily, not anticipating his move. Jack followed.

"Welcome, Nicole! And my friend, Jack! I was going to call you and see if you had plans for the weekend."

"I do have plans." Jack grinned and nodded at Nic.

Carlos smirked. "Ah, well. I got nothing to tempt you then." He clapped Jack on the shoulder and led them into the warm cozy cabin of the boat. "Coffee?"

"I'd love one," Nic said.

"How about a half-n-half?" Carlos asked.

"What's that?"

"Half coffee, half cocoa. That's what I'm having."

"Sounds wonderful." Nic nodded.

"I'll make two more."

Nic sat down on the padded bench circling a table and took off her hat and mittens. Compared to the biting breeze outside, the interior of the cabin was already feeling stuffy to her. It also smelled like fish. She could feel the boat rocking in the wind and waves. She swallowed, took a deep breath, and willed away thoughts of seasickness.

Jack moved with Carlos to the coffee maker on the other side of the room. Their voices were low, but Nic heard every word.

Carlos gestured with his head toward her in a slight movement.

Jack shook his head quickly. "No."

"Anything going on this weekend?" Carlos asked.

"I haven't heard. Check the website. I'm planning on being incommunicado until tomorrow afternoon. At least."

Carlos snorted with laughter and brought Nic the half-n-half. She took the warm mug and pretended she hadn't heard a thing and wasn't blushing either.

The coffee drink was just what she needed. Hot and strong and chocolaty. Perfect goodness. She told Carlos so. He lifted his mug to her.

"The lady has good taste," he said gravely.

"Considering she is with me, there is a sarcastic tinge to that comment, I take it," Jack said.

"Perhaps it is you who has the good taste," Carlos acknowledged, not dropping his serious demeanor.

"I won't argue that. I have great taste." Jack shoved off from the counter and crossed over to Nic. "Shall we?" He held out his hand to her.

Nic took a last gulp of her coffee and nodded.

"Wouldn't your friend like a tour?" Carlos asked.

"I've had her out in the cold long enough today. We better get home," Jack replied.

"And get warmed up." The fisherman nodded.

"What a good idea." Jack grinned at Nic.

The drive was just minutes back to Jack's condo. He asked Nic if she needed to stop by her apartment to pick up anything but she said she thought she was okay for another night, depending on what he had planned.

He looked her up and down.

"You're already overdressed."

She laughed.

He seemed intent on making good on his statement as they waited for the elevator, pressing her against the wall and unbuttoning her coat.

"There's a security camera up there." She eyed the ceiling along the elevator.

"I know," he growled, licking just below her ear.

He pulled off her glove and brought her hand to the front of his jeans. It seemed that the cameras excited him.

She stroked the ridge she felt beneath his jeans, while he tore off his gloves and slipped both hands beneath her shirt, bringing them up to cover her breasts.

Their kisses had become frenzied by the time the elevator doors opened with a chime. Nic jumped and snatched her hand back from Jack.

"It's empty," he said as he backed her into the elevator and up against the side wall. He jabbed at the top floor number with his thumb without stopping his kisses. The doors rumbled closed. "Unbutton my jeans."

Jack kissed down her neck while Nic looked up at where she knew the camera must be.

"What if someone is waiting for the elevator when it opens?" she asked.

"Only one other person and me on the top floor." He didn't take his lips from her neck as he spoke. "And he's in South America." He gave her breasts a squeeze, which made her moan.

Nic kept her eyes on the black glass above the control panel where that security camera must be. *No one ever watches those videos*, she thought to herself and quickly unbuttoned him. He made a low noise in his throat as she curled her fingers around his cock and began steadily stroking him. His fingers tightened around her breasts, almost to the point of discomfort. She found the aching brought by his hands made her squirm. She wanted more.

Her fingers tightened just as his fingers did and she increased her rhythm.

He growled again and nipped at the skin just above the neckline of her T-shirt. "I'm going to fuck you on the floor as soon as we get inside."

She whimpered and nodded and squirmed so that the crotch of her jeans rubbed against her. His cock throbbed in her hand, pulsing with his need.

The elevator chimed, the doors opened, and Jack lifted his head.

Shada stood there.

Jack and Nic stared at Shada. She looked just as startled as Nic felt.

Oh God, Nic thought, *her*.

The elevator chimed again, indicating the door would close. Jack quickly jammed his thumb on the DOOR OPEN button.

"Shada!" Jack stepped away from Nic and she realized that she had been standing there, opened mouth, with his erect cock in her hand. He quickly put himself back in his jeans and buttoned up. Nic winced at how uncomfortable that must be.

Nic yanked down her T-shirt while Jack bent to pick up their dropped gloves. Shada knelt to pick up a glove and bumped heads with him.

"Sorry," the woman said as she sat on the floor rubbing her head. "I was just dropping off some blueprints." Her accent tripped sexily over the consonants.

"You could have called first," Jack said in a low voice.

"I did! Your phone must be off."

Jack groaned. "Yes, it is."

"I didn't want to bother you. I thought you said you would just be busy last night and this morning."

Nic flushed, knowing Jack must have implied that he would have company. Shada must have known it would be her.

Or, maybe not.

She took the gloves that he handed to her.

They stepped from the elevator and joined Shada in the alcove before the two doors to the condos. Shada carried a set of cardboard tubes, obviously holding the blueprints.

"Why didn't you just use your key and put them inside?" Jack unlocked his door.

"I had this feeling that you might be in there and not answering the door. I'm sorry."

Her key? Nic followed the two of them into the condo. *She has a key?*

As soon as the three of them were inside, Shada turned to Nic.

"I'm sorry. I haven't even said hi yet. It's so nice to see you again, Nicole." Shada smiled, her white teeth brilliant against her olive skin. She held out her hand to Nic.

Nic shook her hand lightly before remembering that this was the hand that had just been wrapped around Jack's cock.

She swallowed and tried to gather her thoughts.

"So nice to see you too, Shada. I hope Jack doesn't regularly keep you working weekends."

"Oh, no way. He's always telling me to go have fun for the weekend."

At one of those parties that Carlos mentioned? Nic wondered.

Okay, girl, pull yourself together, she thought. Shada is Jack's assistant after all.

But … the key.

She might have a key, but Nic was the one invited here for the weekend. She walked over to the kitchen and took a glass from the cupboard, pouring herself some water from the filtered kitchen faucet.

"Would you like some?" she asked Shada.

The beautiful woman smiled, shook her head and turned to her boss.

Nic finished the water in her glass. *You might have a key*, she thought, *but I know where the cups are*.

And then she snorted at her own thoughts.

Shada was speaking in that lovely lilting accent. "I will leave for home. I'm sorry to disturb you."

Jack dropped everything he carried and turned to walk Shada out to the elevator. "I'll be right back," he said to Nic.

Shada waved to her. Nic lifted a hand in return.

Then she dropped her glass on the counter and scowled.

Jack was right back, returning as soon as Nic heard the elevator close. He closed the door behind him and came to her in the kitchen.

"Sorry for the disruption," he said as he reached for her.

Nic stepped back, out of reach. "She has a key to your condo?" she asked.

Jack dropped his arms and looked at her steadily. "Of course. She's my assistant."

"I've worked as an assistant before. I've never had the key to someone's home."

He narrowed his eyes. She saw his fingers flex. "You know it's different than that. I trust Shada. She is so loyal, she would never invade my privacy."

Nic nodded and gritted her teeth.

"She could walk in here any time," she said.

"But she wouldn't. As she just demonstrated."

She nodded again. Then she turned from Jack and walked toward his bedroom.

"Where are you going?" he asked from behind her.

"To get my stuff."

"Nicole!" He sounded like he was right behind her. She took two long strides, when he put a hand on her shoulder.

"Don't!" She spun around.

"You knew this would be different. I told you everything." His face had darkened and his jaw was clenched.

"I know. But I'm thinking that, huh, maybe this isn't the healthiest situation to be walking into." She used her best flippant tone.

"You are right. It isn't. I'm seven years older than you. I've had a lot of women in my life. We have some work entanglements. You're right. It's not the easiest situation to walk into. But" —he caught her wrist— "do you really want to walk out?"

He yanked her to him and wrapped his other arm around her waist. She braced her hands against his chest, ready to push back.

"Tell me, Nicole. Right now. Do you want to walk out?" His eyes blazed at her, his hands tight on her body.

She was breathing hard, staring up at him. Her fingers curled against his sweater.

"My head is saying 'Leave right now,'" she said through clenched teeth.

"And what is the rest of you saying?"

"Just because I want to fuck you doesn't mean I should stay."

"You imply that it's your lust that is making you stay."

"Yes."

"Is it your lust? Or your heart?"

She stared at him. She found that she couldn't tell the difference. Her lust and her heart were all wrapped up in a physical and emotional yearning.

But she couldn't tell him that.

His fingers loosened on her wrist and waist. He stepped back, giving her some space.

"Don't go," he said.

She couldn't leave. Not at this point. A key? He had told her about Shada. He didn't have to, but he did. It made sense in a twisted way.

There was a fire between them. A heat that she just couldn't walk away from. Was it just sex? It was the most powerful draw that she had ever felt. It had to be more.

"Okay," she breathed.

He exhaled in relief and pulled her gently to him again. "You have nothing to worry about," he said into her hair. "As I told you, I'm the most unattached man in Seattle."

She wanted to stay. She wanted to know him. She wanted to explore this between them.

But she doubted that last statement.

CHAPTER TWENTY-ONE

He made the dinner that night that he had planned for the night before. They had never gotten around to dinner on Friday, just finished the crackers and dip and Prosecco at some ungodly hour, sitting cross-legged and naked on the bed.

Tonight he prepared Moroccan-spiced salmon and sautéed greens with rice.

While he prepped the food, she took out her phone, turned it on, and moved for some privacy toward the windows.

She sent a text to Evi.

Still @ Jack's. FYI

Just seconds later came the reply.

WELL! I wondered where u were.

Nic typed:

Sorry. I should have let u know sooner.

Yes! You should have. But all going OK?

Yes!

Nic smiled as she hit the send button.

There was a long pause. She was about to put her phone away. Then:

U getting a little cream in ur coffee?

Nic stifled a laugh and typed a reply.

I'll tell u tomorrow. 3pm @ Milo's?

Yep. I want aaaallll details.

See u then.

Stay safe. I can send Saul to rescue ur ass.

Don't need the Marines. All good here.

See u tomorrow then.

Nic turned her phone off again and rejoined Jack in the kitchen. She played sous chef to him, cutting and stirring as he needed, and then sitting back on a stool with a glass of spicy Pinot Noir. She turned the label toward her. Cloudline, from Oregon's Willamette Valley. Tasty.

She had changed into the one other outfit she brought with her: a soft, elastic waist short skirt in gray and a baggy sweater in a darker gray. It was a casual outfit and not really date-worthy. But she hadn't bothered with panties or bra beneath them.

She took a sip of wine, smiling and feeling a little wicked. She looked at Jack over the rim of the glass.

He caught her glance as he plated the salmon. "You know," he said, as he nonchalantly scooped some rice onto each plate, "I'm really glad you're here."

"Yeah?" She played along, hoping for a reason why he was glad.

"Yeah. I'll tell you something." He spooned some of the greens on top of each salmon fillet. "I've never brought anyone to see that bait shack before."

She lowered her glass to the counter. "No one?" she asked, incredulous. "Ever?"

"Nope. You're the first."

"But—" Nic searched her mind for the details she knew of him. He had a girlfriend some years back, besides all of the other women. And what about friends? "Why?"

He shrugged. "I never got a sense that anyone would be interested. Come on. Bring the wine." He carried the plates to the table.

"Why not?" She took the bottle and their two glasses with her.

He pulled back her chair and waited until they were settled, before topping off their glasses. "Well, those interested in my architectural talents didn't care about those early attempts. And those who were interested in me … well … I found their interest didn't extend to my other talents."

She studied him. He picked up his fork to eat, but she didn't miss the cynical twitch of his lips.

"It seems to me that they missed out on the full package of Jack. Their loss," she added quietly.

He met her eyes. All the cynical traces in his features left him. His face softened.

"Have I told you I'm really glad you're here?" He smiled.

"I believe you may have mentioned that." She grinned.

The dinner was incredible. She was hungry, since they had indulged in a late breakfast and then waited for dinner. The salmon, rice, and greens made for a perfect light but fulfilling meal. Since she had helped him in the kitchen, she knew what effort he had put into preparing such a simple entree.

Thinking about his kitchen preparations, she realized something.

"You know last night? When you accused me of dabbing the dip on my mouth on purpose?" she asked.

"Yes?"

"Well, I just realize now that when I arrived, there was absolutely no prep work done to prepare dinner."

"Uh-huh." He took a sip of wine.

"And all those candles in your bedroom were already lit."

"Yeah?"

"You had no intention of making dinner last night, did you? You planned on getting me immediately into your bedroom."

A slow smile lit his face.

They washed their plates together. Nic noted, as she placed the plates and utensils into the dishwasher, that just in these few times, they had already settled into a kitchen rhythm.

Jack turned on the stereo system and led her to the couch. He filled up their glasses and then drew her legs over his lap as they sipped. His hand ran from her ankle up the back of her knee, to stroke the back of her thigh. She didn't mind the casual possessiveness of his touch. He wasn't asking for permission to touch her now. He knew that if she was here, she was agreeing to this much.

His hand skated under her skirt and curved around her buttock.

Her bare buttock.

His eyebrows rose. His lips smirked at her.

"My lovely Nicole. What a vixen you are."

He squeezed her ass cheek.

"You're starting to get the idea, Mr. LaTour," she murmured over the top of her wine glass.

The music was a lazy blues number. Something she had heard before, but couldn't quite remember. Between the sensual music and Jack's touch, she was soon moving slowly, pointing her toes, arching her back, flexing her muscles. She twisted slightly, so Jack could easily caress her ass.

The music made her move.

She swung her leg off Jack and set her glass on the table. Then she rose and began to sway in front of him. She was barely moving, but running her hands up her stomach, lightly over her breasts, and caressing the side of her neck.

Was she tipsy? They had shared several glasses of wine, but she felt that it was her turn to seduce him. He had worked his magic on her last night, for the entire night. It was her turn.

He leaned back against the couch cushions and watched her, sipping his wine.

"Nice," he said. "Keep going."

She swayed her hips. Brushed her cheek with the back of her fingers. Cupped her breasts through her sweater.

"Strip," he said. But she shook her finger at him, turned, and walked seductively toward the windows. It was just ten feet away from him, but she felt separated and able to express herself there.

She faced him, bending over slowly, sliding her hands down her parted legs. She imagined her bare ass beneath the lifted skirt facing the window.

Then, with the next beat of the music, she turned so her back was to him, and repeated the move. Legs spread, bending over, her fingers sliding over her skin, her skirt riding up over her ass.

"Damn," he said. She looked at him between her legs. His eyes practically glowed in the dim light. Only the kitchen light feebly lit the room.

She walked right up to the floor-to-ceiling window and placed her hands on it. She turned back to him and brought her legs together, shimmying, bending her legs with her back against the glass. There she danced, moved, arced toward him. She took the bottom of her sweater in her hands, pulled it over her head, and tossed it to the floor.

Good God, it must be the wine, she thought.

She cupped her breasts, lifted them. Brought her thumbs and forefingers to her nipples and pinched them.

She danced for him.

He rested his head against the back of the couch and took a gulp of his wine, while he watched her.

She felt like his private dancer. Bought and paid for and wanting to give him everything she could.

She pinched her nipples even tighter and moaned. Twisted her hips.

He sat forward, put his glass on the table, and let his hands dangle between his legs.

She ran her hands over her stomach and dipped into the waist of her skirt.

This needs to go. Now.

It was as if she could hear his thought in her head. His commands. But they were her thoughts. Her commands.

The skirt needed to come off.

She eased her fingers into the waistband and slowly, so slowly, pushed the skirt over her hips. Swaying as she did so. She watched him as her hands pushed her skirt down her hips, over her thighs, to drop to the floor. She stepped out of the puddle of fabric.

She was naked.

And loved it.

Nic brought her fingers back up her thighs, along her hipbones, back up to her breasts, then up and into her hair. She lifted her hair and watched him, as she moved her body.

He was sitting forward, intent. She had him.

She swiveled her hips, turning to face the window. She leaned forward, placed her palms on the glass, and arched her back.

He was on her.

His hands pressed hers against the window. His body pressed against the back of her.

"Jack," she breathed, pinned by him.

"You want me," he said. She could feel him fumbling against her. She looked down to see his jeans pushed to the floor.

"I want you," she acknowledged.

He pressed hard against her. Her breasts were pressed against the cool window, hard and aching.

She looked down. There was an apartment building across the street, one story less than this one. In the third floor, she saw an alcoved window. A dim light. The figure of a man standing there.

"Jack!" she exclaimed, stiffening. "There's someone watching."

"I see him," he said behind her, his groin pressing against her ass. "Don't worry. These windows are tinted. No one can see in."

"You sure?"

"Yes, of course. I made sure of it." He bit her earlobe.

She pressed back against him, keeping her eyes on the male figure across the street.

Then she moaned as she felt the heat of his cock against her.

"You want this, don't you?" he whispered in her ear.

"Yes."

"What do you want?" He pressed against her.

"I want you."

"No, Nicole, my beauty. Tell me what you want."

She gazed dazedly at the figure across the street. "I want you to fuck me."

"What? Could you say that again?"

She took a deep breath and spread her legs wider, arcing her bottom toward him. "I want you to fuck me. Please." This time she raised her voice.

"You want me to take you against this window. While that man appears to watch. Don't you?"

She whimpered, flushing that he knew her need right then. But her need overcame her inhibitions. "Yes."

He chuckled and pressed against her again. "Tell me."

She swallowed and put words to her fantasy. "I want you to fuck me against this window, while he watches."

"From behind," he added.

"From behind."

"Why?" he asked. His fingers came around her hips, pulling her to him.

"Because," she moaned, "because I want him to watch how you take me."

"No, Nicole." He moved a finger down between her legs and over her slit. "Tell me why."

She shook her head, confused. *Why did she want to do this? Why was she yearning not only for his penetration, but his taking her in front of an audience?*

"Because I want him to know that I am yours to take," she whispered. Relief swept through her. Relief that she had finally found the truth.

He parted her slit with two fingers and thrust himself into her. She cried out at the sudden intrusion. He forced his cock deeper inside of her in just two pumps. She scratched her nails on the glass of the window and bent her knees slightly, pressing back on him. He pushed deeper into her.

He bent her over further. She pushed her hands against the glass. He pulled her hips back to him, so that her legs were straightened and braced.

Then he really began to fuck her.

His fingers twirled into her hair and pulled her head up, forcing her back to arc and her ass to lift against him. He thrust deeper, harder, faster.

She moaned. All she wanted was more.

"You like that?" he asked, as he took her, his voice rough.

"Yes. Yes," she pleaded.

She opened her eyes. The man was still there. He was standing in the window. From his silhouette and movements, she could tell that he was masturbating.

He could see the two of them, she was certain.

She was glad. The knowledge excited her.

Jack rode her hard from behind, his thick cock imbedded deep into her, before pulling back and going deeper. Her fingers splayed on the window, her knees stiffened.

"Ask me, Nicole," he growled in her ear.

"Please," she whimpered.

"Please what?" He thrust his cock into her over and over, driving her words from her.

She shook her head. "I … I … don't even know what to ask for. Just … please," she gasped.

He laughed and then pounded harder.

Nic watched the man across the street. He was stroking himself hard now, his face upturned, she could tell from the outline of him. He was watching her.

She began to cry out with each hard thrust Jack gave her.

The man was going to watch her come.

Then she did.

She shrieked and spasmed against Jack, driving herself back onto him. Again and again and again.

Her orgasm rippled, then tidal waved through her, picking up speed as it crashed into her. Knocking her almost off of her feet. Jack's stern grip on her hands kept her upright as she came. Her eyes closed, she wailed and her hands slid down on the window.

Jack's arm came around her waist and he pushed hard into her. He moaned and she felt him throbbing inside of her. She sobbed openly with the decadent feeling of being taken. Being given.

Nic leaned against the window as Jack pulled out of her. She slid partway down to the floor before he caught her again.

She knelt there on the floor, shivering and barely cognizant of her surroundings.

Never had she felt something so powerful. So all-consuming. So obliterating of herself.

So freeing.

As Jack lifted her into his arms, she turned her head to look out of the window and across the street.

The alcoved window glowed in the dim light. The man was gone.

* * * * *

Jack made her a late breakfast of scrambled eggs and toast, with orange juice.

She needed the nourishment.

It had once again been a night of frenetic love making. After the moments against the window, he had carried her to his bed and made love to her gently, loving her body from head to toe, lavishing her with his touch and words. Later, deep in the night, she had straddled him and rode him, undulated her hips slowly, both of them half-hypnotized by the low light and the late hour.

He brought the breakfast to bed, rousing her with the scent of coffee.

She moaned as she sat up, her hair in her face.

He pulled it from her eyes, his thumb stroking her cheek.

"Hey, sleepy girl. How about some food?" he asked.

She looked at him. His smile, his unshaven face, his green eyes and the hair dropping onto his forehead. His wide shoulders and tawny chest.

What a nice way to wake up.

She smiled.

"Yeah," she said softly and settled back against the pillows.

They ate, sharing one plate. One bite for her, one bite for him. A nibble of toast between them. Sips of orange juice. Only the coffee mugs were their own.

As they finished, he set the tray aside and moved closer to her.

"I need to take you home today."

"Yes." She thought of everything she needed to do before starting the work week. Paying bills. Cleaning. Laundry. Meeting Evi. She took a quick glance at her watch. She had plenty of time to meet Evi.

"Nicole." Jack seemed to hesitate. She tilted her head, waiting for his words.

"This has been an amazing weekend," he continued. She chilled, hearing a note of finality in his tone.

He went on. "I want it to go on. I want to have you with me. I want to find, to discover, what it is between us." He looked her in the eye. "Can we do that?"

She realized that the note of finality in his voice didn't indicate an end. It was a decision on his part to make a new beginning.

"Oh, yes. Yes, Jack." She couldn't help but throw her arms around him.

He kissed her long and hard, pushing her back against the pillows before pulling back.

"Then, before I take you home, I have something for you." He reached over to the drawer in the bedside table and pulled it open, withdrawing a square box.

From the box, he withdrew a silver bracelet. He held it up for her to see and then fastened it around her wrist.

The bracelet was a series of circles, linked together. From one link, hung a charm. Nic turned the face of the charm to her.

It was inscribed with a swirl of letters. *J. L.*

Jack LaTour.

"Will you wear it?" he asked.

She looked at it around her wrist. It was delicate, but weighed enough so that she could feel it against her skin. "It's beautiful, Jack. I love it. Yes, I'll wear it. Gladly." He leaned in for another kiss.

As they kissed softly, lazily, languidly in his bed, she knew where she had seen this design before. It perfectly matched the circular tattoo on Jack's hip.

His sign. He had given her his mark. She held her wrist against her chest, with the feel of the circles on her skin, as he kissed her. Again. Again. Again.

CHAPTER TWENTY-TWO

"Again?" Evi gasped and rolled her eyes. "I've already lost count."

"So have I," Nic said, cradling her coffee cup in her hands.

"The man's a machine!"

Nic laughed. "I know it sounds that way, but he was gentle too. At the right times. You know" —she set down her cup— "it wasn't just the sex. Although that was amazing."

"Yeah?" Evi took a gulp of her cooling eggnog latte.

"He was affectionate. Funny. Interesting. A good cook. And he really seems to want me with him."

"Everyone wants you with them!"

"You know that isn't true. But it's the feeling that he's so drawn to me that reinforces how much I'm drawn to him."

Her friend nodded. "Chemistry."

"Desire."

"A meeting of the minds."

"Intellectual connection."

"All wrapped up together, like a buttery cream cheese pastry, which I'm going to buy for myself now. You want one?" Evi pushed back from the table and stood.

Nic shook her head.

"He doesn't have you on a diet, does he?" Evi narrowed her eyes.

"Oh, hell no. He fed me well. Caviar, sparkling wine, breakfast in bed … mmmmm, it makes me hungry just thinking of it."

"Well, shit. Sandwiches with your old friend Evi will never cut it again, will it."

Nic smiled. "As long as they're good sandwiches, I'll still have lunch with you."

Evi snorted and turned toward the front of the coffee shop.

Nic shifted in her chair, images from the night before flying through her mind. Looking down on the street below her. The window glass cold and hard beneath her hands. The man across the street. The silhouette of his hand moving against his groin.

She shivered.

Feeling Jack moving into her. Pushing into her. His words. His commands to her, to explain what she wanted and what she felt. Almost daring her to keep going, don't stop, go with what feels good.

She pressed her thighs together and took a big gulp of coffee. She needed to get back to her apartment and do some laundry. She was all out of clean panties.

When Evi returned, she asked to see the bracelet again.

"You know, Saul didn't buy me a damn thing until months into our relationship." Evi touched the silver bracelet, bending her head to look at the delicate links. "I mean besides dinner and beer and a porn video called *Pirates* that he wanted me to watch with him."

"Did you?"

Evi looked at her. "Watch the video? Of course. It was pretty good."

"Did it make for hot sex afterward?"

"Naw, not really." She turned the small charm to look at the initials. "He kept saying 'argh' and 'me matey' and stuff like that. But the rope work was fun."

"Rope? Really?"

Evi grinned and raised her eyebrows. "Aye."

"Jeez. Everyone's getting tied up but me, I guess."

"You should try it. It's very sexy. Did Jack just get this made for you?"

Nic was startled. "Well, yes, I think so. What do you mean?"

"You haven't been seeing each other for very long. I just wondered if he rushed it to be made for this weekend. Or if he's had it around for a while."

"To give to anyone?"

"To give to someone, I guess."

"I'd like to think he meant it for me." Nic heard her voice grow cold and she pulled her arm back.

"Oh! I do think he wanted to give it to you! It sounds to me like he's completely smitten. I didn't mean that he keeps a stash of these to hand out to girls he has a good weekend with. I'm sorry, it came out terribly, didn't it?"

"A little."

"It is pretty. Do you like it?"

Nic smiled. "I love it."

Evi looked out the window onto the quiet Sunday city street. It wasn't raining, but the pavement was still wet. If the temperature dipped low enough that night, it would be slick on the sidewalks tomorrow.

"I should mention something, I guess," Evi said.

"What?"

"Lawrence called me yesterday."

Nic felt her heart sink to the bottom of her stomach. She set her cup down, suddenly not having any room for eggnog. "What did he say?"

Evi shrugged. "He asked how you were. If you were okay."

"What did you say?"

"I said you were getting fucked every which way. What do you think I said? I said you were doing well enough."

"Well enough?"

"Well, I didn't think it was kind to imply that you were having the time of your life with another man. Not so soon. And he sounded sad."

Nic grimaced. "He did?"

"Yeah, he did."

"Did he say anything else?"

"He asked me to call him if I thought you ever needed him."

Nic tapped her fingers on the table. "Don't call him, Evi, okay? I don't need anything. He can't think he's going to be my knight in shining armor and rush in for the rescue, if I ever get my feelings hurt."

"I think he just meant to be helpful."

"He wants to keep his hand in. It's best for us both if we know that there is no possibility of becoming involved again."

"What if the thing with Jack falls apart? Even then, you don't want to see Lawrence again?"

"What if the thing with Jack does fall apart? I've dealt with breakups before. I'll be okay. Breaking up with Lawrence was so final. It was a relationship without a future. Remember, he told me that himself." She leaned in, putting her hand on top of her friend's. "Promise me. You won't call him if I am having a hard time. No matter what. I have you and Saul and friends to rely on. I can't have Lawrence thinking I'll need to rely on him."

"Okay, Nic, okay. I won't call him."

Nic sat back in her chair, blowing out a breath of relief. "I've got to get home. I've been away all weekend and have some things to do before the week starts."

"Lunch this week?" Evi asked.

"Yeah. Let's try for Wednesday?"

"Sounds good. Will you be seeing *him* this week?

"Maybe. Probably. I don't know. Yeah."

"Uh huh. Sounds definite."

Nic grinned and pushed her arms into her coat.

"It's definite, Evi. It's definite."

She jingled her bracelet and hugged her friend goodbye, before walking out the door.

CHAPTER TWENTY-THREE

Frances had the crowd in the palm of her hand. She strode across the stage with one hand holding the PowerPoint clicker and the other tucking her short hair behind one ear. Her voice filled the large darkened ballroom as she passionately made the case for the Tyff Foundation. Stats, financial figures, and photos of smiling beneficiaries filled the screen behind her. She cut a commanding figure with her long legs, aristocratic profile, and crimson fitted business suit.

Nic watched from her chair on the side of the stage. She was up next. She had her presentation ready and her notes in hand.

But Jack filled her head.

He called her every night, describing how he would tuck her into her bed. And then what he would do to her.

She turned on her hip, crossing and uncrossing her legs. Imagining Jack's tongue on her, as he described last night. *Right there. Yes, there.* She licked her lips. *Ah, and there. And then ... and then ...*

"And now I'd like to introduce Nicole Simmons, director of programs for the Tyff Foundation." Frances was gesturing to her.

Oh, right! Nic rose from her chair and strode to the middle of the stage, taking the A/V remote from her boss's hand.

The thought of Jack's flickering tongue was replaced by the hope that the remote in her hand would actually work and show the information she wanted.

"Thank you, Frances. As she was saying ..." Nic continued smoothly into the presentation. She and Frances had practiced it enough times that it came to her naturally. She had a firm grasp on the information and didn't need to look at the notes she left on the podium. In fact, she preferred the more freeing movement of pacing the stage and directing her attention to the audience, instead of the screen behind her or the papers she had prepared.

It wasn't hard to be convincing, as secure as she was in the value of her job and the mission of the Foundation. They did good work. She knew it and she had the facts at hand to prove it.

She was onstage for forty minutes with her presentation. Then Frances stepped on to wrap it up. They received a warm reception and conversed with individuals for quite a while afterward.

As the crowd thinned, Nic felt a hand on her elbow. She turned and gasped with a smile to find Jack there.

"Well, hello! Fancy finding you here," she said.

"And why not? I'm working with the Tyff Foundation too." Jack turned to the man with whom Nic had been talking. "I'm the architect on the new community center."

The discussion continued on the scope of the new project.

Frances finally joined them and the last of the audience faded away.

"Wow, I thought they'd never leave!" Frances sank into a chair with a glass of ice water.

"Good job! You did great!" Nic saluted her with her own glass of water.

"You too, mon cherie. Flawless. I couldn't have asked for better." Frances swigged the water. "And hello to you, Mr. LaTour. Just happened to be in the neighborhood?"

"Not at all. It's been four days since I've seen Ms. Simmons in person and I felt I couldn't let another day pass like that."

"Oh, yes? Isn't he the charmer, Nic?" Frances smirked at her.

"He is. And I'm very glad to see him too."

Jack surprised her then by sliding an arm around her shoulders and leaning in to kiss her cheek. He left the arm around her as he straightened up.

"Will you be bringing Nic to any of the parties soon?" Frances asked, her lips smiling, but her eyes calculating.

"We haven't discussed it." Jack narrowed his eyes.

"You might want to discuss it. I think she would like it."

Nic looked between the two of them. What parties? Carlos had mentioned a party. Was it those kind of parties? The kind that Jack and Carlos and Frances went to? Obviously so.

"Sure. I'd like to go," she said with a smile and a shrug.

Jack and Frances both stared at her. Then at each other.

"Well, there is the Saturday night one. It might be a nice introduction," Frances muttered and looked deeply into the bottom of her water glass.

Jack gave a little groan.

This was starting to irritate Nic. What was the big deal? What kind of party? It's not as if her history were limited to tea parties. She had been to an Ecstasy party in college, for God's sake.

"Saturday night?" she asked.

"Nicole," Jack started, then gave Frances a look.

"I'll go get some more water and head back to the office. Nic, I'll see you back there?" Frances got to her feet and gathered her bag quickly. "Nice to see you again, Jack. Bye to the both of you for now."

Jack and Nic sat down in a couple of chairs.

"So you want to go to a party." Jack leaned back in his chair.

"I want to know what you are talking about, when you discuss these things with your friends."

"Friends?"

"Carlos also asked about what was happening. You said to look at some website."

"You overheard that."

"It wasn't like I was eavesdropping. I was right there."

He nodded. "Okay. The website is for Lush Life, that group of Seattle-area fetishists and swingers. The parties have all kinds of themes. Most of them not to my taste. But Saturday night's might be interesting."

"What is the theme for Saturday night?"

"It's a sex show. With a local dance kinda aerial kinda sex troupe."

"Really? There are such things?"

"It's very well done. I've seen them before," he said.

Nic nodded. "Of course you have. I'd like to see it."

"You sure?"

"I'm sure."

"With me?"

Nic reached over and took his hand. "I wouldn't want to go with someone else."

He smiled. "You are something. And I am lucky."

"Yes, you are."

"Just to be clear, I will know people there." He narrowed his eyes.

"As in women you've had sex with."

He hesitated before replying in simple terms. "Yes."

She looked down at their hands intertwined on his knee. She would be face to face with women that he's known. Intimately.

Those women weren't her. She knew that. He hadn't seduced them. He hadn't pursued them.

He hadn't taken them to the bait shack.

Damn it.

He had taken her to the bait shack.

"I can deal with it," she said finally.

He grinned and pulled her over, so she was sitting on his lap. She looked around but the ballroom was empty.

"Did I say that you are something?" He nuzzled her ear.

"I think you did." She closed her eyes with a purr.

"I appreciate your open mindedness." He unbuttoned a button and slipped a hand inside of her blouse.

"I'm not exactly an innocent. I went to an Ecstasy party in college once."

"You must tell me about it sometime," he said, as he tilted her back against his arm and closed his lips over hers.

CHAPTER TWENTY-FOUR

The box arrived at her apartment on Saturday afternoon. His earlier text had told her just enough.

Wear what's inside for tonight. With your shoes with the chains.

And then a long pause before the next text.

Please.

She opened the box, from a Seattle store she wasn't familiar with.

Inside was a glossy black leather outfit. A short skirt and bustier top with thin shoulder straps. Nestled on the top of the outfit was a rose made out of red leather.

When she opened her apartment door for him that evening, she thought she had managed to make the most of her look. The leather skirt was slit on each side, high on the hip. One of her black thongs was the only thing that she could wear beneath it.

The bustier pushed her breasts up and out. Considering her cup size, it was a generous view.

She had twisted her hair into a messy knot at the nape of her neck and twisted the stem of the leather rose in there, so it nestled against her brown tresses. A little more eyeliner than normal and some mauve eyeshadow to deepen her eyelids. Extra mascara. Clear shimmery lip gloss to balance the darkness of her eye makeup.

Her bracelet was her only jewelry.

She put on the high heels with the silvery chain around the ankles. Her legs looked a million miles long.

A touch of ginger scent on her neck, between her breasts, on the insides of her thighs, her ankles.

"Wow. Holy wow! You look amazing." He gaped at her and then stepped inside and swept her into his arms. He rained kisses down on her until she pushed him away.

"You'll smear my makeup." She laughed.

"Your makeup will be smeared all over by the end of tonight," he promised.

He looked the role too. Black jeans and a tight black T-shirt. Black leather jacket. He looked dangerous.

He is dangerous, she thought.

"Care to join me?" he asked and cocked his elbow toward her.

She knew he was dangerous. Not just him, but the maelstrom he was leading her into. He was the embodiment of the excitement, trepidation, daring, and challenge that she knew might await her this evening.

An invitation to adventure.

"I'd love to." She folded her hand around his arm and folded her reservations away, into the farthest reaches of her mind.

She had to admit to herself that she was a little nervous. His Jeep sped up Aurora Avenue toward the north of Seattle, home to the enormous old estates of some of Seattle's founding fathers. As she had learned over the few years that she had lived here, the descendants of these frontiersmen still lived in the area and many still owned the ancestral homes.

This was one of those homes.

Jack's Jeep turned into the lit driveway of a large estate, sweeping around to the front door. The house was gothic in style, with a turret featured on one corner, a wide porch, and dark gray brick with arched windows. Four stories high and probably also had a basement. Even though night had long ago descended, she could see glimpses of finely landscaped grounds.

A uniformed valet opened the door for her and took her hand to help her out of the Jeep.

"Ms. Simmons." Jack moved next to her, folding her hand around his bicep and curling his fingers over hers.

A good thing that he had such a sure hold over her. The pavement stones leading to the front steps were uneven and as sexy as her shoes were, they weren't meant for hard walking.

"Who owns this house?" she asked, as they walked closer to the front door, her ankles wobbling slightly. The house loomed over them, lit up from every window. She could see people on an upper balcony, laughing with glasses in their hands. People also crowded the front porch.

"Don't ask, darling. You might have heard of his last name." Jack led her into the throng.

Jack was immediately greeted by a woman in an elegant formal-length gown. Nic felt underdressed next to her.

"Jack! Oh my God, it's so good to see you! It's been forever!" She kissed him on both cheeks and then turned to Nic. "Hi! I'm Cindy. Nice to meet ya."

"Cindy. This is my girlfriend, Nicole." Cindy's eyebrows went up in surprise. So did Nic's.

Girlfriend?

"Oh wow. Hi again then! Jack's girlfriend. Wow. Okay. Uh, this is Randy." The woman pulled on the arm of the man next to her. When he turned around, Nic started.

His face was painted to look like a donkey and he wore felt donkey ears.

He held out a soft hand to her.

"Randy, honey, this is my old friend Jack. And his … uh … girlfriend. Nicole."

Nic shook the man's hand. It was as limp as a dead fish, absolutely no life in it. Jack ignored the offered hand.

The donkey-man nodded and looked away, sipping his drink.

At the front door, a uniformed butler took their jackets and gave Jack a ticket to retrieve them. Nic was glad for the tight crowd, as she felt that her lower body would be almost completely displayed, if there were any room to see her.

Glancing to her left, she saw Frances leaning against the doorway to another room. Her back was to Nic and she was dressed all in black with tall black boots lending even more inches to her already domineering height. In any other situation, Nic would have crossed the hall to greet her boss, but, at a sex party, she felt uncertain. Would Frances want to say hello? Would she rather not be reminded of the outside world while she was here?

Frances half turned toward her and Nic ducked her head. Nope, there was no way she could face her boss here. Look at the way her boss was dressed! Look at the way she was dressed!

Jack led her further into the house, greeting a few people quickly here and there, until they got to the bar set up against a far wall of a large greeting room. He got champagne for her and a whiskey for himself.

"You don't have to drink it," he said, as he handed her the glass full of bubbles. "But it looks good on you."

He slid his arm along her back and drew her closer. "I know this is a lot to take in," he whispered.

She looked around, secure against his arm. A lot to take in indeed. Men and women sauntered through the room or stood in small groups, laughing and talking. The women were dressed in everything from head-to-toe black to barely there, less than she wore. One woman was in a sheer sparkling bodysuit. Another woman wore a black catsuit with cutouts for her breasts. Which were huge.

Nic tore her eyes away from the brazenly displayed breasts.

"Who are these people," she whispered to Jack.

"Fetishists," he replied. "There's a little of everything."

"Do you ever dress like a donkey?"

"Not if I can help it." He grinned. "No, never."

"Do you know most of these people?"

He took a sip of his drink. "By sight. To say hello, maybe. Not well."

"But some?"

"Yes." He nodded his head. "A few I know better than others."

Nic scanned the crowd.

There was a pretty perky blonde who glanced in their direction, dressed in a flirty skirt, lacy top, and garter belt with stockings.

There was a severe-looking woman who eyed Jack blatantly over the rim of her glass. No, there was no way that Jack could have—

And there was Veronica. All tall and gleaming blonde, encased in a strictly form-fitting outfit of white latex. She looked like a fetish secretary.

Was she a fetish secretary? Nic wondered.

"Hello, sir," Veronica said, as she glided up to them. She glanced at Nic and then back at him. "Jack."

"Veronica. Hello." Jack sipped his drink again. "You remember my girlfriend, Nicole."

Nic found herself smiling and standing up straighter, as the woman seemed to wilt a bit. Yeah, sure, Jack had fucked this glorious Barbie doll, but he referred to Nic as his girlfriend.

And she had the bracelet.

She took a sip of her champagne, holding up the arm with the bracelet.

"Of course. Hello, Nicole. Nice to see you again." Veronica nodded, blonde waves falling over her face.

"And you, Veronica. You look lovely tonight."

"Thanks." The woman twisted her fingers in front of her.

"Can I get you a drink?" Jack asked.

"You know I don't drink," Veronica mumbled, looking away over the crowd. Her fingers gripped together so tightly that the knuckles turned white.

Jack ordered a sparkling water and handed it to her. Nic was glad that Veronica had something to occupy her fumbling hands. The tension in those hands was unnerving.

"I haven't seen you at one of these parties in a while." Jack sipped his whiskey.

"I came with Erica. She wanted to be here." Veronica blinked rapidly, her mouth first curving into a flash of a smile before fading. Her expressions fumbled as much as her hands.

Nic searched the room. Then she noticed Jack looking up.

Erica was leaning on the railing of the upstairs landing. Her blond hair was swept up high on her head and she was dressed in a white gauze dress, with sheer panels falling to the floor. She might as well have been nude, for the dress hid nothing. Her full breasts, round hips, and long legs were perfectly visible beneath the fabric.

She was gazing down on them. No, Nic realized, she was actually gazing down directly on her. Erica's blue eyes boldly confronted her, not flinching or looking away.

Nic didn't look away either. After several seconds of returning the locked stare, Nic nodded at Jack's ex-lover.

And smiled.

"I'm going to show Nicole around before the show begins. See you at the office on Monday?" Jack's hand was firm on her back, urging her along.

"Yes. Of course." Veronica actually looked like she might be blinking back tears. Nic almost felt bad for her, but not quite. She wasn't that tender hearted.

Jack hurried her through the crowd, taking a big gulp of his drink as he did so.

"That was a little abrupt," Nic said to him, as they navigated their way down a crowded hall.

"You think?" He smiled grimly. "I'm heeding your intuition about Veronica. She might not work out."

What did that mean? Would Jack fire her? And then what? What was the obligation he felt toward Veronica? Toward his ex-whatevers in general?

And Erica? Was Erica here for the party? Or here to watch Jack?

"Do you have to R.S.V.P. for these parties?" she asked.

"Yes. On the website."

Perhaps Erica had known that Jack would be here.

"So, you will be giving me a tour?" she asked, to change the subject.

"We won't go upstairs, yet, but on the main floor is the bar and lounge area where we were. There is a big ballroom at the end of the hallway where the show will take place. There's a veranda along the back that leads to a large lawn. They often have tables and a dance floor out on the lawn, but I doubt they would tonight because of the cold. Then there are the private offices of the owners."

He steered her into a shallow alcove along the wall, out of the way of the crowd.

"I take it you've been here before." Nic took another sip of her champagne, trying to look nonchalant.

"Of course I have. You knew that."

"You seem to know the place well."

"I know the owner of the house. And yes, I've been here for quite a few events. Is that a problem?" His eyes narrowed. "You knew all this."

Nic looked past him at the parade of people in the hallway. The noise level, the laughter, the number of people, it could almost have been any weekend society party. Except that the clothing style ran toward skimpy and revealing. Provocative. There was a charge in the air. Like a dirty joke that only the in-crowd would understand.

Jack was in on the joke.

She wanted to be in on the joke, too.

"No problem." She smiled brightly at him and took another sip of champagne.

She saw his jaw clench. "Nicole," he began. Then stopped.

"Yes?"

He studied her. Then took her hand and kissed her palm. "I'm so glad to be here with you," he said in a low voice. "I've been thinking of nothing else for the last two days."

"Me neither," she replied. She meant that.

"Come on, let's go get some seats for the show."

He took her hand in his and led her along the hallway to the open double doors at the end. They entered the ballroom, filled with chairs arranged in theatre seating, with a raised stage at the front hidden by curtains and swags of scarves festooning from ceiling to walls. Glitter covered the floor like sawdust in a saloon. Liveried men helped the guests find seats as they entered.

Jack and Nic were shown to two seats on the aisle. A waiter appeared at their side with two glasses of champagne. Nic set hers aside, knowing that she should pace herself.

Jack held her hand and caressed her bare legs as they talked. She looked around the room, noting more characters as they entered and took a seat. Men in dark clothing and women in flashy outfits meant to attract attention. One woman sitting across the aisle from them, dressed in a red loose skirt, crossed her leg and Nic saw her leg bared from foot to hip, just as hers would be if she crossed her leg.

She shifted onto her hip and crossed her leg in the same manner, feeling her skirt fall away. She turned more onto her hip, knowing that her bare buttock was partially revealed.

She felt daring. And the more she dared, the more she gained confidence.

Her breasts swelled above her corset with each breath, her nipples barely concealed behind the stiff covering. She found she was having a hard time sitting still. She wanted to rub her thighs together, to bring her shoulders back, so her nipples rubbed against the stiff boning of the corset. To cross her legs again and feel the cooler air on the bared skin of her ass.

Jack stroked her arm and naked shoulder as he spoke to her.

"We'll watch the show here, Nicole. It should be very erotic. Then I intend to have some fun with you. We won't just be observers here tonight."

Nic swallowed. "We won't?"

"That's not what you want, is it? Just to observe? You want an experience."

Jack leaned in close as the lights dimmed.

"Remember," he whispered, "it's a sex show. There will be people in the audience who feel the urge to respond."

She turned to look at the stage, his words sinking in. *The audience will respond?*

Music filled the room, with a thundering of drums. There was a crescendo of strings and percussion. People were still filing in, pushing in closer.

"Come. Sit on my lap. We can give up a chair." Jack pulled her onto his legs, with her feet between his. The chair she had been using was immediately occupied by an older man with white hair swept back from his forehead. Jack nodded to him and the man nodded back.

Nic leaned back against Jack's chest as his arms circled her waist, holding her against him.

She twisted her wrist, glancing down to see his bracelet gleaming in the dim light against her skin.

His bracelet. She was the only one here wearing his bracelet.

She turned slightly to kiss his temple before turning back to the stage.

The music rose, lifting the expectations of the audience. Just at the moment that the audience swayed, balanced, anticipating, three figures dropped from the ceiling, unrolling from flimsy swathes of fabric. Nic caught her breath, as the three hidden figures reached the floor and unfurled into human forms, legs long and lithe, stepping onto the stage. Arms shedded the fabric behind them.

A man and two women twirled into the low lights on the stage. Glimmers of reflections danced over their nude bodies. The three danced around each other, not quite touching, but just barely breezing past, their arms curving through the air. The bare breasts of the women glimmered with shimmery makeup. The bared body of the man blazed with a warm bronzed glow.

Slowly, as the music became more lush and vibrant, the three circled in on each other. Nic caught a brief glimpse of the naked man's organ in the artful lighting, half erect and as much a part of the dance as the limbs of the three. His arms reached for the women, who curled against him and then leaped away.

The dance went on, as the three explored the boundaries of the stage and of each other, contracting together, expanding apart. The two women wove together in a sensual tangle of arms, legs, and long lines. The man came over them, his body seeming to blot out their own, until they burst from beneath his arms and leaped to grasp the hanging scarves, swinging out over the audience.

Nic gasped along with those around her, as the naked women soared over the audience, their fists twisted into the fabric. As they swung back to the stage, the man caught them both, his large hands easily stopping their momentum. The women dropped to their knees at his feet.

Nic exhaled with an appreciative sigh.

She felt Jack's hand trace down her hair and over her back, to graze against the top of her ass.

"You like?" he whispered in her ear.

"I like," she whispered back.

The man on stage cupped the heads of the two women and brought them to him. Reverently. Commandingly.

The women brought their fluttering hands to his legs, stroking him. Then to his torso, caressing him.

Nic saw their mouths came to his organ. Both of them began to caress his cock with their lips, as their hands wove over him.

The man threw his head back and gazed to the ceiling as the women seemed to worship him.

Nic had never seen anything like this. Not porn, but art. Not crass, but graceful. So beautiful, that one could only appreciate the aesthetic. She could feel the benediction in the women. She could sense the barely controlled movements of the man. The more they attended to him, the more power he gained. And the more he was humbled by it.

His hands shook in their hair.

Yes, Nic thought. This is what she felt with Jack. The entanglement. The power flowing between the two of them. Until it filled them both.

The man bent to kiss both women and then lowered them both onto the stage. The three of them became a tangle, limbs entwined, all three moving as one entity. Nic could tell that he was fucking them both. She could see his cock spearing between their legs, but which in turn and who with who, she couldn't say. All three of them wound their wrists through the hanging scarves as they undulated against each other, until they were bound together.

Jack's hand slid up the inside of her leg and nudged her thighs apart. She kept her eyes on the act on the stage, the lights spinning over them. The audience was hushed. Only the music could be heard.

His fingers found her thong and pulled it aside. He stroked her wet slit. Nic leaned back, her head on Jack's shoulder. She spread her legs, so that one foot was on each side of his leg.

"Good," he whispered. "Watch them. Feel me."

He stroked her again and then his finger was inside of her. His thumb was on her clit.

Nic arched on his lap, her hands pressing against her stomach. While she felt the urge to protest, to push away from him, at the same time she pushed down on his finger. Her eyes skittered from the stage and over the people around them.

"Don't look away. Watch them." He fucked her with his finger, drawing her wetness from her to bathe her pussy lips. His thumb ground against her.

The three performers had increased their tempo. Nic could hear the soft cries of the women and the harsh moans of the man. She saw his buttocks rising and falling, tightening against his conquests.

Oh my God, she thought. *I'm watching people fucking each other on stage.*

She shivered and moved with Jack's finger inside of her.

On stage, the man's hand gripped the hair of one woman. A woman's lips fastened around the swollen nipple of the other woman. The man's glistening cock withdrew from one woman and then plunged into the other.

Then they rose.

With their arms and legs twisted into the scarves, the three of them suddenly began to rise above the stage, still a party of three united into one. They still fucked, sex and lips and nipples and glistening moisture, moving together as they rose. The music rose as they did. The audience raised their heads to watch the movements above them.

Nic glanced from the aerialists to the audience. People were moving against each other. Kissing. Stroking. One woman was on her knees fellating the man seated before her.

Nic raised her eyes to the performers again. They moved above her, the sex raw and needy and urgent now, suspended in midair.

She stifled a cry and turned her face to Jack's neck. She began to climax, tightening and smothering her reaction. She trembled and felt her wetness gush over his hand, her cries swallowed in her throat.

"So beautiful," Nic heard the white-haired man beside her say.

"She is. And she's mine." Jack slowed his thumb on her.

Nic felt a hand smooth over her hair. She opened her eyes, realizing it wasn't Jack's.

One of Jack's arms was around her, holding her. His other was between her legs.

She turned her head to look over her shoulder. The white-haired man smiled at her, a lock of her hair between his fingers.

"Jack is a lucky man," he said.

Nic was speechless. This man had just watched her orgasm on Jack's lap.

On her boyfriend's lap.

She swallowed.

"Yes, he is," she croaked.

The lights slowly brightened and a wave of applause rose from the audience. Nic looked up to see that the three performers stood on stage, the scarves draped around them. They took their bows.

She straightened up on Jack's lap and clapped her hands. Never mind the fact that she had to bite her lip to keep her teeth from chattering and that her legs were still trembling from her climax.

Jack's arms were tight around her.

"My dear," the man next to her said. Nic tried to stifle the blush she felt creeping up her cheeks. She turned to look at him.

"You are welcome to my home any time." The man touched his forefinger to her cheek, before he rose and walked away.

The room was emptying now that the show was over. Nic felt drained.

"Well, Nicole. Looks like you got yourself a permanent invitation to the Lush Life." Jack nuzzled her hair and turned her to curl against him. "You come beautifully, do you know that?"

She didn't know that. She just knew that she came with his slightest touch. She felt a mixture of unabashed pleasure, some shame, and an increasing sense of wonder at that.

* * * * *

The room was almost empty.

Chairs were askew. A few pieces of clothing were abandoned on the floor. Nic remembered seeing the sexual activities of the people around her, mirroring the performers on the stage.

What power those actors must feel, she thought. *To inspire the audience to join them like that.*

"You okay?" Jack murmured against her cheek.

She tilted her head back to look at him and smiled, as she drew her finger down his cheek. "I am so very okay," she said.

He smiled in return and lifted his fingers to her cheek. She saw that they glistened with her juices. She could smell her scent on them.

As his fingers came to her cheek, she licked her lips. She kept her eyes on Jack's face, as he traced circles over her cheek. She could feel the design he was making on her skin and she closed her eyes to savor the sensation.

Right here in the middle of a crowded room, she had orgasmed on these fingers. The man sitting next to them had watched her come and had thought her beautiful in the middle of her ecstasy. In the midst of her vulnerability, she had felt beautiful. Sensual. Discovered.

Jack pulled her to her feet and kept hold of her wrists in one of his hands as he led her from the room.

The mood of the party had morphed. The barely suppressed sensuality was laid bare now, with people groping each other against the wall and laughing as they shared champagne. Nic caught a glimpse of the male performer, who moments earlier had been wildly fucking two girls on stage, now standing in the center of a group of people, making what seemed to be casual conversation while absently stroking his half-erect penis. In another corner, a man had his hand hidden beneath the skirt of a woman, the rotating movements obvious in their purpose. The woman had her head back against the wall, her eyes closed and lips parted.

Jack led her quickly along the hall to the wide staircase by the entrance. The staircase itself was the scene of more couples of every sexual persuasion, groping and kissing and fingering each other. At the top of the stairs, two women reclined on a loveseat, their tongues twining and hands searching.

Nic scarcely had time to record these views, because Jack was rushing her so quickly along. He turned into a short hallway and opened one of the three doors there. He hung a Do Not Disturb sign on the outside doorknob before pushing the door shut.

The room was small, dark, and held only a short-armed settee and a large gilded mirror on one wall. Recessed lighting in the ceiling cast mostly shadows.

Jack turned her to face the mirror and gripped her shoulders from behind. She looked in the mirror to see his face pale over her shoulder. His shadow loomed behind her.

"See your reflection?" he whispered in her ear. His voice was rough.

She shivered at the harshness of his tone, but nodded.

His hands reached around to unfasten the hooks at the top of her corset, between her breasts. He opened it partway, then yanked the corset apart. Her breasts pushed through the opening, bared in the mirror. His hands cupped them from behind, squeezing them, pushing them together.

She moaned and leaned against him, her own hands pressed against him behind her back.

His teeth bit softly at the side of her neck as he played with her breasts. His fingers pinched and plucked at her hardening nipples.

Nic could barely see herself in the mirror, the room was so dimly lit. Her breasts pale beneath his hands, her face lifted, her eyes dark, her hair cascading around her, having worked loose from its knot. The red leather rose that had rested in her hair was lost.

Jack, with his black garb and dark hair, was nothing more than a figure behind her.

His fingers wove into her hair and pulled her head back. His lips found hers, assaulting her. She sagged against him.

God, what was he doing to her. He groped, he savaged, he took her tits and lips. And she responded. Arching against him, offering him more. Parting her lips, lifting her breasts. Silently pleading with him to take what she offered.

He stepped back, pulling her with him, and then pressed his hand to the middle of her back, indicating that she was to bend over the arm of the settee.

She did, all too willing to do whatever he asked at that point.

In fact, Nic dimly realized her only craving was to give him just what he wanted.

She pressed her hands onto the seat of the couch and bent down low, the cushioned arm against her hips. Jack pushed her skirt easily up to her back and yanked her thong to one side. She heard the sound of his zipper and then felt the head of his cock pressed against her wet opening. She whimpered and spread her legs.

"Before I take you," he rasped against her ear, "you should know that this is a two-way mirror. There might be people watching us."

Nic gasped and looked at the mirror. She could see nothing, no hint of movement in the silvery depths of the mirror, only an image of her bent over, her naked buttocks bared, and the vague shadow of Jack standing against her.

"Look at the mirror, Nicole. Don't look away."

She fixed her eyes on the mirror, on his reflection there, on whoever might be standing on the other side.

His fingers stroked her wet slit once, twice, then spread her apart. With one smooth motion, he was inside of her.

Long smooth thrusts deep inside of her. He pushed in harder and then ground against her, his hips against her ass, her own hips pressed to the settee's arm.

Long caressing strokes, opening her before him as he bore into her. She could feel the width of his cock tunneling, stretching her.

He increased his speed, a little at a time. She kept her head raised and her eyes on the mirror, as he took her from behind. She had to brace her arms on the settee by the time he was pounding against her, his hips hitting her buttocks, the impact of him jarring her entire body.

He ran his hand down over her back and then gripped her hips, pulling her back onto him as he drove into her. Each time harder. Each time deeper. She cried out as he pounded into her. His fingers bit into her flesh as she felt his frantic need rising. His breathing was ragged.

He growled. "Take it, Nicole. Let them watch you. Take it, slut."

She whimpered, shocked at his words. And owning them. She was his slut. She felt the title descend on her like a badge of honor. One she wanted to earn. That she was earning. Now. Bent over and being fucked by him like a bitch in heat. His bitch in heat. His slut.

When he shouted and she felt him come into her again, she kept her eyes on the mirror. Her chin raised. It was her that he found his release in. Her that he desired. Her that he filled with his seed.

She lifted her chin higher, her eyes bright and clear. She looked in the mirror. She smiled.

* * * * *

He pulled from her with a groan, leaving her feeling aching and exposed. Nic stayed in place, her feet spread wide, bent over the arm of the short sofa, her skirt still pushed up over her ass. Catching her breath.

Jack came around and dropped onto the settee in front of her. His spent cock shone with his release and her wetness. He reclined against the cushions, brought one hand to her cheek, and gently guided her to him.

He didn't have to say anything or give any instruction. She bent down and held his cock with her hands, licking him. The taste of their fluids together was intoxicating. She relished the taste, and the duty, licking gratefully until he was clean.

"Come to me, Nicole," he said then, quietly.

She stood and slid around the arm of the settee to settle on his lap. He pulled her skirt down, fastened her corset, and kissed the flushed swell of her breasts. He put her to rights and then cradled her on his lap.

"My lovely, you were perfect. Amazing. Gorgeous. You were riveting." Caresses accompanied his words.

Nic glanced at the mirror, feeling a little shy about the experience now. "Do you think they are still watching?"

He stroked her hair, giving a quick glance to the mirror. "Perhaps, to see how the scene plays out. But the main show is over. I expect most people have drifted away." He ducked his head to look her in the face. "How do you feel about what we just did? Being displayed like that? Being" —he hesitated, searching for the right words, it seemed— "being called a name like that?"

"'Your slut?'" She grinned at him. "I loved it."

"And that?" He lifted a shoulder toward the mirror.

"I … I loved that too."

"You like to be watched. I could tell from your reaction to the man in the window the other night."

"I like to be watched, when you make me feel beautiful and desired. If that makes sense."

He nodded, smiling. "You are an exhibitionist."

"I am not!" She was indignant. "I've never been the kind of girl to prance around in showy clothes and make a spectacle of myself." She kept her voice to a whisper, but had to proclaim her objection.

"You are a very modest exhibitionist." He nodded again. His lips twitched with a smirk.

"Well, I am, aren't I?" She lifted an eyebrow.

He gathered her close, kissing her cheeks, her nose, her lips. Then he lifted his head to look at her. "You are clever and lovely and funny and personable and have a thousand other grander characteristics, than simply being labeled an exhibitionist. You are too complex to ever be one thing. And I expect that for the first time, you are comfortable being exhibited. Perhaps because you are with me."

They sat for a short while, before he moved her off his lap and stood to straighten his clothes.

"We need to leave. The room will be in demand."

"Oh!" Nic looked at the leather sofa, suddenly realizing that it would be used again that night. That it might have been used already before them. She wrinkled her nose. "Um, ick."

"Don't worry." He grinned and pulled her to her feet. "A cleaner will be in here fifteen seconds after we are gone."

"You really do know what's up around here."

"I do. But now it is time to go. When we get home I have something to give you."

Moments later, as the Jeep pulled away, Nic looked a last time over the imposing gothic house. Her eyes fastened on a second-floor window.

Veronica stood in the window, watching them. Next to her stood the ghostly figure of Erica.

Nic suddenly felt certain that Veronica and Erica had been in that other room, watching her and Jack through the two-way mirror.

A flash of heat seared through her. It was wicked, it was almost catty, but she was glad.

She bit her lip, suppressing a smile, and turned away from the gazes of the blonde sirens who stood all alone, looking out of the window of a home hosting a sex party.

When they reached Jack's condo, he undressed the both of them, leaving their clothes scattered over the carpet. He pulled her into bed with him, against his chest, and lifted her hand, catching her bracelet with one finger. He drew his finger along it, looking from her to the silver links and then back to her. His finger lifted the charm with his initials on it.

Then he reached into his bedside drawer and withdrew a tiny box. Inside the box was another silver charm. On the charm was a simple engraving of the gothic mansion.

Her first sex party.

He linked the charm onto her bracelet with a pinch of the metal ring, assuring her that he would do a better job of it tomorrow.

He kissed her, gently and romantically. His fingers traced her face, his lips met hers in tender touches.

She fell asleep listening to his whispers of admiration and desire. Just on the edge of sleep, in that wavering place between dreams and reality, she was certain she heard him whisper thc word *love*.

CHAPTER TWENTY-FIVE

Nic took her coffee from the smiling barista and found a table for two, off to one side of Milo's coffee shop. She was waiting for Evi, who had just texted that she would be a half hour late. Wonderful. Nic had already ordered her coffee.

She needed to catch up with her friend. It had already been four days since the party at the north Seattle mansion. She had withheld all details until she got together with Evi in person. She promised a wild tale. Between their schedules, the meeting hadn't been possible until today.

No eggnog latte today, though. She added a half packet of Sugar in the Raw to her nonfat latte and sipped the bittersweet scorching drink.

The heat felt good.

She was just scrolling down the list of new e-mails on her phone, when a shadow darkened the top of the table. Nic looked up to see Erica, she of the art gallery debacle and ethereal entity at the Lush Life party.

"Hello, Nicole." The pretty woman slid into the seat opposite her.

"Uh," Nic managed, her phone still in hand.

"I'm not stalking you or anything." Erica waved a manicured hand in the air between them. "I just happened to stop in here for coffee." She lifted her own cup in evidence. "And saw you."

"Okay." At least Nic managed a halfway coherent word this time.

"It was so nice meeting you at the art gallery a few weeks ago. I'm sorry that I ended up ruining your evening."

Nic had been willing to be polite with the intent of getting rid of her, but the woman was going to go the fake-regret route. Nic was putting a stop to this now.

"Hey, look." She grinned and shrugged. "You didn't ruin my evening. Jack and I had an awesome time. And it certainly led to some even more incredible times together. Like last Saturday night." Nic gave the word 'times' a suggestive emphasis. "So no apologies. It's all good. Jack told me all about you. He and I are in a really good place now. But hey, thanks for saying hi. I'll tell Jack you said hello."

She turned her attention back to her phone.

Erica didn't leave. Instead she sighed heavily.

"There are things you don't know about Jack."

"Of course there are. We are still discovering each other." Nic tapped on an e-mail and opened it, hoping that Erica would see that the conversation was over.

"Have you discovered this?"

Erica laid her arm in front of Nic, pulling the sleeve back.

On the inside of her wrist was a tattoo. A ring of woven linked circles. Identical to the tattoo on Jack's hip. Except in the middle of this circle was the elaborately scripted initials. J.L.

Jack's symbol. Tattooed on Erica's wrist.

And on Veronica's wrist. Nic suddenly remember the brief glimpse of a circle tattoo on the other woman, the first time she met her.

They all had the mark. The tattoo. All of Jack's women must have that tattoo on their wrist.

Just like her bracelet.

Nic began to pull her arm back, meaning to hide the bracelet in her lap, but Erica grabbed her wrist. Nic stiffened at the cold touch of her fingers.

"I see he gave you the bracelet. That's the first step."

"First step?" Nic snatched her arm away, rubbing at the spot where those cold fingers had chilled her skin.

"First is the bracelet. Then when he owns you, he makes you get a tattoo. And then, when he makes you his favorite girl, he makes you get a tattoo on your buttock. So that when he fucks you from behind, the tattoo on his hip will line up with the tattoo on your ass. It's a little creepy, don't you think?" Erica smiled sweetly as she raised her coffee cup to her pink lips.

"You have the third step?" Nic choked on the words, not wanting to ask the question but not able to stop herself.

Erica nodded.

"Jack and I are different."

"He told me the same thing," Erica said.

Nic looked away, looking anywhere but at the gorgeous blonde sitting across from her. The one with Jack's marks permanently inscribed on her body.

"Look, Nicole. I didn't tell you this to hurt you. I thought you should know. Jack isn't always truthful, as I know from experience." Erica reached out to touch her arm again, but Nic flinched away.

"Don't," she hissed. "Go away."

Erica bit her lip. "You should know what you are getting into. I've been in relationships like this before, but he managed to get under my skin. You haven't experienced anything like him. I'm just so sorry that Jack LaTour is your first experience."

"I've had other boyfriends."

"He isn't your boyfriend." Erica shook her head. Her eyes reddened, as if she was trying to hold back tears. "He can't ever be anyone's boyfriend. He isn't capable of it."

"Fuck you." Nic grabbed her bag and stood.

Erica looked up at her. "It's just a warning. I'll give you my phone number in case you ever want to call me."

"No fucking way. You are seriously messed up. And I'm not a dumb shit. I know what I'm doing."

"I'm sorry, Nicole. I really am. You and I aren't the only ones he's messed up."

Nic was about to launch another string of curses, but she swallowed her anger and stood up straight. "No, I'm sorry, Erica. I won't be a member of your little club." Then she swung her jacket over her arm and stalked out of the coffee shop.

Once on the sidewalk, she texted Evi:

Can't meet today. Migraine. I'll call tonight.

She threw her phone into her bag and made her way through the drippy, dreary weather back to her apartment.

She could cut and run. They had only been together six weeks, if that. She could get over him. She would be fine.

She and Jack were different. She could feel it. She had to have faith.

She thought of how Jack had held her, of his words, on Saturday night. The sex at the party had been fantastic, daring and exciting. Some of the best she had ever had. But it was afterward, in his bed, caressing her as she felt asleep. That was the Jack who loved her. She had heard him say it.

She would see him on Friday, just two days away. Until then, she wouldn't mention Erica. But on Friday, she would definitely ask some questions about Erica and bracelets and tattoos.

She flexed her wrist, feeling the bracelet against her arm. The initials J.L. on the charm. She had been so proud of her bracelet at the party.

She was still proud to wear it.

Wasn't she?

Damn it all to hell.

CHAPTER TWENTY-SIX

Nic plucked at her bracelet as the elevator rose to the fifth floor. Jack was waiting for her at the open door to his condo. He took her overnight bag from her in one hand and scooped his other arm around her waist, pulling her up to his kiss.

"It's been days," he whispered in between kisses. "I can barely concentrate on work, thinking of you like I do."

"I'm sympathetic. It's hard to look at a computer screen, while I'm daydreaming of staring at the mirror while I feel you moving into me from behind." She smirked.

"You liked that, didn't you. Dirty girl." He lightly slapped her bottom.

She turned to him as soon as they were inside his condo. He dropped her bag on the floor and caught her, as she threw her arms around his neck.

More kisses ensued as he walked her backward further into his place. He pressed her against the kitchen counter, his hands in her hair, his tongue in her mouth and his erection obvious against her hip. He ground against her as he kissed her.

"This is your fault," he growled in her ear as he bit at her earlobe.

She tilted her head back to look at him, leaning her elbows on the counter. "I saw Erica on Wednesday."

His growl stopped. His grinding stopped. He stepped back from her, looking stunned.

"Erica? Like … that Erica?"

"Yes. Your Erica."

His jaw tightened and he looked wary. “She’s not my Erica.”

“She says otherwise. And she has the tattoos to prove it.”

He groaned and looked up at the ceiling. “I was going to explain all that.”

“But you didn’t.”

“No. We were having such a good time together. I hated the idea of bringing up any unpleasantness. Why haven’t you mentioned it on the phone over the last two nights?”

“Because I wanted to talk about it in person.”

“You didn’t sound mad.”

“I don’t know enough to be mad, but you better explain.”

“What did she tell you?” He looked cautious.

She walked around the kitchen counter, got a glass from his cupboard and poured herself a glass of water. “Okay. Here it is, Jack. I don’t have to tell you anything. You get to do all the talking tonight. I’ll just ask a few questions here and there.” She took a long sip from the glass.

She strolled toward the sofa, discarding her coat on the floor as she did so.

Falling back against the cushions in the corner of the sofa, she folded her legs beneath her and sipped her water again. Jack followed her across the room and stood at the end of the sofa.

“So? Talk,” she ordered, with a tight smile.

His face darkened and a muscle worked in his cheek.

“I’ll talk, but are you listening? With an open mind?”

She shook her head. “Remember. You are the one talking tonight.”

He was not used to being spoken to this way and she could tell he didn't like it one bit. She wasn't mad, at least not yet, but she was harboring a bitchy resentment. Why did dating him have to be so difficult? Why couldn't he just be a guy with a few ex-girlfriends?

"Okay." He threw up his arms. "Where do I start?"

She sighed. "I'll make it easy on you and start with a question. You obviously haven't had to explain yourself very often."

"I've never had a girlfriend who questioned me like this."

"Let's start there then. Am I your girlfriend?"

"Aren't you?"

She gritted her teeth and said nothing.

"Yes, Nicole. I think of you as my girlfriend."

"Erica says you can never be anyone's boyfriend. That you aren't capable of it."

"Erica doesn't know me. You know me better than she ever did."

"How long were you with her?" Nic asked.

"Three years, from when I first took her on, until I released her a few months ago."

"What do the tattoos mean?"

He sighed. "May I sit down?"

She gestured grandly with one hand. "Please do."

He sat, turning to face her, with his arm on the back of the sofa. The low lights shadowed his face.

"I started the tattoos years ago, when I first took on one of these women. There are many who give some mark of ownership to these kinds of women and she craved one from me. I gave her a charm bracelet that I bought at an ordinary jewelry store. But we were together for several years and she wanted something more … permanent."

"Like a tattoo."

"Like a tattoo, yes. So I designed a tattoo and we went together to get it on her wrist. That made her happy."

"I was under the impression that you hadn't had any serious relationships besides an early girlfriend."

"These aren't serious relationships. At least not from my perspective. I don't share anything about me, Nicole. I just use them for sex and care for them as a friend. There are some intense feelings having to do with the sex, but nothing approaching a boyfriend/girlfriend relationship. During all these years, I've never had just one woman at a time. I've always carried on multiple relationships, simultaneously. The women all understood that. Most even liked that aspect. Being part of a cadre."

"Jack's club." Nic remembered the way Erica had tried to include her in that group.

"If you like. The tattoos were a part of that. It gave them a sense of belonging. An identity. The way a sorority girl might get a tattoo of the symbol of her house. Having a name tattooed on you isn't that unusual."

"And the top girl got the tattoo on her ass?"

Jack winced. "Erica told you about that, too? Quite chatty, wasn't she?"

"Oh, she wanted to be my new best friend."

"Yes, the bottom tattoo. Shada was the first one to have that. It was necessary, because I needed to keep her apart from the other girls. They needed to know that she was special to me and my priority. I helped her out of an abusive relationship and she needed some extra care at that time."

Nic pictured Shada's sweet smile and her dark kind eyes. For the first time in a few days, she had a tiny spark of gratitude for what Jack did for this one girl, at least.

"How many have had the 'top girl' tattoo?"

"Three. Shada, another woman, and then Erica. I gave her the tattoo just nine months ago, but gave her up four months after that."

"Who was the other woman?"

Jack made a face. "She's long gone. No longer an issue."

"Sounds like you buried her under six feet of cement."

"That is a tasteless joke, Nicole." He glared at her.

She realized she perhaps had pushed him too far.

"You're right. It is tasteless. I'm not in the best of moods at the moment." She sipped her water and looked out at the view of Seattle. "How many women out there have these tattoos? The wrist ones?"

"Sixteen," he said, without hesitation.

She gaped at him. "Seriously? I thought it was just your employees and Erica."

He shrugged. "Several have moved on to happy relationships with other people. A few have moved away. I'm in touch to some extent with all of them." He brushed his hand through his hair, shifting restlessly on the sofa. "It wasn't something I did lightly, these tattoos. It was a responsibility to accept this woman and to make sure she was safe and content. To publicly, or at least within our community, let people know that she belonged to me."

He leaned toward her slightly, looking her fully in the face. "I'm thirty-four years old, Nicole. Any man would have had relationships by this point in his life. Probably even an ex-wife. I have had relationships, but it has been a long time since I've been intimate with a woman with more than my body and my control."

She kept her eyes locked with his and nodded slowly.

"Do you want to know about the bracelet?" he asked.

"Erica said it was a first step. A bracelet for beginners."

He narrowed his eyes. "She lied."

"What do you mean?"

"Since that first woman, I've never given a bracelet to anyone. And never one like this one." He reached for her arm and touched the chain around her wrist.

"What about your girlfriend?"

"I gave her jewelry at times, but not anything like this. Not anything that resembled the tattoos."

"Why did you give it to me?"

He moved closer to her, taking her hand in his and keeping his thumb on her bracelet. With his other hand, he tentatively tucked her hair behind her ear.

"I don't know if I can explain. I don't know if I really know myself, but I'll try." He held out his hand, silently asking for a sip of her water. She handed him the glass and he took a deep drink.

"I gave that first woman a charm bracelet. I've never given anything remotely similar to another woman. Until you. I have feelings for you, Nicole. Some of them are similar to what I've felt toward the other women in my life. Sexually, I want you more than I've ever wanted anyone. I want to know you inside out and to be so far inside of you that you can feel me existing in your core."

Nic flushed and curled her legs up against her.

"I also want people to know you belong to me." His eyes flickered over her face. "Not in the way these other women belonged to me. At least not exactly like that. It is more than you being identified as simply "mine." It's more that you are a part of who I am. So yes, it is a mark, like the tattoos are. But it means more than those tattoos ever did. I am filled with pride when I see it on your arm. I love thinking of you during the day, at your work or doing your laundry or tucked into your bed, wearing my bracelet. I may have felt some satisfaction that these other women agreed to wear my tattoo, but with you, I am ecstatic that you have agreed to wear my bracelet."

"Erica said that you forced some women to get the tattoos."

He looked at her intently. "Do you think that's true?"

"No."

"How do you know?"

"Because I think almost any woman would be thrilled to have your mark."

"I hope you know that I would never force someone to do anything against their will. That is not the kind of person I am. I like being given to, even in extreme situations. Some force, yes, perhaps. But not like that. Never like that."

She nodded and then asked the question that had been lurking at the back of her mind for the past few days.

"Will you want me to get these tattoos at some point?"

He hesitated and then slowly shook his head no.

"I don't want you to mark your skin for me. I want it to be so plainly obvious that you belong to me, that there is no need for that kind of thing. In the way you walk, in how you are at my side when we are out, in how you speak about me. Everyone will know that you are mine. The bracelet is just a symbol of that. Not an identifier."

He came even closer, his hand sliding through her hair to cup the back of her head. He took the glass from her fingers and set it down on the table, then tilted her head back so her eyes met his.

"Will you be mine, Nicole? Will you be mine, as I am already yours?"

His. Would she be his? Was he hers? Would this work? Wasn't it too soon to think like this? Her mind raced with answers and affirmations, denials and questions.

Then she let it all go.

"Yes," she breathed, without thinking, without effort, the response as natural as the beat of her heart.

His lips met hers to seal the vow. Then he said clearly what she had dreamily heard him whisper the other night.

"I love you, Nicole Simmons."

* * * * *

He led her to his bedroom. He undressed her slowly, revealing each inch of her skin to be kissed and caressed with his fingertips, until she stood naked at the foot of his bed.

She reached for the buttons on his shirt, but he held her hands together.

"Do you trust me, Nicole? It's important that you do."

He was still so full of secrets, it seemed. And a past that she didn't understand. Complications that he found difficult to explain. She had questions that still weren't answered and trepidations about what their future might hold. She knew that she might end up being emotionally hurt by him.

Yet she wanted to risk it. For the reward, she could sense, would be worth the risk. Worth the hurt.

He loved her. She didn't just believe his words. She could sense it in him. He would never willingly hurt her.

In the bedroom, or in any location, she knew that she could trust him to keep her safe.

"Yes," she said.

He brought her to the bed and laid her down on the silky covers.

"For tonight, let me dictate what happens. Go with it. If you need to at any time, just tell me to stop."

She began to sit up. "What do you mean?"

"Lie down, Nicole. Trust me." He ran a hand down her shoulder and over her breast, stomach, and hip as she laid back. "I'll tell you what I will do before I do it. I promise. Just stay here for the moment."

He walked to the large armoire and pulled open the doors. Inside were a series of shallow drawers. From one, he pulled several lengths of red material. Then he came back to the bed.

"With your permission, I would like to tie these on your wrists and ankles."

"What? Why?"

"This is where the trust comes in. I promise you, I won't let any danger come to you, but it will be so worth it. Trust me?" He wrapped a piece of the fabric around his fists, pulling it taut between them.

She thought of Evi and ropes and pirates. *Aye.*

"Okay." She brought her arms up over her head and stretched her legs out, lengthening her torso.

He loosely tied the end of one of the red velvet strips to her wrist, showing her the end of the length that she could catch and pull with her fingers, to release the knot if she needed to. He repeated the action on the other wrist and then her ankles.

Then he crawled up on the bed to tie the other ends of the strips to the four posts, at the end pulling her legs apart to secure the last ankle.

The ties were tight, but not so tight that she couldn't squirm and pull at them.

He smiled at her as he came around the bed and doffed his clothes. When he was nude, he came back to stand next to her. His cock was already half-hard.

He put his hands on his hips and surveyed his work.

"Damn, Nicole. You were made for this. Sexy bitch."

He then commenced playing with her.

She had never been helpless before while someone tormented her. And such sweet torment! He touched her. He flicked her nipples. He ran his fingers over her stomach.

He licked her pussy lips, while scratching his fingers on the inside of her thighs. He slid up her to suckle her breasts, then moved up her again to tease her mouth with the tip of his cock, just smearing his pre-cum on her lower lip. Back down, he lay between her legs, spread her pussy open with his fingers, and then touched, circled, talking to her about what he was doing, what he saw in her. He pushed his fingers into her; first one, then two, then three. He pulsed them inside of her, watching her intently as she writhed.

"What do you want right now?" he asked.

"Please," she gasped.

"Ask for it."

"Jack! Please!"

"Beg me." His voice was low and he continued to pulse his fingers inside of her.

She moaned and twisted, feeling the fabric pulling at her wrists, preventing her from turning or moving away from those damn fingers. The restraints on her ankles kept her from spreading her legs wider. She tried to press down harder on his fingers, and then tried to close her legs, but couldn't. She was becoming desperate as he played her, teased her.

"Jack!" she cried.

"Beg me."

"Please, Jack, please! I am begging you!"

"Explicitly. Tell me what you want. Beg me." His voice was maddeningly cool, while hers was raspy and panting.

She groaned and arched off the bed as much as she could. Then she fell back, squirming again.

"Please, Jack, push your fingers deeper into me. Please!" She gasped, unable to think clearly enough to form the words she needed.

"Again, Nicole. Beg me again."

"Ahhhhh!" She gritted her teeth, grasping at the words. Concentrating.

"Jack." She focused her eyes on his face. "Please finger fuck me until I come. Touch that magic spot inside of me and watch me come undone. Force me to orgasm." She swallowed. "Please, I beg you."

He smiled and did as she asked.

She thrashed on the bed, yanking at her bonds. He made her lick his fingers clean and then started on her again. Four fingers this time, until she was shrieking and bucking on them, feeling the burn of him stretching her while he also caressed her g-spot to another climax. She screamed her thanks as she came, feeling the pull of the restraints. He cradled her head in his hands while she sucked on his cock, him kneeling over her. Roughly telling her how he saw her, her grace and sexuality and wanton need for him. He fed her sips of water through a straw as she recovered, only to start in again.

She lost track of time, relying only on him to begin the next set of activities. Again and then again he played her, making her beg, moan, scream, and come.

She wondered if she was losing consciousness. At one moment he was between her legs, his mouth on her. Then she closed her eyes and tumbled through a series of shockingly intense responses. When she opened her eyes, he was kneeling by her head, bring her mouth to him. He was everywhere around her, touching every part of her. She felt him inside her body, his lightening touch sparking through her. She felt him inside her head, his whispers, his control, his presence occupying her.

The restraints kept her safe. Otherwise she might have lost all control, convulsing on the bed, her arms and legs flailing. The strips on her ankles and wrists held her in place, maintaining the control that she needed while she ceded her own control to him. He delivered sensations, affirmations, and orgasms, while coaxing entreaties and pleas from her.

At some point he turned her over, securing her again and raising her ass with a firm cushion under her hips. He brought his palm down on her ass as she pulled at her bonds, her head raised and cries falling from her mouth at the spanking, more from shock than any real discomfort. Heat radiated from her bottom throughout her. Each whack made her tighten and grind her clit against the cushion. She never yelled for him to stop. She never screamed out a denial. She screamed in shock and intense pleasure. She didn't fight it.

Then he fucked her. Kneeling between her tightly tied spread legs, he entered her from behind, his hips hitting against her heated bottom. She sobbed, rolling her hips up to him, her hands in fists and yanking again on the restraints. She cried her thanks as he thrust into her, cried her gratitude at the mercy of the restraints holding her, cried her pleasure as he released his own pleasure into her, filling her not only with his seed, but with his life.

She collapsed then, her hair tangled around her face, her body covered in a sheen of sweat. She was barely aware of him untying her. He drew the strips of fabric from her ankles and wrists, rubbing her pressure points. He gathered her naked spent body to him and drew a sheet over them.

"Mine?" he whispered, stroking her hair.

"Yours," she replied in a hoarse whisper.

CHAPTER TWENTY-SEVEN

"I can't believe you did that!" Evi gasped and then laughed. "Nic gets so carsick. You were really taking a risk."

Nic smiled and rolled her eyes. "It was close, Evi."

Jack was telling Evi about Nic's green face after he sped down a long circular ramp into a parking garage. Etta's restaurant was popular for Sunday brunch and every parking spot within blocks had been occupied, when he gave up and pulled into the underground garage.

Nic picked at her french toast, taking a few bites now and then. Her stomach was still jumpy. A sip of her mimosa helped settle it.

Evi had jumped at the chance to meet Jack, when Nic called her earlier that morning. She was waiting for them when they finally arrived, giving Nic a huge hug, kiddingly scolding her for being so unavailable that week, and then shaking Jack's hand, casting her eyes up and down his figure.

Jack dug into his smoked salmon and eggs. The trip down the parking lot rabbit hole obviously didn't affect him.

"Nicole speaks so well of you, and often," he said.

"She should. I've been her best friend for years. I'm very protective of her."

Nic almost rolled her eyes again, but thought better of it. Instead she pursed her lips at her friend. "Evi treats me like a sister. In all the bad ways, along with all the good ways."

"Uh-huh." Evi chewed on a piece of toast. "So I already know how you two met and where your first date was. And the second date that ended with you, Jack, walking off. How you took her to the bait shack, which was sweet."

"Evi," Nic said, putting a warning note in her tone.

"I can't imagine what else she has told you." Jack gave Nic a sideways glance, one eyebrow raised.

"Oh, she tells me everything. Eventually. But we do need to get caught up. It's been almost two weeks since I've seen her in person. Where have you been keeping her?"

"In bed," Jack said with a straight face. Evi laughed and Nic grinned and felt herself blush. His comment wasn't far off the mark.

Jack and Evi conversed easily, sharing a wicked sense of humor. Jack took Evi's teasing well. That was a rare talent in itself.

Jack paid for brunch and went to get the Jeep to pick Nic up outside, not wanting to subject her again to the curlicue ride back up the ramp.

"You okay?" Evi bumped Nic's shoulder with her own, as they waited inside the entryway of the restaurant. "You're quiet today."

"I'm tired. Not enough sleep."

"Too much sex?"

"A lot of sex. Never too much." She smiled.

Evi leaned in closer. "He's good at it, isn't he? I can tell."

"He's fricking amazing at it." Nic shook her head in wonder. "I can't even tell you."

"You better try and tell me some of it. Please? Pretty please?"

"I promise, at least a little. Coffee tomorrow."

"I bet he likes it a little rough." Evi leaned toward the window, searching through the rain for any sign of the Jeep.

"Oh boy, does he."

"Kinky?" Evi gave her a sharp glance.

"Definitely."
"In a good way, I hope."
"Definitely."
"Can I get photos?"
"Definitely not."
"You're no fun. Is he big?"
"Nicely proportioned."
"Mmmm."
"Don't fantasize about my boyfriend."
"I'm not. Just about his cock. I've told you all about Saul's cock."
"His masterpiece, as you refer to it." Nic looked around to make sure no one was eavesdropping.
"Oh yes. God was generous to my Saul."
Jack pulled up in front of the restaurant and Nic gave her friend a quick hug. "Bye, Evi. I'll tell you all about it tomorrow."
"See you at Milo's at eleven then."
Nic hesitated. "Let's meet at the Starbucks closer to work."
"Why? We love Milo's! It's our place."
"I'll tell you about that tomorrow, too."
"I get the feeling you've got more to talk about than cock size and kinky sex."
A woman nearby obviously heard that, because her mouth fell open in comical surprise. Nic smiled sweetly and pointed to Evi.
"Sorry about that. I can't take her anywhere."
Evi looked over at the woman, as she followed Nic out the door. "I may have a dirty mouth, but it's this girl here who's the sex fiend. You wouldn't believe the kinds of things she's done."
Nic grabbed her arm and yanked her through the door. "Bad Evi! Bad!"
Evi laughed and hugged Nic to her. "You love me. You know it."

"God help me, I do."

"Go, my child!" She waved Nic toward the Jeep. "Go and be bad!"

* * * * *

Nic leaned against the wall, waiting for the rickety old elevator to arrive at the basement level and carry her and her basket of clean clothes back up to her floor. Her phone buzzed in her back pocket but she ignored it. Evi had been texting her dirty jokes all day, since leaving her in front of Etta's restaurant. Nic suspected that Saul was supplying her with the jokes.

Some of them were pretty funny.

What do Tupperware and a walrus have in common? They both like a tight seal.

Nic laughed to herself remembering that one. Dumb, but funny.

What do you call a lesbian dinosaur? A lickolotopus.

She was still smiling when she opened the door to her apartment, entered, and flipped the bolt behind her. Her phone vibrated again. She dropped the laundry basket and pulled it out.

More texts from Evi. She was on a roll today.

Except there was one from an unknown number. She tapped that one and it bloomed open on the screen.

How was brunch? You didn't eat. Tummy filled with Jack's cum?

She had to read it three times, her eyes flying over the letters, before she realized what she was looking at.

Someone had sent her this text. Someone who had seen them at brunch.

As she reread the text again, another came in, appearing below the first one.

You have pretty eyes. Especially with Jack's cock in your mouth. Has he taken you in ass yet? He loooooves that.

She shivered. Was it from the same phone number? It had to be. Why? Why would someone send these texts to her?

The phone buzzed again and she looked down at it to see another text come in.

I could come to that crappy apartment of yours and tell you about all the things Jack likes.

She dropped the phone with a cry and ran to the window, pulling down the blinds. She ran into her bedroom and did the same thing to the window there. She turned around, looking for other things she should do. Lock the windows? She was several stories up.

Lock the door!

She ran into the other room and saw that the door was already bolted. Of course, she always bolted the door, as soon as she came in.

Call Jack.

She had to tell him. She sat down on the couch and put her head in her hands, trying to slow her breathing.

"It's okay," she repeated over and over. It had to be okay. Just because some stupid bitch wanted to scare her or make her feel bad didn't mean that person was actually dangerous.

It had to be Erica.

Nic felt a flash of anger at the woman. Why couldn't she go away, just take that tattooed ass of hers someplace far away?

She looked at her phone on the floor. Her lip curled when she thought of picking it up.

She had to. It was the only phone she had.

So she did.

The phone buzzed as soon as she had it in her hand.

She screamed and threw it across the room. It landed harmlessly on the carpet.

She had to. She had to get it. She had to call Jack or someone. Evi? No, it had to be Jack. She had to calm down and call him. Her hands were shaking. She wouldn't be able to tap in the right numbers. Why hadn't she put Jack on speed dial yet? The cell company. She should call them and see if she could get the number blocked.

That thought helped calm her. She ignored the phone for the moment and returned to her bedroom to get one of the bills from her cell phone company.

Then she came back to pick up her phone.

The last text had been from Evi. That also helped. Maybe the bitch texts were over and done with.

First she had to call Jack. He answered his phone right away.

"Hey, baby, how's the laundry?"

"Jack, I'm getting creepy text messages."

His voice went from playful to serious in an instant. "What do they say?"

"They refer to us. Someone has seen us places."

"What number are they from?"

"I don't know. It's blocked."

"Can you forward them to me?"

"Yeah, just a minute. If we get disconnected, I'll call you right back."

She forwarded all three texts to Jack's number and then had to call him back.

"Shit," he said.

"Yeah. I'm a little freaked out."

"I don't blame you. The door's locked?"

"Yes. Definitely. And the blinds are down."

"You're staying with me tonight."

"I have to work tomorrow."

"It doesn't matter. I can take you to work on my way to the office."

She groaned. "What a bother this is." Then she added, "Do you know who it is?"

"No. But based on what you told me about your conversation the other day, I have my suspicions."

"I thought so too."

"Stay there. I'm going to straighten this out. I'll pick you up in an hour."

"I can just meet you at your place."

"I will pick you up in an hour," he repeated, his voice stern. "Stay there."

"Okay. I'm going to call the cell phone company and see about getting this number blocked."

"Good idea."

"I'll be ready when you get here."

He sighed. "I'm sorry about this. I know you must be frightened."

"Not really frightened," she said, pushing away the thought of how she had screamed when the phone had buzzed in her hand. "Pissed off. Unnerved. But I'll be okay."

"See you soon, baby." He dropped his stern voice and spoke softly to her. "I'll make this problem go away. I'll take care of you."

"Thanks, Jack."

"I love you." He hung up, not waiting for her reply.

She hadn't said the same words to him yet, but she was ready to. It was time.

*   *   *   *   *

Two hours later, Nic paced the floor of her apartment, circling the couch. Her bag was packed and by the door. She had called the phone company and gotten a block from restricted calls.

Her blinds were still drawn. Her phone sat silent on the coffee table.

She picked it up and quickly texted Evi.

> *I'm staying at Jack's tonight. Still plan on seeing you at Starbucks at 11 tomorrow.*

Evi's texts had died out in the last hour. She must have run out of jokes.

Nic almost wished she'd send a joke now, but instead she just received a reply.

> *Can't get enough of him, can you? Slut. See you tomorrow. Have fun.*

At least that made her laugh.

Even Evi was calling her a slut.

Finally, her phone rang.

"Hi. I'm out front. Are you ready?" Jack said.

"You're a little late."

"I know. I'll explain. I'm sorry."

"I was worried."

"Good. I'm glad you worry about me. Now come down here."

"Bossy man. I'll be right there."

He pushed the Jeep door open for her as soon as she left her building. She slid into the seat, tossing her bag onto the back floor.

He leaned in to kiss her and then started off. Night had fallen an hour ago and the streetlights streaked over his face so quickly, that she couldn't get a good look at him.

"Is everything okay?"

"I'll tell you when we get to my place."

Ten minutes later, she was following him into the elevator from the dark parking garage. That's when she saw the long bloody scratch down the side of his face.

"Oh my God! Jack. What happened?" She touched his cheek. He flinched away.

"Does it look that bad? I haven't seen it yet." He felt along the scratch.

"It looks like serious."

"You can clean it for me when we get upstairs, while I tell you what happened."

Nic seethed. That bitch had scratched him. He must have gone to talk to her and she attacked him.

Once inside, Jack retrieved a wet cloth and antiseptic ointment from the guest bathroom. Nic knelt next to him on the couch and dabbed at the cut, cleaning away the blood. She held back her words, even though she was still boiling inside, thinking of what Erica had done to him.

"It doesn't look as bad, once it's cleaned up. Just drew blood in a few spots." She dotted the scratch with the ointment and then sat back on her heels, tossing the ointment tube onto the table. "You went to see her."

"I had to."

"You couldn't call?"

"It was something that had to be done in person. I still do have some influence over her, no matter how angry or deluded she is."

"What happened?"

He sighed and leaned back against the cushions. "I drove to her house and she answered the door. She pretended she didn't know what I was talking about. She said she never called you and didn't know where you lived.

I told her she was a liar and had never been worthy of being mine. That I made a mistake in ever offering the first tattoo to her, and that I must have been under the influence when I gave her the second one. That's when I got this."

He gestured to the side of his face.

"Jack. She sounds disturbed. What did you do when she attacked you?"

"I grabbed her, of course. I had to get her under control. So I made her kneel."

"Kneel?"

"That was how she used to listen to me. She liked to kneel on the floor. I knew it would center her and she would listen."

Nic ground her teeth together, but said nothing.

"And then once she was calmer, I" —he broke off, glancing at her— "I'm just telling you all this in the interest of full disclosure."

"Go on."

"I made her strip."

"What?" He made her strip? He was with her when she was naked? Why couldn't he just yell at her like a normal man?

"It's what she knows, Nicole. And then, I told her that she was no longer under my protection. That she was never to contact you in any way ever again. That she would never hear from me again. And that I would arrange for enough money to be transferred to her bank account, so she could get the tattoos removed. I told her that she better do it within the next six months, as I will have someone check."

"Not you?"

"Not me. I'm not seeing her again."

Nic nodded, somewhat satisfied. "Was that it?"

"No. I made her repeat what I had just told her. I ordered her to apologize to me and then I ordered her to write an apology to you." He lifted his hip to pull a piece of paper out of his back pocket.

"You didn't have to do that. I don't really want the apology."

"Read it or not. The point was reinforcing who was in control. And making sure she realizes how badly she behaved."

"Did she say anything else?" She picked up the folded piece of paper and turned it over in her hands.

"She said, 'goodbye, sir' as I closed the door."

Nic opened the paper. A few lines were written in a thin, slightly wavering handwriting.

I'm sorry for the texts messages. I was out of line. I hope for a happy future for you and Jack.

"Heartfelt," she said.

Jack shrugged. "I wasn't expecting Shakespeare."

"Since that's all settled, I don't have to stay here tonight. I can stay at my apartment." She wasn't sure that staying with him during the week was a healthy habit to start.

"Please stay here, Nicole. I want to feel you next to me."

He looked exhausted, his body limp against the couch cushions. His eyes were closed.

She knelt down and slipped the shoes off his feet, massaging first one foot, then the other. He didn't open his eyes and she wondered if he had fallen asleep. After many minutes, he spoke again.

"It's draining to have to discipline someone like that. I was so furious at what she had done, I almost wanted to slap her back when she attacked me."

"I'm glad you didn't."

He opened an eye and looked at her. "I am known for my self-control. It would not have been appropriate." He opened the other eye and watched her as she massaged him, his feet resting in her lap. "I kinda like you down there. Sexy."

"Perv." She smiled.

"You must like it too or you wouldn't have gone so willingly to your knees."

"I do."

"I've noticed just how quickly you like to kneel."

"Not like her," Nic said sharply.

"No. Not in any way like her." He leaned forward and put a hand under her chin, tilting her face up to his. "Only in Nicole's way. Thank you, darling." He kissed her softly on the lips.

"For the foot rub?" she asked, when he pulled back.

"For calling me right away. For not having a fit that I went to a former sub's home, made her strip, and asserted myself over her. For caring for my severe injuries." He grinned. "For walking up to me that day at your office and sticking your hand out and introducing yourself."

She lifted herself up to kiss him, wrapping her fingers around the back of his head to pull her to him, stroking his lip with her tongue. Then she knelt back and ran her hands down his legs. "Want me to make you feel even more thankful?"

"As a matter of fact ..." He began to unbutton his pants. "I do."

She did stay the night. In fact, she stayed at his condo every night that week.

CHAPTER TWENTY-EIGHT

For Nic, the week was uneventful. At least as far as work, daily life, and irrational gorgeous stalkers. The sex, however, was extremely eventful. And plentiful. She couldn't get enough of Jack and craved him inside of her as soon as he pulled out. He seemed to feel the same.

One night he didn't say a word as he walked in the door of his condo, where she waited for him. He just pushed her face down over the table by the window, yanked down her yoga pants, and fucked her hard and fast. She didn't complain. She fucked him back, just as aggressively.

He also made her coffee every morning. Washed her hair in the shower one night. Gave her a bruising hickey on the inside of her thigh that she wore like a badge of honor for days. If only she could have showed it off like she did her bracelet.

She made him a risotto dinner with wild mushrooms, one of the few dishes with which she was confident. He mixed their laundry together to send out to the service he used. She made a little corner for her cosmetics on his long bathroom counter. He dropped her off at work every day with a kiss and greeted her with open arms when he next saw her. Unless he was bending her over something to fuck her.

She visited his office again at his invitation and coolly nodded to Veronica as she walked in. She went straight up the stairs to his office, stopping by Shada's desk.

Nic noticed the tattoo on Shada's wrist now. On the wrists of all the girls in the office. She told herself it was nothing more than employment I.D. Somewhere in the back of her mind, a voice kept reminding her of just what the tattoo did mean. She shut the door on that voice whenever it got too loud.

After talking with Shada, she went into Jack's office, closed the door behind her, and gave him a blowjob on her knees, in front of the windows looking down on Cherry Street. When he came, she tilted her head back, looking up at him as he filled her open mouth. The rapture on his face was her reward.

She wore her bracelet every day, never taking it off. Jack loved to finger it around her wrist when they cuddled together on the couch.

Every night was filled with sex and affection, sometimes lovemaking, sometimes hard fucking, sometimes a little kinky play. One night, he laid her over his knee on the edge of the bed and alternately fondled her pussy and ass, between glancing but sharp slaps on her buttocks. Another time, he cinched her wrists behind her back with one of his belts and had her kneel on the bed, with her head down and ass raised. Then he played with her. Another night he pushed her legs wide apart and sucked and nibbled on her clit, until she exploded in orgasms.

Some nights, she thought she might lose her mind. She would be so out of it, delirious with need and pleasure and sheer mental, emotional, and physical exhilaration.

By Friday night, she was exhausted. As she trudged to his condo from the bus stop, she almost wished just for a hot bath and a pizza.

He arrived home at the same time she did and they greeted each other with a close hug and warm kiss.

"Tired?" he asked.

"Very."

They ate soup and bread and shared a bottle of wine. After the dishes were put away, he sat on the couch and she curled up at his feet, resting her head on his leg. He stroked her hair, sipping his wine with his other hand, until she fell asleep.

She woke when he gently shook her.

"You've been asleep for two hours, sleepyhead," he said softly.

"Oh wow, I'm sorry." She ran a hand over her face, blinking rapidly.

"How are you feeling?"

"What? Oh, fine. I'll never fall asleep now, though."

"Good. Follow me." He stood up.

"Huh? What?" She shook her head, trying to clear her mind.

"Come on. Time for bed."

"I know I won't be able to fall asleep."

"Silly girl. I'm not talking about sleep."

He walked to his bedroom, disappearing from sight.

Good God. He wanted her again.

She straightened her legs beneath her and crossed to the bedroom, wavering slightly as she fought for balance.

Nic paused, leaning against the doorjamb. He had stripped off his shirt and was laid out on the bed in just his pants. Her sleepiness wore off in a hurry as she let her eyes linger on him from his bare toes to the top of his dark tousled hair.

"Come here, baby." He patted the bed next to him. "I promise not to molest you if you don't want me to."

She slid onto the bed beside him, running her hand up his chest, through the wiry black hair there. She could see a few silver hairs as well.

"What if I want you to molest me?"

"You aren't tired of me yet?"

She shook her head. "Not at all."

He gently nudged her onto her back, his hand stroking up her arm to grip her wrist as he kissed her. "We can't go on like this," he said in between kisses. "We'll wear each other out."

"I can't believe I can still walk after this week."

"Me neither. I've used you well." He laughed against her neck.

"I'll say."

He pulled her shirt up and kissed over her stomach, making her giggle. Then he had her skirt unfastened and down around her knees, pulling it off and dropping it on the floor. Her panties quickly followed.

He pulled her legs apart and kissed the fading hickey on her thigh. "How does this feel? Still tender?"

"No."

"Hm. I'll have to give you something else to feel over the weekend." He bit into the soft flesh of her other thigh.

"Ouch! Stop that!" She tried to pull her leg away, but was laughing as she did so. He never bit her cruelly, but the bites he did give her were thrilling.

"Mmm, no I won't stop. We need matching marks here, I think." He gripped her thighs harder and reapplied his teeth to her.

Nic tried to still herself, but couldn't stop squirming. His teeth increased the pressure, making her gasp and flail her legs.

He pulled back with a long hard suck on that spot. "Can't have you thrashing around like that. You'll kick me in the head." Jack crossed to his armoire and Nic's heart skipped a beat. She had seen a few of the things he kept in that armoire. The ties. Belts, both leather and fabric. One night he had pulled out a long silver chain before he seemed to reconsider and replaced it in the drawer.

There were lots of drawers in the armoire and she had only seen what was in a few of them.

"Let's see what I've got here," he mused, opening and closing drawers.

She could protest, saying she would hold still, but he knew as well as she did that she loved being restrained. It increased her arousal tenfold when she was helpless to escape him and his touch. Whether the touch was soft or hard.

He pulled two cuffs from a drawer and turned to her. "Do you think you are ready for these?"

She gulped. The cuffs were metal and lined on the inside of the rings with soft furry material. "I can't escape from those, can I? The way you showed me to untie the fabric strips."

"No. I won't lock them with the key, but I will latch them and you won't be able to unlatch them easily. But you couldn't escape the belt on your wrists the other night."

She hadn't even thought of escaping the belt.

She bit her lip. He waited for her answer.

"Okay. Yes, I'm ready for those."

He smiled. "I already knew that."

He lifted one of her feet and slipped the cuff around her ankle. It closed with a click that made her jump, but the soft padding was comfortable on her skin. The cuff had weight but wasn't as heavy as it looked.

A short chain extended from the side of the cuff and ended in a metal latch. Jack brought the latch to a little metal ring set into one of the posts at the bottom corners of the bed.

He looked up at her, latch in hand. "Okay? I'll only ask once."

She nodded, her heart thudding in her chest.

He clicked the latch closed around the ring.

It wasn't that she hadn't noticed the rings set in the bedposts. She knew what they were for, but so far he had just used soft restraints that he tied around the posts. Like normal people. Now she could see that this was a bed that had been specially modified for bondage.

Bondage that he practiced with ...

She slammed that door in her mind.

He took her other foot and clicked the cuff around that ankle. Without asking this time, he latched the cuff to the other post.

"Lie back."

She laid back on the bed, stretching her arms up over her head, arching her back and pulling on her legs, testing the give of the chains. She had already learned in this week that this was the first thrill of being bound, feeling how much, or how little freedom, was given to move. She tried to close her legs and found that they were held wide apart with little give. Since her arms weren't bound, she could move her upper body freely and she could bend her knees. The ankle cuffs just prevented her from closing her legs.

Jack took immediate advantage. He slid his hands under her hips, gripping her thighs, and pulled her down to the end of the bed, so that her knees were bent upward, her legs still spread wide. She clutched at the covers as he moved her, squealing in excited alarm.

He knelt on the floor.

Then he fastened his lips onto that same spot on the top inside of her thigh and began to suck.

Hard.

She gasped and arched her back, twisting her fingers into the sheets. "Jack," she cried. He was serious about giving her another matching mark.

He didn't let up. His teeth scraped against her skin, sending a jolt through her.

She yanked at her legs, but the cuffs were doing the job that he intended. Her involuntary response just might have resulted in him being kicked in the head.

She couldn't help yanking at her legs, trying to close them. The frustration mixed with the excitement to stoke her even higher. She cursed, feeling the bruising beginning on that spot, the rush of blood that would pool and turn purple.

He gave a last hard suck and then closed his teeth firmly on her flesh. This mark would be framed by the imprint of his teeth.

She cried out as he moved up to his next target. Here, he was gentle. For now, anyway.

He nuzzled his mouth against her, lightly licking her. She heard his appreciative murmurs and giggled to herself, as she imagined he was having a private conversation with her pussy.

"What are you laughing at?" He lifted his head, sounding bemused.

"I'm not laughing. I just had a tiny, funny thought."

"You really are distracted tonight. I better give you something to focus on."

He returned to his work, kissing her mound. He licked along each side of her lips, dipping his tongue into the crevice at the bottom of her slit.

She moaned as he aroused her little by little. When his fingers opened her pussy lips and his tongue more determinedly swirled over her, flicking her folds, and his thumb began to circle her clit, she began to twist and whimper. Her hands wandered over herself, caressing her own cheek, cupping and squeezing her breasts, pinching her own nipples, trailing across her stomach, stroking his hair, and scratching up the inside of her thighs.

"Jack," she groaned, not able to stop moving.

"Mmmmmm." He didn't seem to be listening to her.

She couldn't focus, there were too many things going on. What he was doing to her with his mouth most of all, but her mind darted to her fingers on her nipples, the lick of her lips, the feel of the sheets bunched up beneath her, and the wetness she felt on the inside of her thighs. Even the lights in the ceiling seemed to flicker and buzz.

Her attention wanted to fly off in all directions, even as her physical arousal increased with each passing second.

"Jack. Please." She called to him.

"Mmmm, I'm getting you there." His reply was muffled.

"No. Please. I need your help."

He lifted his head. His lips and cheeks glistened with her wetness. "What's wrong?" he asked, frowning with concern. "Are you okay?"

"I need … I need you to help me." Her hands fluttered over her body, not able to keep still. "I need … I need my wrists cuffed. Please. It's too much. I can't …"

She should have realized that she didn't need to explain.

He smiled at her. "Sure, baby."

He got to his feet and crossed to the armoire. As he turned from her, she could see his erection tenting the front of his pants and she couldn't help hissing her breath between her teeth.

He returned with a matching set of cuffs.

"You think I'm ready for these on my wrists too?" she asked.

"I know you are."

He closed the cuffs around her wrists and she saw a quick glimpse of her bracelet, before the click. He latched them to the rings in the bedposts at the head of the bed.

She was spread-eagle on the top of his bed. Held like this, she had little slack. She looked up at each wrist cuff, twisting her hands. There was no discomfort, the furry lining in the cuffs cushioned her.

She was firmly secured to his bed.

He didn't ask if she was okay, but he did hold her gaze for several seconds, giving her the opportunity to back out, before he nodded and turned away.

From under the bed, he pulled out a firm foam cushion and slid it under her hips, raising them slightly.

"Just for my convenience, of course," he said with a grin and then returned to his play.

This time, she was all his. Now that she was firmly restrained and couldn't flail about, couldn't touch herself, all she was aware of was his mouth, his tongue, his teeth, and his thumb. Her focus narrowed as she closed her eyes and blotted out the ceiling lights. She stopped pulling at the cuffs, just tugging at them a little. Her focus narrowed even more, not onto a physical place like her pussy, but in her mind. Just him. Just him. She was conscious only of a pinpoint of light in her mind. She gasped, trembling, the mantra of his name echoing in her head as sparks traveled up and down her spine. His thumb increased its pressure on her clit, his fingers held her lips spread open as he speared his tongue into her over and over and … Jack … and again and … Jack … and …

She arched up, her body taut as it pulled hard on the cuffs. With a screaming sob, she reached orgasm. The restraints kept her safe and secured to the bed and able to give herself fully to the sensations soaring through her. He kept his thumb on her, rounding her clit over and over, not letting up, not releasing her from her spasms. It was all she knew. Her cries were distant to her ears, the feel of the cuffs was a vague hold. All she knew was that pinpoint of light that had exploded behind her closed eyes, and the abandonment of her body to Jack.

With whimpering sobs, she came back to awareness and opened her eyes. Her pussy was still contracting, little pulses of pleasure zipping through her pelvis.

Jack rose up over her and she caught her breath at the sight of him. His gaze was heated and heavy. His lips wet and parted. His chest was gleaming with a sheen of sweat and the muscles of his shoulders were flexed and hard. She felt her heart pounding inside of her, echoing the throbbing in her pelvis.

She twisted her wrists in the cuffs, suddenly so wanting to touch him, but couldn't. Her palms were damp and she could feel the lining of the cuffs sticky around her wrists.

His hands stroked her cheeks gently, but his hot gaze gave her enough warning. She knew him well enough to know that his gentle touch alternated with his rougher touch. He had been gentle with her for quite a while.

Sure enough, his hands floated over her skin and settled on her breasts.

"Breathe, Nicole," he said.

She took a deep breath, her breasts swelling beneath his hands. At the apex of her breath, his fingers tightened around them, squeezing hard. She released her breath with a startled rush.

His hands relaxed as she took several shallow breaths.

"Again."

She breathed in deeply, ready this time. As her breasts rose into his palms, his fingers closed around them, digging into her soft flesh, gripping her tightly. She whimpered but held her breath, her eyes locked with his. His hands shook slightly, trembling, almost causing her to lose the breath she held. He grinned wickedly at her.

"Good. Good. Hold it," he said and gripped her tighter.

She groaned, feeling lightheaded, and finally released her breath with a great whoosh. His hands left her aching breasts immediately, but then returned to gently massage them.

She panted, looking down at the red marks of his fingerprints. The throbbing had never left her pussy from the last orgasm and now she felt added heat. Why did she love this so? His calm authority matched with her helpless thrills. The mix of pleasure and discomfort that lifted her higher than any soft touch by itself could have.

How did he know just what to do to her, and when?

Experience, giggled that mean inner voice. She slammed the door again on it and winced at the echo.

"You okay?" he asked, seeing her wince.

"Oh yes," she said with a sigh. She twisted her hands again in the cuffs, feeling the slight prickle of the sweat-dampened padding against her inner wrists.

"Good, because I'm not done." With that, he gripped her nipples in a hard pinch and pulled them, twisting, demanding her complete attention again. Which he got. Again her mind pulled in to focus only on him.

He brought the tip of his cock against her opening, closed his fingers tightly around her hips, and pushed hard inside of her.

She cried out as she felt him burrow deep inside of her body, without mercy, forcing her body to accept and accommodate him. She felt her channel tight around him, molding to the shape of his cock. Her entire body seemed to shift, becoming the sheath for him, perfecting itself to hold him in a custom-made fit.

He didn't stop to let her adjust, or wait for her to catch up to him. Instead he drew himself out and then thrust in again, smiling at her cries. He was half kneeling between her legs, holding her with his hands, and taking her body for his pleasure.

He pounded into her and she released herself to him, unable and unwilling to resist in any way. She took him inside of her over and over, giving him her body as he demanded it of her. His grunts as he thrust himself into her were her reward. The look of intense, hard-won pleasure on his face was also her reward. The more he took from her, the more she felt rewarded.

The pinpoint of light. The mantra of his name. The existence of him as a part of her.

She cried out his name in wonder as he took her. He moaned her name in reply. Sweat trickled down his chest as his exertions increased, as his thrusting turned to complete rutting. Need, want, pleasure, distress, pain, ecstasy … all swirled into that pinpoint of light that she focused on in her mind. The pinpoint that was only him.

Pleasure.

His name.

Discomfort. The wrist cuffs bit into her as he jerked her body.

Pleasure. Jack. Pleasure. She cried out over and over. *Yes. Yes. Yours.*

"Mine," he declared to her. It was not a question.

Yours. Yours. Yours. She wasn't sure if she said it aloud. Her pussy throbbed around him, as he seemed to swell inside of her.

He growled, snarling.

He was close.

Pleasure. Pain. Throbbing in her core.

Pain.

Pain.

Her wrists.

Pain.

"Jack," she screamed.

His neck was strained, his head lifted, every muscle taut as he working himself into her.

"Jack!" she screamed again, panicked.

Her wrists were on fire. She jerked against the cuffs and the pain flared even more.

"Jack! Help!" she screamed again.

He froze. His eyes focused on her face. "What? What?"

"My wrists! Something's wrong! My wrists!"

He leaped from her and she was aware of the burn as his swollen organ pulled from inside her. The burning of her wrists terrified her.

She screamed she didn't know what. Words.

He was fumbling with her cuffs, detaching them. First one and then the other dropped to the bed.

She started to pull her hands to her, but he seized her forearms and lifted them so he could see.

"Nicole!" he yelled and the fear in his voice terrified her further.

The pain in her wrists was almost unbearable and she wasn't able to form words anymore. Just trailing screams.

He dropped her hands and she lifted them to her face.

Her wrists.

Red. Bloody. Sizzling flesh. Blisters.

She shrieked.

He had her in his arms and then in the bathroom, holding her wrists under running water. He was yelling something, but she couldn't hear him as she watched her blood swirl down the sink drain.

His yells. Barked directions. His fingers gripping her forearms and holding her hands beneath the water, when she just wanted to sink to the floor. The sound of voices. Another pair of hands on her. She heard a scream and knew it was her but, she couldn't feel herself anymore. Horizontal. She was lying down.

"Nicole. I'm here. Nicole." She could hear Jack's voice close by, but she couldn't call to him.

"Nicole." His voice broke.

She couldn't move. She couldn't feel.

She was gone.

CHAPTER TWENTY-NINE

For a while, it seemed she was indeed gone. Then for a long while, she was barely there. There were bright lights and lots of voices, but they didn't seem to be talking to her. There was a terrifying pain in her wrists, and then it was gone. There was cold and she shivered and then heat and she sweated.

There was that pinpoint of light in her mind again, but Jack wasn't there to fill it. She moaned, trying to say his name.

A hand cool on her hot forehead. "Shhhhh, dear, it's okay now." A woman's voice.

A man's voice. "The medication will make you feel sleepy."

She started to complain but his words were a promise and she slept instead.

CHAPTER THIRTY

Nic opened her eyes to the sun. It lay softly over her, shining through a window, reflecting off white walls. The sunlight was as comforting as the blanket tucked around her. She closed her eyes and slept some more.

When she opened her eyes again, the sun had shifted, not shining so directly through the window.

Her arms lay on either side of her, the wrists wrapped in thick white bandages.

An image of her bloody and blistered wrists flashed through her mind. She moaned, bringing her arms up. Her wrists. What must they look like under the bandages.

"Hey there."

It was Evi, in a chair next to the bed. The hospital bed. She was in the hospital. Of course.

"How are you feeling?" her friend asked, scooting her chair closer.

"Woozy. My wrists," she trailed off.

"They'll be okay, but you've got some nasty burns. It will take a while to heal."

Nic moaned.

"Do they hurt? I can call the nurse."

"I don't feel a thing. Not in my wrists," she said. "You haven't called my mom, have you?"

"Please. I know better than to do that without your permission."

"A few days, okay?" She tried to focus on her friend.

Evi nodded. Her face was more serious than Nic had ever seen it, not the hint of a smile or a trace of teasing in her eyes. "He hurt you."

"No." Nic looked around. "Where is Jack?"

"I don't know now. They wouldn't let him in to see you last night."

"Why?"

"Security tends to frown on half-naked swearing men who declare themselves to be a boyfriend. He was convinced to leave. They told him that if you gave permission when you woke up, he could see you then."

"I give permission."

Evi sighed. "Are you sure?" She leaned toward Nic, her voice lowered. "They let me in because I said I was your best friend. And I had your information—work and insurance and stuff. But Nic," she grimaced, "they implied that he hurt you." She whispered, "There are bite marks."

Nic nodded. "I know. I wanted them."

"Shit."

"It sounds weird now, but it didn't seem weird then. There's just one bite mark. One new bite mark. The other is just a hickey."

Evi held up her hand. "Okay. Hickeys I get. What about the cuffs?"

"You know about that?"

"Everyone does. The police brought them in because the doctors wanted to see what was causing the burns."

"Police?"

"Well, duh, Nic. Girl brought in unconscious, naked, and injured. The paramedics saw the cuffs. And whatever else there was in the room."

Nic groaned and looked away.

"Look. I don't think he hurt you on purpose. You guys were playing some kinky games that got out of hand."

"Something went wrong, Evi. There was something on the cuffs. You should have seen the look on his face. He was horrified, absolutely horrified."

"I'm sure he was. The police might not be so sure. They want to talk to you when you wake up."

"I'm awake."

"Do you want me to tell them you're awake? You could feign sleep for a while longer."

Nic was quiet for a moment, thinking of what she should do. "I want to see Jack."

"I'll call him and let you know you are awake. Nic, I should tell you." Evi hesitated. "I called Lawrence."

"Evi! You promised!" Nic shook in her bed with sudden fury. "I can't see him. He can't see me like this."

"He wants to see you."

"No!"

Evi sighed. "He's been in the waiting room down the hall since the middle of the night."

"Fuck, Evi!"

"Well, I was terrified. There were questions and police and I could hear you screaming in the E.R."

"Who called you?"

"Jack. As he was following the ambulance to the hospital."

"Call Jack. I have to see him first. I have to … I need him."

Evi's jawed clenched, but she nodded. "Okay. Close your eyes and pretend to be asleep for a little longer. I'll go outside and call Jack."

Nic closed her eyes and pretended to be asleep. For a few minutes. And then she really was.

* * * * *

She got a nap in but then Evi was back, gently shaking her awake.

"Hey girl."

"Hmmmm? Did you get a hold of Jack?" Nic struggled to open her eyes and moved to sit up. As she braced her hand on the bed, a bolt of pain shot up from her wrist. She gasped.

"What is it? Your wrists? I'll get the nurse."

"No. Wait. I just need to sit up. God, that hurt." Nic fell back against the bed.

"Well, stupid, this is a hospital bed. You don't just sit bolt upright." Evi pressed a button on a control panel and the head of the bed lifted to a sitting position.

"Oh right."

"Modern technology. Ain't it amazing?"

Nic smiled. Evi was starting to sound like her old self. That was reassuring.

"What time is it?" Nic asked.

"Ten in the morning."

"Can I have some water?"

"Oh yeah. I should have thought of that." Evi held the glass for her, as Nic sipped through the straw.

Nic swallowed the cool water and thanked the gods for creating such nectar. So soothing as it trickled down her throat.

"Jack?" she asked, as soon as she was done with the water.

Evi pressed her lips together. "I've left messages. He hasn't called back."

"Do you have my purse?"

"Yeah." Evi crossed the room to a closet and brought Nic's purse to her. "The paramedics brought it in with you."

Evi rummaged around until she found the cell phone. Nic looked at it. No messages. No texts.

Where was he? Why wasn't he here? Why wasn't he answering his phone. Nic felt a flutter of worry in her stomach.

Also a smoldering of anger. He should have flooded her phone with messages, worrying about her, but there was nothing.

"Right. Okay then. Who am I supposed to talk to?"

Evi smiled. "There's my in-charge friend. Two cops showed up about five minutes ago. Do you want them in?"

"Yes. Let's get this over with."

"Um, Nic," Evi grinned. "How about I clean you up a little?"

"What? Me? Oh." She brought a hand to her face.

"You've got makeup smeared all over. And your hair. It's like someone took an egg beater to it."

Evi got a wet cloth, washed her face, and used the brush in Nic's purse to smooth her hair. Nic found that her wrists didn't ache if she kept them perfectly still, but any flexing sent stinging pains shooting up her arms.

First a nurse came in and checked her IV. She looked over the bandages and assured Nic that there wasn't any extensive damage, just a lot of healing to do. She let Nic know that the doctor would be in to see her in an hour or so, and turned to leave.

"Do you know anything about my bracelet?" Nic asked her.

"A bracelet?"

"I was wearing a bracelet when I was brought it. I think I was."

"I'll check on that." She left the room.

Nic asked Evi to stay during the police interview.

Nic thought she hid her nerves really well, but the cops were pros at picking up on lies. She knew that. So she tried not to lie. Much.

Yes, it was consensual. All of it.

She didn't know what had caused the burns, but she was certain that Jack LaTour had not put it there.

She and Jack were in a relationship, yes. And yes, it was exclusive.

Yes, the cuffs were consensual.

Yes, the hickey was consensual.

Yes, the bite was consensual.

Yes, the marks on her breasts were consensual.

As they ticked off their questions, she felt her face heating up. They were so clinical, asking about such intimate moments she had shared with someone else.

Yes, she knew what was in the armoire.

Yes, cuffs.

Yes, restraints.

Yes, lubricants.

Yes, belts.

She hesitated and then lied. *Yes, she knew about the whip.*

She said yes to every item they listed. Even the ones she didn't know about. Masks. A ball gag. A crop.

Videos.

They asked what was on the videos. She said she had seen the DVD discs in the armoire but had not watched them.

And the photos? Yes, she knew there were photos. She had not seen them.

Evi's eyes grew bigger as each item was verified.

Nic went emotionally numb as the interview went on, but she got through it. They seemed satisfied with her answers. It was the substance on the cuffs that interested them.

They told her that initial indications were that lye powder had been sprinkled on the cuff linings. It would have had to have been deliberate.

The cops finally left.

Deliberate. It had been deliberate. Someone had done it. Not Jack. No, never Jack.

She looked at her bandaged wrists.

"Evi, I really need to see Jack."

"I know. But in the meantime—" Evi tilted her head toward the doorway.

"Yeah. Okay. I'll see him."

*   *   *   *   *

"Hello." Lawrence knocked as he peeked in. "May I come in?"

Nic had been nervous about seeing him, but once she saw his smile, his welcomed face, and his warm eyes, all of the tension flowed out of her.

Her smile was genuine.

"Yes. Please do."

He circled her bed to take the chair that Evi had vacated, but first he leaned in to kiss her forehead.

"How are you feeling?"

"Okay. As long as I don't move my wrists."

His lips twitched. "Evi says you have a long path of healing ahead of you."

She nodded. "I'm not looking forward to that."

He was silent for a moment, his fingers barely touching her arm. Then he took a breath. "I'd like to help you with that."

"With what?"

"Your healing. I can make sure you have a quiet place, with expert care, and all the help you need. And Evi visiting constantly, as much as you like."

She sighed, touched by his concern. "I don't think so. I think I need to be here."

"But—" he started, stopped, then went on. "They don't know who did this yet."

"I think I know."

"Your boyfriend."

"No! Not him."

"I mean that it happened because of your boyfriend."

She didn't reply. She didn't want to affirm his statement, but she couldn't deny it either.

He stroked her upper arm. "Nic, I have a friend with a place in Mexico. On the east coast. Private. It's beautiful, warm, and far away from here. You could spend a few weeks there. Resting. Reading. Healing. I can bring in the best doctors or nurses, whatever you need." He tilted his head, watching her. "I would be with you."

She sighed again and looked at her lap. Then at her wrist.

To get away. To clear her head. Just for a few weeks.

She glanced at her purse on the table next to the bed. She hadn't heard a chirp or a buzz from her phone.

Sun. And Lawrence, to take care of her. No exes. No threats. No having to pull the blinds because someone might be watching. No listening to the man you love describe how he stripped and dominated another woman. No fear.

No thrill. No ecstasy. No Jack in her mind, in her heart, in her body.

She wasn't sure she was up for that kind of thrill at the moment.

But Jack knew how to soothe her too. To stroke her hair and her body and whisper his love and admiration.

He couldn't keep her safe and the danger was his fault.

She felt tears prickling the corners of her eyes.

"Let me think about it," she said in a low voice. Lawrence squeezed her shoulder and sat with her until she fell asleep again.

CHAPTER THIRTY-ONE

Evi helped her put her shoes on, having assisted with every bit of clothing she had brought from Nic's apartment. It was hard to get dressed when you couldn't bend your wrists.

The trauma doctor told her that she would need to change her bandages every night and apply ointment. He prescribed pain medication, but suggested that she switch to something over the counter as soon as she could handle it.

The nurse reported back that there was no mention of a bracelet from the emergency room documentation.

Evi helped steady her as she stood up.

There was a knock on the half-open door and it swung inward.

Jack.

"Well, crap," Evi muttered.

He looked like hell, dressed in gray sweatpants and a rumpled white T-shirt. Stubble marked the lower half of his face.

"Can I come in?" His voice sounded dejected, flat.

"Yes," Nic said and sat back down on the edge of the bed.

Evi groaned and moved past Jack to leave. "She's been discharged and I'm taking her back to my place. Don't take long."

He nodded.

He studied her and she let him, not offering a seat to him or smiling or welcoming him in any way. His eyes traveled over her face and then dropped to her heavily bandaged wrists. He paled.

His lips moved, but he didn't say anything out loud.

"You haven't called," she said.

"I couldn't. I was busy."

"Weren't you worried about me?"

"I was out of my mind with worry. Terror. But once I saw that you would be okay, at least for the time being, there was something else I had to take care of. Quick."

"Erica."

He sighed. "May I sit down?"

She nodded.

He was quiet for several moments and then leaned forward, his hands clasped between his knees.

"It wasn't Erica," he said, looking at her steadily.

She wasn't expecting that. Disbelief drove her next questions out of her head and she just stared at him.

"It was Veronica," he continued.

"The whole thing?"

"The texts, the spying, and yeah, the cuffs. She stole my condo key from Shada weeks ago, returning it after she had snuck in and sprinkled the lye powder on my favorite cuffs."

"Why?"

He shrugged. "The same reasons Erica had, I guess."

"But why did Erica admit …"

"Because she didn't know what else to do when I confronted her. I didn't believe her denials. So she confessed."

"But you …"

"Yes. That was one of the things I needed to take care of quick. I needed to fix things with her."

"How—" She broke off. "Never mind. I don't want to know that part."

He nodded. "No. You don't."

"And Veronica?"

"She can't bother you anymore."

"Can't?"

"She's gone away. I've arranged for some people to take care of her."

"Did you see her?"

"Of course."

"The same thing that you did with Erica?"

He shook his head. "More severe. She was punished."

Nic grimaced.

"She seriously hurt you, Nicole. That can't be permitted."

"Let the police deal with it."

"You've got to be kidding."

"I had to talk with them."

"I know. How did that go?"

"You aren't in any trouble, at least not from me. I said everything was consensual."

"It was."

"Yes. It was."

He hung his head down, staring at the floor. She knew he must be exhausted. That he must have been worried.

But—

"I can't see you anymore, Jack." The words were out of her mouth before they had fully formed in her head, before she knew she would say them.

He just nodded. "I know."

"You know?"

He stood. "I never should have become involved with you. I should have known it wouldn't work. When it came to you, Nicole, I didn't know what I was doing. I thought it could be normal."

"We could have—" she began but he cut her off.

"When I was dealing with Erica, when I had to deal today with Veronica, I knew just what to do. I knew exactly what had to be done. I knew how to handle them, how they would respond. I knew what to expect. I'm in my element with women like them.

With you?" He looked at her, his eyes vacant, tired. "With you, I didn't know what you would do at any time. I didn't know how you would respond, what you would say, what I would do. I was winging it. And look what happened." He gestured to her wrists.

"This wasn't your fault."

"But it still happened."

She nodded. "You talk about your control over these women. Erica and Veronica and the rest of them. But you can't control the way they feel. And you can't control their anger." She looked up at him. "You couldn't stop them from hurting me."

He looked stricken, as if he realized for the first time that his control was not absolute. "It won't work between us," he said.

Nic felt small. He didn't want her, or at least not enough. She had been a novelty for a while, but he wanted what he knew. What he really desired. And it wasn't her.

He rubbed his eyes. "I'm exhausted, Nicole. I know I'm flubbing this badly."

He knelt down in front of her and put his hands on her knees. "You are an amazing, accomplished, and compelling woman. You deserve better than me. Better than letting me tie you up on my bed."

"I thought I was getting better than that from you."

"I thought you might be, too. But I think I was wrong."

"Erica was right."

"About what?"

"You aren't capable of being a boyfriend. You're too one-dimensional." Her words were bitter.

He nodded. "You might be right."

She looked down at his hands on her knees. They sat like that in silence for several seconds while she wished him away. Not just from the room. From her life. From ever having been in it. From the past eight weeks.

"Bye, Jack," she said. It was an effort, but her voice was strong and clear, although she didn't look up at him.

He stood. "Bye, Nicole." No kiss. No touch on her hair. He turned and left the room.

She wouldn't cry. She kept repeating it to herself until the tears dissolved without ever wetting her cheeks. At that point, Evi was beside her again.

"Come on. Let's go home."

The nurse insisted on delivering her in a wheelchair to the curb, where Evi pulled her car around. As Evi put her bag into the trunk, the nurse handed her some paperwork. Then she gave her two other slips of paper.

"This form is to report the loss of your bracelet, honey. I hope we can find it for you. And this one" —she pointed to the smaller piece of paper, little more than a business card— "is just in case you need it. Take care."

Evi helped her settle in her seat, and while she walked around the car, Nic looked at the card the nurse had given her. It was a hotline number for abused women.

Evi pulled into a pharmacy and told Nic she would get the prescriptions filled and be right back. Nic crumpled up the lost-and-found report and the card into a ball.

"Here. Throw these away for me. I don't need them."

CHAPTER THIRTY-TWO

Three days later, Nic was rolling down a runway in a private jet with Lawrence.

She brought her fingers to her mouth as she looked out the small window. The bandages around her wrists had been swapped out for a smaller version, that was not so bulky.

The plane lifted and they banked over downtown Seattle, heading south.

As the plane leveled out at cruising speed, Lawrence touched her foot with the toe of his shoe. He was sitting in the large seat across from hers.

"You okay?" he asked.

She shook her head. It was no use saying she felt fine. She was still subdued from the whole experience, still in discomfort from her injuries, and still hurting from not hearing a word from Jack since he walked out of her hospital room.

She turned away from Lawrence's searching gaze.

Nic had been staying with Evi and Saul since she was discharged and she was undoubtedly glad to be out of that household. Evi had fulfilled every definition of a best friend. She had bathed her, fed her, and held her when she cried. Still, the house was small. And *Fast and Furious* was a loud movie.

She needed some quiet.

She had called Lawrence yesterday and agreed to his offer of time away. She insisted that it didn't mean that he needed to accompany her. She would only stay a week, but he said he needed to be there at least for a few days to get her set up. He could work long-distance from the villa anyway.

The arrangements were made in a whirlwind of passports, plane arrangements, and coordinating medical care and household help. She wasn't privy to the details, but she knew it must be costing Lawrence a small fortune. Or at least a registered percentage of his annual income.

She owed him, but she was too tired to think of it now.

A flight attendant approached, offering drinks and announcing that a meal would be ready in an hour. Nic asked for plain water. Lawrence agreed to the same.

They cruised through the air over Oregon and into California before Nic unbuckled her seat belt and got to her feet. Lawrence stood to help her.

"I just want to go freshen up."

"I'll help you."

"No, I can do it. Thanks. But I can do it."

He let her go, but he didn't sit down as she picked up her bag and made her way back to the bathroom.

Her wrists still hurt. She was off the hardcore pain meds, but still needed over-the-counter pain reliever regularly.

She popped one and looked at her face in the mirror.

She had looked better.

Dark circles, pasty skin, and pale lips. She looked like the vitality had been sucked out of her. Even her eyes were a paler blue.

She tried to smile. It looked like a grimace.

She hadn't worn makeup since Evi had washed the smeared stuff off her face in the hospital.

Just before the police asked all those questions.

Time for a touch-up, she told herself.

She looked through her bag, shifting things gently so as not to overextend her wrists. Her makeup bag was at the bottom.

She put it on the steel counter next to the sink. The last time she'd seen it, it was on Jack's bathroom counter, in the corner she had claimed for herself.

Frances had arrived at Evi's house the day after she left the hospital, carrying her overnight bag that she had left at Jack's, the makeup bag included in it. She said that Shada had brought it to her. Frances didn't say much, just perched on the edge of Evi's couch after declining a mug of tea.

"Take a few weeks, rest, heal up. We can hold down the fort until then."

"Thanks." Nic forced a smile. She refused to ask about Jack.

"It's for the best, Nic," Frances said as she left.

Nic unzipped the makeup bag.

Foundation was beyond her. She looked past that for some mascara.

There was a piece of paper there. She pulled it out and unfolded it.

My heart breaks for both you and Jack. I am so sorry what happened to you. Jack has never been better - happier, vibrant, alive - than when he was with you. Please be well, Nicole. And please, someday, come back to him.

It was signed *Shada*.

She closed her fingers around the note, crumpling it.

Jack.

Her heart gave a lurch, the first feeling she had felt in days. Since Friday night in fact.

She smoothed the note out on the counter. *Shada.*

Come back to him.

She couldn't. Not now. If he had been happier, vibrant, and alive a week ago, so had she. But that was gone now.

She folded the note and put it back in the makeup kit.

Leaning toward the mirror, she carefully applied a little mascara and some clear lip gloss.

Happy. Vibrant. Alive.

She wasn't there yet.

But she would get there.

She zipped up her makeup kit and smiled at herself in the mirror again. Still not her best look, but better than before.

She then she turned away from the mirror and made her way back to her seat. She smiled at Lawrence and held out her hand to him.

He took it and joined her in the seat next to her.

"Nic," he said and kissed her fingers.

"I think that I am very glad you're here," she said, and leaned in to kiss him on the lips.

The rest of the plane trip, she laid in his arms while he stroked her.

And little by little, she felt life returning to her.

THE END

I hope you enjoyed this story, I know I enjoyed writing it for you. The story of Jack and Nic isn't done yet. Stay tuned for the next book in the Circles trilogy - Broken Circles.

If you have a moment, please consider writing a review on Amazon with your honest opinion of this story. I always appreciate feedback. Yes, I do! Really!

To see what else I might be up to, please visit my website at
www.elisecovert.com
On my website, I include a song playlist to accompany each novel or novella.

This novel was first edited by Jim Thomsen and then a final edit by Alan Riehl/Riehl Faith Productions

The cover art was produced by Kari Ayasha of Cover to Cover Designs
www.covertocoverdesigns.com

Elise Covert is the Seattle-based author of steamy romances. She writes sexy stories for smart readers. Elise can be found lurking on Facebook at Elise Covert - Writer or at her website, www.elisecovert.com.

Made in the USA
Middletown, DE
28 October 2014